For I
My "beta reader"
with grateful
appreciation!

The True

Pretender

ARTEMIS
—PRESS—

Anne Cleeland

For Billy's mom, who is true; and for all others like her.

Chapter 1

Epione paused, the sewing needle poised in her hand, and strained to listen to the two women who were speaking in the next room.

"Four dead, now—*four*. And the authorities do *nothing*." The outraged customer in the milliner's shop was speaking in low tones to the shop's proprietress, Madame Dumonde. "*C'est infâme*; the English do not care about us—they care only about their own."

"I think you overreact," Madame soothed. "I do not see any connection at all, between these victims. I think it a coincidence, only. "

But the other woman was not to be placated. "*Quant à moi*, I will take my girls and stay with my sister in Hampstead, until the murderer is captured. I will take no chances." She

1

added in ominous tones, "You should close the shop, Madame; it is better to lose a few days' profit than to be murdered."

But Madame Dumonde was made of sterner stuff. "Come now; you must see that I cannot close the shop. We need only be vigilant, and take care not to be out-of-doors after the sun sets."

Thoughtfully, Epione bent once more to piece together the capote bonnet—the brims were not as pronounced this year, *merci le bon Dieu*— and pressed her needle through the stiff taffeta with the aid of a thimble. A shame that Madame did not scare easily; it would be a pleasant diversion, if the woman chose to close the milliner's shop for a few days. Perhaps Epione could take a trip, somewhere; she'd never traveled anywhere, after all, and it would be oh, so agreeable to be elsewhere, until the scandal died down—she lived in fear that someone might recognize her, despite having changed her name. In a strange way, these recent murders had been helpful, in that they had replaced her sister's scandal as the prime topic of conversation.

Pulling at the thread, she made a wry mouth at her own foolishness. She was a practical girl, and the practicalities were as they were; she had no money, no prospects, and now she must once again readjust her dreams, after the bitter, bitter news from the banker yesterday. With a stifled sigh, she rested the half-completed hat in her lap, and flexed her fingers for a moment, wishing she could keep her mind from thinking about her disappointment. You were a little naïve, to think that anything would come of your *tendre* for Sir Lucien, she admitted to herself; it comes of living in dread that someone will uncover your shameful secret, and of hoping that some kind man will rescue you from your difficulties—like the hero in a fairy tale.

But her life was no fairy tale and in truth, it had been a stroke of good fortune to have found this very agreeable job that so suited her abilities. Nevertheless, a diversion would be much appreciated; she couldn't shake the feeling that there was something unnatural in the sameness of her days, something simmering just below the surface—although it may only have been her constant fear that at any moment, someone might enter who would know her true identity, and recoil in horror.

The customer's voice could again be heard, giving advice to the milliner. "You must lock your doors—and have you a dog?"

"A cat, instead," Madame replied.

There was a dismayed pause. "*Quel dommage*—I can't imagine that a cat would be of the least use."

With an amused smile, Epione gave herself a mental shake—she was overreacting, to think that there was something brewing, beneath the tedium of her days. Although once again, the strange man was standing in the doorway across the street, and watching the shop.

Out of the corner of her eye, Epione glanced out the workroom window in the fading light, to see that the man still leaned against the bricks across the way, his wide-brimmed hat pulled low, so that it shielded his face. He'd been there during the last hour yesterday, too—she'd noticed, because he was directly in her line of sight.

Madame's customer had moved over to the purchase desk so that Epione could now see her through the workroom's open doorway. "You must admit it is all very alarming, Madame. This latest victim was an instructress from *l'Académie*—a woman, this time; the three before her were men."

"Is this so? Was she—" there was a suggestive pause.

"I have not heard; I think not."

Madame could be seen to shrug, as she toted up the woman's purchases. "Who can say why she was killed? A woman, with a dubious reputation; *a bourgeoisie.*"

Epione noted that Madame's voice held a trace of dismissal, because obviously, an *aristo*'s murder would be of far greater interest than that of a mere *bourgeoisie.* Amongst the French *émigré* population that now lived in London, the old castes were still revered despite the Revolution, so many years before. Indeed, Madame Dumonde's attitude toward Epione would undergo a dramatic change were she to learn that Epione was herself a daughter of the *ancien régime,* and indeed, from one of its noblest houses. Not that Madame—or anyone, God willing—would ever know of it; after her sister's scandal, hers was a name that could inspire only shame.

4

Epione slid another glance at the watcher-across-the-way, as she deftly tacked the dyed feathers into place along the hat's peak. He is not the murderer, she assured herself; murderers wouldn't stand at their leisure in an exclusive shopping district. And even at this distance, she could see that he was a handsome man—it seemed unlikely that a handsome man would be inclined to go about killing people. Nevertheless, as she clipped off a thread, she resolved to exit out the back door, tonight.

Madame's customer directed her footman to gather up the packages, but paused on the threshold to issue one last warning. "The victims may be unconnected, but the authorities believe it is the same murderer. If it is not a madman, then perhaps it is an aging Jacobin, who holds an old grudge."

But Madame only tilted her head in amused skepticism. "A Jacobin wouldn't murder an instructress, one would think. Or a stabler."

"*C'est cela*," the woman conceded. Nevertheless, she drew herself upright and announced, "The English authorities must be held to account; I will go to Bow Street this instant, and press them for more information."

"As you wish," Madame replied, with just a hint of amusement in her voice. "As for me, I must hope everyone would rather buy hats, than hide in their homes."

The customer left in her carriage, and Madame observed her departure through the window, standing in place long after the woman

5

was gone, as though lost in thought. Although it was an hour before closing, Epione stood, and passed through the doorway into the showroom. "Would you mind very much, Madame, if I left early today?"

Immediately, the woman was pulled from her abstraction, and faced Epione with some alarm. "What is it, Epione? Are you ill?"

Epione hid a smile; despite the woman's brisk exterior, she was almost over-solicitous, when it came to her sole employee. "No, Madame; I have an errand to run, is all."

This, of course, was not exactly true; instead, Epione was hoping to avoid the watcher-across-the-way. As strange as it seemed, she had the uneasy feeling that it was she that he watched—although why a milliner's assistant would incite such scrutiny was a puzzle. She wondered, for a moment, if it had anything to do with the extraordinary news of the château in France, but this seemed unlikely; if the watcher was indeed her supposed cousin, there was no reason for him to stay back, lurking in the shadows.

As she packed away her materials, she considered her cousin's letter—this "cousin" she'd never heard of, despite the fact that in all *aristo* families, careful track was kept of any surviving relatives. The letter divulged that her cousin was to inherit her father's estate in Normandy, and that he wished to meet so as to discuss the matter with her.

It all seemed very far-fetched, and in truth, she had little interest; she'd wanted nothing more than to remain here in London, patiently waiting for Sir Lucien to come and fall in love with her. But yesterday, the banker had burst this particular bubble; Sir Lucien had unexpectedly married, the man informed her, unaware that the words had made her heart freeze. A whirlwind courtship with a foreign woman—apparently he had a penchant for foreign women; just not this particular one.

You are foolish, Epione, she castigated herself. To have thought that he'd visit you to see how his stipend was spent, and then come to the realization that his dead wife's sister was the right woman for him. Foolish, especially after everything that had happened—the horrifying scandal that had made her assume another name, so as to sink into shameful obscurity.

Epione paused before her reflection in the gold-gilt mirror as she pulled on her gloves—which should have been mourning-black, but she didn't wish to give away any clues. Perhaps she should indeed meet with this "cousin," and see what he had to say—perhaps he would be the hero from a fairy tale, and would rescue her from her difficulties. With an indulgent smile at herself, she pinned on her hat, and took her pelisse from the hook. The past few days had brought all manner of unsettling news, and she must ignore this ridiculous feeling that it was something more than a coincidence. You are being fanciful, she assured herself as she blew out the candle; no one has the slightest interest in you.

Slipping quietly out the back door, she turned to walk briskly down the back alley and closed her hand around the trimming shears in her pocket—until they captured the murderer, it would pay to be cautious.

Epione smiled and nodded at the tailor who stood at the back stoop of his own shop as she passed by. Monsieur Chauvelin was a bachelor, some ten years older than herself, and although he was rather stiff and unfriendly, he always made an effort to nod to her, as she came and went. She thought that perhaps he admired her from afar, but was too shy to engage her in conversation—which was just as well; Epione was kind by nature, and didn't wish to dash his hopes.

The lowering fog brought a bite of chill, and made her breath form a cloud as she stepped along the damp, uneven cobblestones. The news of Sir Lucien's marriage had forced her to face facts, and the facts were, at present, a bit grim. I must come up with a plan, she thought with resolution; I cannot live out my life as a milliner's assistant, scraping by and ashamed to show my face. And I would like a husband—now that the prime candidate is no longer available—so to this end, I should probably look to settle elsewhere.

Epione had never lived anywhere but London—her mother had fled the Terror when she was a baby—but she knew, instinctively, that she'd rather live somewhere a bit more peaceful, a bit less crowded. Perhaps she could find a quiet town—after all, as long as there were women who craved frivolous hats, she could always support herself—and look for some kind man to marry her. He'd have to be English, of course; no self-respecting Frenchman would take her, not after what her sister had done.

With a lighter heart, she quickened her step. She would find a nice, obscure village in the English countryside, and sink into English obscurity. She would then write to Sir Lucien; write, and request that the stipend be sent to her new address until she could find her feet, and also take the opportunity to congratulate him on his marriage. There was always the off-chance that his banker was mistaken.

"You avoid me." The words were French, and said in a mock-accusatory tone.

With a startled gasp, she glanced up to see the watcher-from-across-the-street, only now falling into step beside her, as though they were old acquaintances. He was tall, with brown hair, and a dark stubble of beard which made a stark contrast with the white, charming smile he bestowed upon her, his eyes alight with humor. Rather than make a denial, she stammered, "I—I don't know why you watch me; it makes me uneasy." She glanced around to see if there was anyone near enough to offer aid.

With an easy manner, he tilted his head in acknowledgment. "Have no fear—I am not the murderer."

Fairly, she pointed out, "I imagine that is precisely what the murderer would say—and I would rather speak English."

This surprised him, and he turned his face to hers. "Why is this?"

"My English is better," she lied. He was indeed handsome—dark and handsome; it quite took one's breath away.

After giving her a skeptical look, he continued in English, "It would be best if you do not return home, just yet."

Startled, she paused, but he made a gesture with his hand. "Keep walking, *s'il vous plait.*" He slid her a mock-defiant glance, at his use of the French phrase.

She complied, mainly because he was a force unto himself, and she was having trouble putting two thoughts together. "I—I don't understand; who are you? Am I in danger?"

For whatever reason, he had to think about his answer for a moment. "I think there has been a misunderstanding, and that yes, you may be in danger. Do you have a pistol?"

This seemed alarming, and she glanced up at him again. "No—should I?"

He indicated her pelisse. "What is it you hold in your pocket?"

"Oh—trimming shears." She could feel her color rise.

"*Eh bien.*" He gave her a nod of careless approval. "But a pistol would be more to the point. Shall I give you one of mine?"

Aware that she should—perhaps—be screaming for help, instead she could not suppress a smile as she shook her head in exasperation. "Who are you? Please—I have half a mind to call the Watch." It would be a shame, though—handsome and charming didn't come her way very often, working in a milliner's shop.

He ducked his chin in regret. "I would rather not say—not yet; but you should not call the Watch. The British authorities are searching your rooms, as we speak."

She stopped dead in her tracks and stared at him. "*What?*"

He stood before her, his brown eyes searching hers thoughtfully. "I think there has been a misunderstanding, only; but I would not go home, if I were you—not as yet."

With a knit brow, she regarded him for a long moment. "And why would I need a pistol, if it is the British authorities?"

With a sigh, put his hands on his hips, and contemplated his boots—apparently he had little patience with formalities. She noted that he had a sword at his side—unusual, because he did not appear to be a military man. The sword had a foreign-looking, hooked hilt, but she only glanced at it for a moment before he raised his gaze to hers. "If I tell you too much, then I may bring more trouble to your doorstep—assuming it is all a misunderstanding."

She thought about this, and found that she very much wanted to continue this strange and alarming conversation, despite everything. "Can you give me a hint, do you think?"

"Josiah." His gaze was suddenly sharp upon her face.

Epione shook her head, disclaiming. "I do not understand."

He nodded, rather gravely. "Yes—it is probably why you are still alive."

Aghast, she stared at him. "Why—whatever do you mean?"

"You are supposed to speak English," he reminded her in mock censure, as he took her arm. "*En-avant*, walk this way."

In an attempt to gain some semblance of control over the situation, she protested, "You must see that I cannot—I've no idea who you are, or why you are saying these things to me—"

"Hold! You there—"

With an unhurried movement, Epione's companion pulled her into a doorway, and then calmly drew a pistol at the man who hailed them, firing off a round as she gasped in dismay, and the report echoed loudly off the bricks around them.

With a curse, the other man scrambled for cover behind a stack of crates. As though nothing untoward were going forward, her companion turned to take her hand, and bow over it with his charming smile, sweeping his hat before him. "*Au revoir,* Mademoiselle d'Amberre; we will continue this conversation at another time." He then turned and bent over the door—apparently to pick the lock—and then exited into the building without a backward glance, whilst Epione stared after him in dismayed astonishment at his use of her true name.

Chapter 2

After her strange companion made his unorthodox exit, Epione stood in the doorway for a confused moment, trying to regain her bearings. The man who had hailed them approached cautiously, with his pistol at the ready. He was tall and blond, dressed like a gentleman, and she gauged he was a few years older than she. "Where is he?"

"Oh—he has left." She indicated, rather inadequately. "Through the door."

The young man pocketed his weapon, and then offered his hand to her. "Are you all right, Miss d'Amberre? Shall I find you a place to sit?"

Tiens, thought Epione with surprised annoyance; another one who knows my name. "No—no need. But who are you? Who was he?"

Her hand in his, he helped her step from the doorway, and then faced her with a small bow. "I am your cousin, Robert Tremaine. I was waiting outside your residence, hoping to speak with you about my letter. I became alarmed when you were late, and so I came to the millinery, to look in on you."

Except that she wasn't late, she was early, and his story did not ring true—not to mention he hadn't yet relinquished her hand. Gently removing it from his grasp, she asked with some puzzlement, "Mr. Tremaine—I beg your pardon; did I forget we were to meet, this evening?"

He stood before her in the fading light, and she noted that he seemed in no hurry to begin the journey to her Soho rooms. With a self-conscious smile, he confessed. "No; when you didn't answer my letter, I thought it might be best to meet with you in person. Forgive me if I have overstepped— although it was a good thing I was here, it seems."

But Epione could not take this rescue at face value, particularly since her rescuer seemed suspiciously inclined to stall. If the startling revelations she'd just heard were true—if the British authorities were indeed searching her rooms—then this fellow must be in league with them, which would cast his unexpected tale of kinship in a more ominous light. Trying to decide what was best to do, she asked, "Who was the other gentleman? Are you acquainted?"

"I do not know him—did he offer you insult?" He met her eyes, the expression in his own sincerely concerned.

14

For whatever reason, she decided that this was not the truth, and that the two were, in fact, acquainted—that, and her so-called cousin certainly didn't seem very French. "No—I didn't have an opportunity to discover what it was he wanted." This was, in turn, an untruth, but she found she had a perverse desire to protect the handsome, dark-haired man. I am undoubtedly one of many, she thought with a touch of humor; it is the reason handsome, dark-haired men never have to answer for their sins. "You are very persistent, Mr. Tremaine."

She began to move toward the street—she wanted to test him, and in any event, it seemed best to be away from the alley, with its unexpected hazards. Perhaps she should indeed obtain a more formidable weapon; the trimming shears— with hindsight—seemed wholly inadequate.

In response to her movement, her escort promptly fell into step beside her, and offered his arm. "Forgive my eagerness to meet you, Miss d'Amberre. I acted with such haste because I wanted to speak with you before you left the country."

She glanced up at him in bewilderment. "Left? Left for where?" Apparently she'd traded one incomprehensible conversation for another.

His blue-eyed gaze guileless, he paused, and turned to her in surprise. "You have no plans to travel? I was mistaken, then."

But Epione was determined not to allow yet another strange gentleman evade explanation, and so she kept walking, despite his best efforts to slow her down. "I don't understand; what is so urgent, Mr. Tremaine? You indicated that your claim to my father's estate has already been verified." Then, so he wouldn't believe she harbored a grudge, she lifted her face to add, "Please allow me to offer my sincere congratulations; I am relieved to hear it will be turned over to the rightful heir, after all these years." At the time of the French Revolution, many aristocratic estates had been seized by the Jacobins as *biens nationaux*—belonging to the state. She'd no memory of her father or of the land, since her father had fallen victim to the Revolution when she was an infant. But now that France was trying to restore the monarchy, some efforts had been made to return the seized properties back to the original owners—or, more properly, those relatives of the original owners who had managed to avoid the guillotine. Still, when Epione had heard the older *émigrés* discuss the matter, they were cynically doubtful that much of value would be returned—the monarchy would be no more generous than the Jacobins, when it came to wealthy estates.

Therefore, it was with some surprise that Epione beheld the surprising news in Tremaine's letter; her father's estate—*Desclaires*—was slated to be returned back to his family, even though by all accounts it was a premiere property.

Her companion bent his head in a self-deprecating gesture and smiled, so as to invite her to share in his discomfiture. "I confess I am almost embarrassed—my claim is so attenuated that I didn't even know of it." He took another glance around at their surroundings, and it occurred to her he was very watchful, despite his casual air. "Have you ever seen it—*Desclaires*, I mean?"

"No; I left as a baby, when my mother had to flee The Terror."

"Never visited, then?"

His friendly gaze rested on her, but she had the impression he was watching her reaction carefully—although she had nothing to hide. "No—I'm afraid I've never been outside of London." Best not mention her newly-formed plan to depart to an obscure corner of the country and find a husband; despite his amiable mien, her so-called cousin made her wary.

He nodded, and was seen to gather his thoughts. "I wanted to meet with you, Miss d'Amberre, because I have a proposition which may benefit the both of us."

For whatever reason, Epione was suddenly of the opinion that she shouldn't trust anyone on this strange day, no matter how appealing they might appear, and so she allowed her skepticism to be revealed in her tone. "What sort of proposition?"

Almost imperceptibly, she could sense him re-assess, and after a moment's hesitation, he met her eyes in a frank manner. "Look—you've had a scare; it can wait until tomorrow, and I shouldn't have imposed myself on you in this way. May I beg you to spare me a half-hour in the morning, perhaps?"

They began to walk again, and Epione knew it was no coincidence that she'd been suddenly sought out by these two gentlemen, who were apparently working at cross-purposes. Neither one had raised any undue alarm within her breast, but on the other hand, she should take no chances until she discovered what was afoot—not to mention that French *émigrés* were being murdered, one after the other. "I am certain I can be excused for a half-hour, if you come by the shop tomorrow—my employer is very accommodating." Although this may not be the case in this instance; on those occasions when a visiting gentleman had shown an interest in the pretty milliner's assistant, Madame had ruthlessly interrupted to send Epione on an errand.

In the end it didn't matter, because her cousin proposed an alternate plan. "Perhaps I could escort you to work in the morning? That way you won't have to impose upon your employer."

"I shall look forward to it, Mr. Tremaine." Then, because he hadn't mentioned it again—which seemed a little strange—she asked, "Will you report the other gentleman to the authorities? He could have hurt you."

There was a small pause. "Yes—I should do so. It wouldn't do, to allow such lawlessness to go unpunished. I will see to it, after I escort you safely home."

They walked to her rooms, which were located in a modest row of buildings chosen by Epione because, hopefully, no one in the working-class French neighborhood would recognize her.

She lived one floor up from her landlady, which was both a bane and a blessing in that the older woman was a bit intrusive, in the best tradition of lonely widows. At present, Madame Reyne was engaged in her favorite pastime of sweeping the front steps, which was merely a subterfuge to disguise her intense interest in the comings and goings. Upon viewing Epione's approach with a personable gentleman, the broom paused, and the woman raised her brows in an arch manner, the implication making Epione blush.

Her companion gave no sign of self-consciousness, however, and instead nodded in a friendly fashion to the woman before bowing over Epione's hand. "Until tomorrow, cousin." He waited, while she let herself into the front door, and then walked away with a wave of his hand.

Rather than parry Madame Reyne's inevitable questions, Epione hurried up the stairs to her rooms and turned the bolt, standing for a moment to listen to the silence. Satisfied that she was alone, she quickly crossed to pull out a drawer in her writing desk, then another, and another. Letting out a breath, she sank slowly into the chair. The desk had indeed been searched, although if she hadn't known to look for it, no doubt she wouldn't have noticed.

"Josiah," he'd said, but she did not understand the reference. And if it was indeed the British authorities who'd done the searching, then her "cousin" was working with them—there was something about his manner; about the way he'd

19

reacted so quickly and deftly to whatever she'd told him.

The clock ticked quietly on the mantle, and Epione considered the unhappy fact that her past had come back to haunt her with a vengeance. It was the only rational explanation; they must know who she was, and think her a traitor, like her sister. With a heavy heart, she lit a candle against the gathering darkness, and would have been grateful for a cat, even though it would not have been of the least use.

Chapter 3

"You do me great honor, sir," Epione said with as much sincerity as she could muster, "but I'm afraid I must decline your offer."

She sat beside Tremaine on a park bench in the misty morning light, listening to her first proposal of marriage and wishing it were a bit more meaningful. As it was, she could only wonder why the British authorities would go to such lengths, and why her father's estate played such an important part in this charade.

Her unexpected suitor smiled at her, his posture relaxed. "I suppose I'm not surprised— you are not the sort of girl who is going to jump at such an offer—but I must beg you to think it over. I know it sounds—well, almost medieval; but you must admit it would be the fairest and most expedient solution."

"You are very generous, Mr. Tremaine." She tried to keep a note of irony from her voice, but was not certain she was entirely successful. This extraordinary turn of events should have been a balm to her bruised heart, but as it was, she could only be wary, and a bit bewildered by all the sudden interest—particularly that shown by the nameless handsome man who spoke in vague warnings, and picked a fine lock.

Tremaine didn't seem to notice her tone, and continued in his earnest manner, "It just seems so unfair—you are the only remaining linear descendant, but because you are female, I inherit the estate, even though I am but a distant relation. I think a marriage between us is worth considering; it would not be the first marriage of convenience, contracted to maintain a legacy."

She watched the ducks swim in the quiet pond, thinking over what she knew, and what she did not, and wondering what he knew, in turn. "What is the relationship between us, sir? I confess I've never heard my mother speak of you."

"I am your second cousin, once removed." He shot her an amused look. "Or so I am told. Apparently, our family is lacking in male heirs."

"As are all the others," she conceded. "It is an unfortunate consequence of these terrible times." Thinking she may as well try to obtain some answers on these strange and convergent matters, Epione pointed out almost apologetically, "You do not seem French, Mr. Tremaine."

"No—I have little memory of France," he answered readily. "After the Bastille, my father sent my mother and me to England, as a temporary measure. Then, when he was imprisoned, she returned in an attempt to bribe him out, but the Jacobins were in full cry, and instead they were both guillotined."

She nodded in commiseration. It was a common tale amongst the *émigré* community; many had died due to the sheer incomprehensibility of what was unfolding—the belief that surely, matters could not be so far gone—until it was brought home with the crash of a blade that indeed, they were. Epione had lost her father and her older brother to that blade, leaving her mother—wholly unsuited to the task—to flee to a strange country with two small daughters, a heart filled with bitterness, and no funds; it had not turned out well. And although Epione was inclined to be sympathetic to Tremaine's story, she was almost certain that none of it was true. Perhaps the British authorities thought she'd be so dazzled that she wouldn't ask questions, but Epione was not one to be dazzled—not after all she'd been through.

Tremaine continued his recital, as his gaze rested on the far shore. "I was adopted out to an older couple in Cornwall—both dead, now. I suppose I should take back the old name— d'Amberre." With an amused glance at her, he concluded, "And here I thought I was slated to live a quiet and uneventful life in Cornwall."

23

Delicately, she probed, "It does seem very strange; *Desclaires* was awarded to a high-ranking Jacobin—or at least, that is what my mother always said. She was very bitter about it, and there seemed little hope of a restoration."

But he was too clever to be caught up in the particulars of his implausible story, and shrugged to indicate a puzzlement equal to hers. "Then it seems there has been a change of heart; the Congress in Vienna may be making an attempt to redress past sins."

She nodded as though this explanation was sufficient, even though it wasn't. Perhaps he was hoping that she was ignorant of the true situation, but the close-knit *émigré* community was intensely interested in the doings across the channel, now that Napoleon had been defeated and was exiled on the island of Elba. The victorious allied countries had convened the Congress of Vienna to determine how best to restructure Europe, with England determined to restore the French monarchy, even though many were unhappy with such a plan. Even with the best of intentions, however, the Congress was unlikely to return valuable land to disinterested heirs—not in these turbulent times, when all the various factions were grasping for any advantage.

Epione turned to Tremaine with an apologetic smile. "I should go, before Madame wonders what has become of me—she worries, if I am late."

She made to rise, and her companion did not demur, but offered his hand to assist her. "I just thought I'd raise the idea. I can't feel right about it—I'd never even heard of your father's estate, and yet I'm to be awarded it for no better reason than my gender. Since we are both unattached, I thought I'd do right by you—and as an added incentive, we would leave our very uninteresting lives and hold sway over some fine vineyards, on the coast of Normandy."

Teasing, she raised a brow at him, as they began to stroll toward the street. "Speak for yourself, Mr. Tremaine; I lead a fascinating life."

He laughed, appreciating the irony in her tone. "My interest has always been in mining, rather than agriculture, so it would be quite the turnabout. Still, I imagine I could pick up the reins, if I put my mind to it."

Thinking to bring the conversation around to the politics of it—which *must* be the motivation, as otherwise the charade made no sense—she noted with some doubt, "Does it concern you that you may travel to France only to be caught up in yet another war?"

She had the impression he was suddenly wary. "About the French succession, you mean?"

Glancing at him with a hint of surprise, she shook her head. "No—I meant that Napoleon might escape, and make another attempt at conquest. He is not one to give up so easily, and the quarreling about the succession only gives him an opening."

This was not a far-fetched fear; there had been persistent rumblings in the *émigré* community that shadowy interests were working to aid Napoleon in an escape—although it was almost unthinkable that he would be able to raise another army, after the misery of the past eight years.

The possibility persisted, however, because there was no clear concurrence as to who should rule France. The last King and Queen had been executed during the Revolution, and the direct heir—the young Dauphin—had died in a French prison, many years ago. As a result, there were a plentitude of "pretenders"—those who held a claim to the throne due to the ancient and convoluted relationships that connected the peerage in Europe.

The British and the Catholic Church—who wielded the most power at the Congress— were intent upon establishing the closest relative in the royal Bourbon line as Louis the Eighteenth—even though he'd been but an uncle to the Dauphin, and much of the populace was well-sick of the Bourbons. The British, however, were given enormous help in this aim by Tallyrand—a French bishop who was Napoleon's former minister. The crafty Tallyrand was now working to aid the British, in the hope of becoming Louis the Eighteenth's new Prime Minister.

Other factions—less inclined to allow the monarchy and the Church to regain their former power—argued that Napoleon's young son should rule, under the regency of his mother. And yet another faction championed Louis Philippe, the Duc d'Orleans from the junior branch of the royal Bourbon family, who'd spent most of his life traveling in exile. Due to all the fractured divisions, there seemed little hope that France would unite behind Louis the Eighteenth—the dead Dauphin's uncle—and the circumstances were ripe for a tyrant like Napoleon to rise again. Sadly, Epione reflected that despite the turmoil and horror of the recent past, many lessons remained unlearned—*plus ça change, plus c'est la même chose*.

"Promise me you'll think about it—we would do well together, I believe." Tremaine bent his head so that she could feel the full force of his engaging smile from beneath the brim of her hat—one of her best creations, as she'd suspected that matrimony would be proposed—and Epione reflected that she was half inclined to marry him out-of-hand, just to discover what it was all about. Instead, she shook her head in bemusement. "It does seem medieval, to marry someone for such a reason. And I cannot imagine that you are as unattached as you claim, Mr. Tremaine; I would feel badly, were I to cut out some hopeful Cornishwoman."

He hesitated, weighing what to say, then admitted, "I have recently suffered a disappointment; it only strengthens my desire to build a relationship on good-will, and mutual trust."

Intrigued, she sensed this was perhaps the truth—for once—and offered, "I am sorry for it; indeed, I have suffered the same."

He raised his brows at her, and she caught a flash of surprise in his eyes. "Is that so? Then I suppose we could find a measure of solace in each other."

As the morning mists had now cleared, she unfurled her parasol against the sunshine and asked with real curiosity, "Can you speak of her? Or is the wound too fresh?"

He glanced up, to consider the street ahead for a moment. "Our differences were too much to overcome." He paused. "She is foreign-born."

But this touched a nerve with Epione, who retorted with exasperation, "*Tiens*; what happens to rational men, when they meet foreign women? What is so alluring? I cannot begin to understand it."

"You lost a suitor to a foreign woman?" He seemed genuinely surprised, as though she had gone off-script, although why he would know of such things was unclear.

With a sigh, she shifted the parasol to the other shoulder, and confessed, "No—not truly; he was ineligible, and never a suitor in the first place. Mainly I was hovering in the background, hoping."

He tilted his head in an expression of sympathy. "Bad luck."

"Yes—at least you were able to put it to the touch. Is there no hope, then?"

He glanced at her in amusement. "You are not supposed to be championing her, you know; I am doing my best to secure your consent."

"I do not know what it is you are endeavoring to do, Mr. Tremaine." She allowed her tone to hint at her disbelief.

But his next words were thoughtful, and held a measure of wistfulness that was–as far as she could tell—authentic. "No; I wouldn't mind marrying, upon my word. Several of my friends have married—all at once, it seems. I envy them their happiness."

Since it seemed they had wandered into being more-or-less honest with each other, she ventured, "Is there any chance you can you tell me what this is truly about?"

But she was to be disappointed, as the blue eyes turned to meet hers, utterly sincere. "I know it seems far-fetched, but believe me, I am hoping to share your father's honors with his only remaining daughter." He made a self-deprecatory gesture. "And I have other motives, also; you must admit it would be easier to establish myself as the next Vicomte d'Amberre with you by my side. I am alive to the delicacy of the situation, and how I would be considered a mushroom of the first order, over there. If you were my wife, I would have instant credibility."

This, of course, was true, and she hadn't considered this aspect of his unlooked-for proposal. On the off-chance that he was telling her the truth, she mentally steeled herself. "I have to confess that my reputation would not help you, in this aim. I'm afraid a cloud of scandal hangs over me, and I would not be welcomed by any self-respecting Frenchman."

"Your sister; yes, I know."

Astonished, she stared at him. "You—you know of Marie?"

He nodded. "Yes; I researched the family in order to find you, of course, and—well, there was no missing the newspaper accounts." In a sympathetic gesture, he touched her hand with his own. "You cannot be held to blame for her actions, certainly."

This was unexpected, and made her think that perhaps something else was at play— something other than her sister's unholy scandal. Still off-balance from his casual disclosure, she shook her head. "You do not realize how important such things are to the *aristos*. My family is tainted—my sister was an infamous traitoress, who met a very bad end; they believe such things run in the bloodline."

But her companion was unfazed, and offered with all sincerity, "Then I give you a chance to leave it all behind, and create a new identity in a new place."

This gave her pause, because up to now, she had considered the whole matter as contrived and almost laughable. Now, however, he'd mentioned the one thing that could tempt her— well, aside from the other one thing, and Sir Lucien was no longer in play. She could leave this place of shame and misery and return to France, to start anew.

With a mental shake, she reminded herself that the whole tale was in doubt; the handsome dark-haired man had spoken of a misunderstanding—one that brought danger to her—and he'd correctly predicted that her rooms would be searched. Therefore, she should proceed on the assumption that nothing this man told her was true, and that indeed, she may be at risk.

Matching him in guilelessness, she smiled apologetically. "I wish I knew what to say; you offer me a fairy-tale ending, and it all seems too good to be true."

Her companion shrugged his shoulders in a disclaimer, and then bent over her hand to take his leave. "I am no prince, but—as I said— marriages of convenience have been arranged for far less."

"I will think on it, then."

He offered his disarming smile. "The sooner the better, if you don't mind—can't let them give the land to anyone else, can I?"

"No, I imagine not," she agreed, and wondered to whom he referred.

Chapter 4

"Tell me of this young man—he is *un Français*?" Madame Dumonde was discreetly interested, her dark eyes sliding toward Epione as she rearranged the hats that were on display in the window—even if not sold, they would be rotated out, every few days, to give the impression they were going fast, and that shoppers needed to strike quickly.

"So he says." Epione kept her own conclusions to herself, as she pleated a ribbon with nimble fingers.

"My spies tell me he is very handsome, and he escorted you to work this morning." This delivered with an arch look that invited confidences.

Willingly, Epione smiled at her teasing. "Yes—he is good-looking." Her eyes lifted to contemplate the empty doorway across the way, as there was handsome, and then again, there was *handsome*. "It turns out we are distantly related, which is why he sought me out." She'd decided not to mention the marriage proposal, and the dazzling prospect of a French château, as she'd come to the conclusion she needed more information from the picker-of-locks. Unfortunately—despite its being the appointed hour—that gentleman did not haunt his post. However, Epione did not allow this setback to cause her dismay because she was convinced—for reasons which were unclear—that she would see him again, and soon.

"Is that so—you are related? Well, that is a surprise—he so fair, and you so dark. Does he stay in town?"

Epione flexed her fingers—tired after the day's work—and reflected that Madame was showing a rather uncharacteristic curiosity, which may stem from the fear of losing her sole employee to matrimony. "I would think so, but I do not know his plans."

The bell rang, and Madame went to greet the Comtesse Toray's dressing maid, who came in on a regular basis to choose a variety of hats to take home so that milady could make decisions at her leisure—some of the old *aristos* would never deign to be seen in a shop, under any circumstances. As their voices murmured in the salon, Epione tacked the ribbon on a veiled brim and then held the hat up—contemplating it for a moment with a critical eye—before pulling off the ribbon to start again. The proportions were off, and she'd learned long ago that it was best simply to start over.

Her thoughts were interrupted by the Comtesse's maidservant, who entered the workshop and approached with a measured step to stand before her, ramrod straight, with her hands folded before her. Often, the servants were every inch as aristocratic as their betters, and sometimes, even more so. With a dry smile, the woman greeted her. "Mademoiselle."

A bit surprised, Epione took the needle from her lips, and nodded in response. Usually, the maidservant did not deign to speak directly to her, but relayed any communications through Madame. And it was apparent the woman was unused to smiling, as she gave the impression of a rather stringy gargoyle in this attempt to be friendly.

"Milady is so very pleased with your fashions, Mademoiselle. She asks that you make a home visit, so that she can discuss designs with you, and express her appreciation in person."

This was an unexpected accolade, and Epione was taken by surprise. "Oh—why, that is—"

"How very splendid." Madame interrupted from her position in the doorway, and cast a significant glance at Epione. No doubt this request would lead to a lucrative order, with more to come—the Comtesse was by far the shop's best customer.

The maidservant bowed her head, acknowledging Madame's obsequious attitude as her mistress's due. "The carriage awaits outside; you will accompany me, *s'il vous plaît*."

Amused that it was taken for granted she would accept the invitation, Epione debated what was best to do. On one hand, she was reluctant to stray from her designated post in the event the handsome man made his much-anticipated return, but on the other, she couldn't very well refuse. In the end, she nodded and rose to her feet; it would take but a few hours at most, and with any luck she would be served a decent meal—always a consideration, in these uncertain times. With a show of gratitude, she pulled the thimble from her thumb, and surreptitiously brushed the thread-ends from her lap. "Willingly—which materials shall I bring?"

Considering this, the servant paused for a moment, her expression unreadable. "A sketchbook, perhaps; I believe Milady only wishes to discuss designs, this evening."

Epione gathered up her things and bid goodbye to Madame, who stood behind her desk and bowed her head in acknowledgement, her hands clasped rather tightly before her—so tightly that her knuckles showed white. Why, she is nervous, thought Epione with surprised amusement. Perhaps she is afraid I will disgrace her—and she has forgotten to ask me about the Del Valle order, which is just as well; it is due tomorrow, yet sits in a forlorn state on the worktable, only half-done.

Once they were outside, the footman duly produced the step, and then handed them inside the carriage with solicitous care. Epione smiled a greeting at Monsieur Chauvelin, the tailor, who watched without expression from his shop window. *My stock will rise with that one,* she thought with amusement—*perhaps yet another offer of marriage will soon be forthcoming.*

With a slap of the reins, the carriage rattled down the cobblestones and they were away, Epione enjoying the novel sensation of riding in a carriage and having an adventure—although it seemed there'd been no shortage, of late. As Epione wasn't certain how long the journey would take, she made a good-natured attempt at conversation with the imposing servant. "How long have you served the Comtesse, Mademoiselle?"

"Many years," the woman answered. "From before the Terror." After a pause, her eyes slid to Epione, a gleam of malice contained therein. "Milady knew your mother."

Taken aback, Epione stammered, "Did she indeed?" Feeling the color flood her face, she quickly changed the subject. "And do you have family here?"

"I do not."

Epione decided she'd rather watch the scenery pass by than plow ahead with this awkward conversation, and saw that they were coming into a more remote area, as dusk began to descend.

It was a pleasing landscape, and Epione resisted the urge to lean out the window to admire it. The *émigré* community was insular, and as a result, she'd rarely traveled outside the immediate environs of the Soho district. Indeed, there had always been the sense, amongst her family's acquaintances, that the world would soon be righted, and they would all return to their lands in France —despite the ever-increasing evidence that this was not to be the case. As a result, the general attitude toward their host country was one of slightly contemptuous tolerance; the sting of losing one's land and heritage was intensified by the fact that one had to take refuge in such an inferior country.

Epione had been embarrassed for them, as it was beyond ungrateful—England had taken them in, and had defeated the enemy, for good measure. Epione would gladly have taken up English citizenship, and indeed, this had been her most fervent desire until she'd discovered two days ago that some foreign woman had beaten her to it.

After deciding she liked the prolonged silence less than she liked the conversation, Epione ventured, "Is it much further?"

But before any response could be made, the carriage suddenly jolted, and both women were required to brace themselves so as not to tumble onto the floor.

"Fool!" The maid straightened her bonnet in annoyance, and then composed herself, keeping one hand on the strap as a precaution.

As the carriage seemed steady once again, Epione tried to pick up the threads of the discussion. "Does the Comtesse have a special occasion in mind, or does she seek an everyday hat?"

For whatever reason, the question ignited a gleam of humor in her companion's cold eyes, as they turned to her. "A very special occasion—a Coronation."

"Oh—a bit premature, perhaps." The poor King of England was mad, but Epione hadn't heard any rumors that he was near death. It seemed in poor taste, if it was a joke.

"It is always best to be prepared." The woman rendered her dry little smile, and turned to gaze out the window again.

"Perhaps a velvet turban, then." Epione wasn't certain how old the Comtesse was, as she seemed to purchase all variety of Epione's creations—she was clearly one of those women who could not possess enough hats. If she was of the same generation as Epione's late mother, though, a turban was probably most appropriate— although a prie-cap with an ostrich feather could work, if it were fashioned out of an elegant fabric.

As Epione debated whether it would be too impolite to ask her customer's age, the maid suddenly frowned and leaned forward, peering out the window into the gathering darkness. Epione followed her gaze, but saw only the branches of spreading trees, silhouetted against the fading sky as the carriage gently rocked along its journey. "Are we lost?" she asked, half in jest.

"I do not understand this," the woman muttered. "It is not right."

Nonplussed, Epione regarded her companion. "Are we headed in the wrong direction? Where does the Comtesse live?"

The woman stilled at the question, and rigidly kept her gaze out the window. "Just a bit further," she replied in a clipped tone. "We will arrive soon."

"Well then—that is excellent." Epione settled back into the cushions, her mouth dry and her heart leaping into her throat. As she turned her gaze out her window, she assimilated the alarming fact that the maid had no ready answer to the question of where the Comtesse lived. In light of recent events, Epione decided that an escape was probably imperative, and the sooner the better. Out of the corner of her eye, she gauged the distance to the opposite door and then—taking a breath—she lunged to open it, and leap out into the roadway, as the maidservant cried out in alarm behind her.

Chapter 5

Epione leapt outward quickly, before she had a chance to reconsider, and tumbled onto the packed-dirt road, scrambling to her feet and lifting her skirts with both fists as she raced toward the shadowed hedgerows that were set back a small distance from the roadway. She could hear the footman's shout, as the carriage drew up to a crunching halt, but she didn't stop, instead searching frantically ahead for a break in the hedges, and an avenue of escape.

"Stop, stop—*parbleu*, Mademoiselle."

She recognized the voice immediately, and whirled around in astonishment to face the silhouette of a horseman, pulling up at the edge of the road to face her.

40

"*Nom de Dieu*, but you are an enterprising girl." The handsome man contemplated her for a moment whilst she drew ragged breaths, and struggled to make sense of his presence here.

"Wait here, if you please." He then turned the horse and trotted toward the carriage, which seemed ominously silent, a hundred feet down the road.

Epione lifted her petticoat to examine a scraped knee, and tried to decide the best course of action. If she was to be murdered like the other *émigré* victims—which had been her first, panicked thought—it seemed an overly-complicated scheme; not to mention she'd been casually left alone by the handsome man, who did not seem to be at all menacing. Caution was advised, though; she'd already been deceived once this evening by the maidservant, and she should not assume he was dedicated to her well-being, either. It would be best, perhaps, to start walking along the hedgerow on the off-chance that someone would appear; if there was a witness, surely he wouldn't do her in, if this was his intent.

With this course in mind, she began walking quickly along the shadows of the hedges, heading toward the city lights that glowed in the distance and stumbling occasionally on the uneven ground. She continued as rapidly as she was able for several long minutes, then heard the unmistakable sound of a horse, falling into step behind her. Balling her hands into damp fists, she kept walking, and hoped he wasn't planning to shoot her where she stood.

41

"Where do you go?" The question was casual.

"I don't understand any of this, and it would be foolish to trust you." Mainly she was trying to convince herself of this; paradoxically, she did trust him. And it had occurred to her—in retrospect—that he must have substituted his own man for the driver and commandeered the carriage, which was surely something to be toted up in his favor.

They walked in this fashion for a small space of time, he silent behind her as she doggedly made her way forward, her path ahead lit only by the moonlight. Finally, the silence was broken. "It is a long way; may I beg to give you a ride, Mademoiselle?"

The meek tone made her smile, despite everything, and she stopped to face him, although it was too dark to read his expression. As he hadn't attempted to abduct or murder her whilst he had a clear chance, she was cautiously optimistic that this was not his aim. "What will happen to the maidservant?"

He bowed his head. "You will not see her again, *je vous assure*."

She glanced over toward the deserted roadway, and debated what was best to do. "Will you tell me what this is all about?"

Again, he bowed his head—this time regretfully. "Not as much as you'd like."

They faced each other for a moment, and then she sighed and gave in, since there seemed little choice, and she could feel a blister coming on. "*D'accord;* what should I do, Monsieur?"

"Here." He leaned down and held out a hand, then pulled her up so that she scrambled to sit behind him on the startled horse, who did not help matters by nervously backing in a circle during this procedure.

After she was aboard and the horse settled, he asked, "Have you any injuries, Mademoiselle?"

"A few scrapes is all, nothing to signify."

He prodded the horse forward, and after hesitating for a moment, she put her hands at his waist, since there seemed nowhere else to put them. "I must thank you, I think. Who was she, and where was she taking me?"

"It is not yet clear, but we will find out."

This remark did not bode well for the supercilious maid, but Epione found she could dredge up little sympathy. "Was I to be killed, like the others?"

He thought about this for a moment, one hand on the reins and the other at his hip, as the horse settled into a rhythmic walk. "Perhaps, perhaps not; I think there has been a misunderstanding."

Epione sighed in exasperation. "So you keep saying. What sort of 'misunderstanding'? The maid said she knew my mother, which means she knows who I am."

But this disclosure was not news to him, and he answered easily, "Yes, they all know who you are."

Her eyes narrowed. "Who is 'they'? Madame? Who else?"

"Too many—it would be best to trust no one."

"Except you, I suppose?"

"Except me," he agreed.

"And who—exactly—are you?"

He shook his head with regret, the hooked sword at his side clicking against the saddle in rhythm with the horse's steps. "I would rather not say. The less you know, the better it is for you, *sans doute*."

Epione decided she would take a direct approach on the forlorn hope the maddening man would answer a question, for a change. "If they know who I am, then does all this have to do with my sister?"

"I would imagine." Absently, he flicked the reins.

"Then it seems unlikely that it is all just a 'misunderstanding'," she countered. "I would like to know who you are, and who my cousin is, and what-is-what; I will not take the chance that I am aiding the enemy."

This statement seemed to garner his lackadaisical attention, and he glanced over his shoulder at her. "Who is the enemy?"

Her brows rose, as she contemplated the back of his head. "Napoleon, of course. Why? Who do you think is the enemy?"

He tilted his head so that she had to move her own head to avoid his hat's brim. "I agree the enemy is Napoleon—among others." He paused.

44

"I will tell you one 'what-is-what'; your cousin is not your cousin."

But this was no revelation to Epione, who ventured to look around her escort's shoulder so as to view the road ahead, now that she was getting used to the experience. "No, I know he is not. I like him, though—despite how nearly everything he tells me is a lie. And I imagine he is not truly the heir to my father's estate in France, is he?"

"No. Instead, you are the heiress."

She laughed aloud at the absurdity of this. "Am I indeed?"

"*C'est cela*. You must not marry your cousin, though."

Epione found that—once she let go of any attempt to make sense of it—she was rather enjoying herself, walking along on this quiet road, with the horse twitching its ears back to listen to them speak. "No—I did mention that nearly everything he tells me is a lie, didn't I? Except for the foreign girl who broke his heart, I think."

Her escort cocked his head in acknowledgment. "The foreign girl, she is not to be trusted."

So—apparently all the players in this little drama were acquainted, and were indeed working at cross-purposes. It was all very interesting, and she couldn't help but be diverted, thinking about the foreign-born girl. "That's what I thought—that even if she agreed to marry him, he could never trust her. I didn't say it, of course." She knew she shouldn't be speaking of such things with this stranger, but it seemed entirely natural, as they rode along the road with her skirts bunched up around her legs, and her hair coming down from its pins.

Apparently, he had no compunction about plain-speaking, either. "You must be wary of him; he seeks to take possession of the land by marrying you—it is very important to him. He may try to seduce you, so as to take your choices away."

But she shook her head in disagreement. "No; he hasn't the heart for it."

"Men always have the heart for it. If I may say so, you are naïve, Mademoiselle."

She quirked her mouth at this pronouncement, and belatedly decided she should put an end to this rather shocking and improper topic. "Well then, Monsieur—I thank you for your efforts to protect my virtue at the cost of my naiveté."

For whatever reason, her teasing comment seemed to pierce his amused nonchalance, and his tone became slightly irritated. "Where is your man, in all this? Why is he not the one protecting your virtue?"

A bit startled, she disclaimed, "You are mistaken; I have no man."

He did not respond, and she thought for one horrified moment he knew her secret—but that was ridiculous; no one knew her secret. Nevertheless, she changed the subject. "Are you seeking to seize the estate, also?"

He raised his head to contemplate the stars for a moment. "It is a fine estate—and the land is in good heart. I confess I am tempted; I have been landless a long time."

Exasperated, she gave up trying to get a straight answer from him. "Now what is to happen? I cannot return to the shop, yet I must make a living, somehow."

But his answer surprised her. "You must return to the shop tomorrow, just as always. It is very important."

This seemed even more farfetched than all the other farfetched things he'd said to her, and she struggled to make a response, torn between disbelief and suspicion. "What on earth shall I say, when Madame asks of my visit with the Comtesse?"

He shrugged, clearly amused by her bewilderment. "*Quant à ca*, you will say nothing. She does not dare ask."

She contemplated this pronouncement in shocked silence for a few moments. "I am half inclined to flee into the night."

He shook his head, gently remonstrating. "Do not; you must claim your land in France."

Eying the back of his head with some skepticism, she ventured, "I suppose you will not tell me why my father's estate is so important."

She could hear the smile in his voice. "You suppose correctly—I am surprised you have not learned this by now, Mademoiselle."

"Well then, will you at least tell me your horse's name?" She dared to tease him; it had not escaped her notice that he hadn't offered his own name.

"Blue Fly, is his name. He is an English horse, with no love for Napoleon."

"I thank him for his service, then."

He indicated the horse's ears with a careless hand. "He heeds your voice—do you see?"

"I do. But he is the only one, it seems."

He placed a hand briefly upon hers at his waist, and chuckled as they walked forward into the dark, starry night.

Chapter 6

They continued their leisurely progress toward the center of London, and Epione began to entertain a suspicion that her companion was in no hurry to deliver her home. Hopefully, he was not bent on abduction, as she didn't know if she had the wherewithal to stage yet another escape.

After a small space of time, he broke the companionable silence. "Tomorrow night I would like to search the milliner's shop, *s'il vous plaît*."

She digested this request in silence. "I don't think I should allow such a search, Monsieur. Someone once told me I was naïve, and that would seem the height of naiveté."

He thought about it for a moment, and appeared to concede her point. "Then allow me to explain; our mutual enemy Napoleon is looking to bring about another war."

Assessing this blunt statement, she admitted, "I have heard rumors, but surely it is unlikely? After all, he is a dangerous prisoner, and closely guarded."

"It is almost a surety," her companion advised her, as though they spoke of nothing more pressing than the weather. "And I believe the woman in your shop—and others—are working to aid him in this aim."

Epione caught her breath in shocked dismay. "Madame? *Tiens*—can it be true? Is this why you say they know who I am?" A few short months ago, her sister Marie had been shot to death in her back garden, and the rumor quickly spread that she was passing British state secrets to Napoleon's supporters. The combination of Marie's death and the resulting scandal had caused Epione's mother—never a strong woman—to take to her sickbed, and succumb to grief. Shortly afterward, her stepfather met his own demise after being attacked outside a low tavern—some said by those seeking a measure of revenge for Marie's treachery. Epione had thus been left wholly alone, to make her own way in the hope no one would ever wonder what had become of Marie's younger sister.

"Can it be true?" she repeated in wonder, her brows knit. It was astonishing, but on the other hand, it would explain why she'd been treated so well by the otherwise rather cold shop owner. If Madame was a Napoleonite, she would honor

Marie's service to their nefarious cause. "But if that is the case, why didn't they make an attempt to recruit me, thinking that I'd be willing to follow in Marie's footsteps?"

He cocked his head. "No such attempt was made?"

"None—never a mention of politics." She paused, thinking this over. "Which is rather strange, when you think of it—given Napoleon's abdication, and the Congress of Vienna. Everyone else was talking of it."

Idly flicking the reins, he offered, "It is my belief they wish to keep you close for some reason; their purpose is not yet clear to me."

"A misunderstanding?" she prompted, reminded that this was his theory.

"Perhaps. It makes little sense; you are ignorant of these events, yet you are at the center of them, for some reason. How did you come to work there—was your sister involved?"

"No—it was after Marie died. Madame came to my door, one day." Epione shifted, and subtly tucked her skirt beneath a knee, where it was rubbing against the horse. "I trimmed hats to supplement the stipend—to supplement my income, and she offered me the position in her shop. It seemed a godsend, at the time." She paused, then admitted, "I suppose I should have been suspicious; she was very generous."

He nodded, as though this confirmed his theory. "Why would Napoleon's people wish to keep you close, in such a way?"

51

"I've no idea," she admitted. "It is difficult for me to believe that this is truly their aim." Reminded, she added, "And if it is, then what was their object tonight, in trying to abduct me? There was no need—I come in to work at the shop every day. It makes little sense."

But he had a ready explanation. "They are aware that your cousin courts you."

Epione thought of Madame's probing questions, and could only agree. "And that makes them nervous?"

"So it appears."

Having come to her own tentative conclusion, she ventured, "My *faux* cousin is a spy for the British, perhaps?"

"I would rather not say; the less you know, the better for you."

She made a soft sound of derision, and then caught herself before she rested her chin on his shoulder. "A bit late for that, I think. And you? Why are you watching me?"

With a twitch of his wrist, he flicked the reins in amusement. "You are indeed naïve, if you think you can trick me into telling you."

She leaned to address the side of his face, and pointed out reasonably, "Unfair; I am not trying to trick you, I am asking you, straight out. You are French, I think."

"I am French," he agreed. "As are you."

"I don't feel very French," she admitted, leaning back to her place behind him. "And I am ashamed of my family."

He placed a sympathetic hand briefly on hers again. "An unfortunate legacy. Throw them off, and find yourself another family."

Yes, she thought a bit sadly; that had been the plan—even though she'd done little to pursue it. She'd just assumed that Sir Lucien would come to see how she did—after an appropriate mourning period—and it would all work out from there. To the good, though, she'd hadn't had much time to bewail the failure of this plan since yesterday, when she'd noticed that a man was watching her through the workshop window.

When they were a few blocks from her building, he indicated they should dismount so as to walk the remainder of the way, which was greatly appreciated by Epione, who was worried about the appearance of impropriety. "Allow me to braid my hair, if you please. I've lost too many pins to keep it up, and that way it won't look quite so bedraggled."

He leaned against Blue Fly, and watched without comment as she raked her fingers through her thick, dark hair, and firmly pulled it into a single braid down her back. She'd lost her bonnet when she took her tumble on the road—a shame, as it was one of her favorites. "I wish I could take off my shoes; I'm nursing a blister."

"Take them off," he suggested. "It is dark, and your skirts will hide your feet."

"I cannot spare the stockings," she confessed. "Stockings are very dear."

53

He moved to place his hands at her waist. "Then we will put you on the horse, and if anyone asks, we will say you have twisted your ankle."

She looked up at him, meeting his eyes as the shadows from the street lanterns flickered across the planes of his face. Oh, she thought; oh—he is breathtaking, and very mysterious, which only makes him all the more appealing. I must remember I know nothing about him, and keep my wits about me.

He lifted her rather easily whilst she braced her hands against his shoulders, and then he guided her foot into the stirrup since she wasn't certain what to do, having never been on a horse before this night.

"Hold on, here." He guided her hand to the pommel, then lifted his face to hers, tilting his head back so he could see her from beneath the brim of his hat. "Ready? We will go slowly."

"I am, thank you."

He turned, and led the horse along the street for the remaining distance. She held on and watched him as he walked, having the impression that he was preoccupied, for some reason—although a pensive state of mind was to be expected, considering the grave matters they'd discussed. She wondered if he was a spy, like Tremaine—although he certainly wasn't trying to feed her a false tale; instead, he wasn't telling her anything at all. And his aim in coming to her aid was still not clear.

She thought about it, as she watched him, and decided that he reminded her—he rather reminded her of the young men who had gathered in the *salons* when she was growing up, to drink and play cards and draw their swords at the slightest provocation; confident young *aristos* who adopted a negligent air, and openly mocked their bitter elders. She would not be at all surprised to discover that he was one of them, although apparently it was not something he wished to discuss.

He halted the horse before her building, and then came around to lift her down. "Stay late at work tomorrow, if you would; I will come after the woman has gone."

She met his eyes in amusement, as he set her on her feet. "Why do you need me? You are a picker-of-locks *par excellence*."

"I would like to ask you questions about how the work is done."

She nodded, aware that this raised the alarming possibility that the milliner's shop was a false front, serving an ulterior purpose—truly, an astonishing thought. "Until tomorrow then. You should go; if you come to my door, my neighbors will gossip."

But this was the wrong thing to say to him, and he grinned and swung her up easily into his arms. "You forget, *ma belle*, that you are injured."

She laughed, as he carried her up the steps. "I suppose it is a lost cause, anyway. I've no hat, and no ready explanation for my state of disrepair."

"Then tell them nothing, and let them draw their own conclusions."

"As you do," she teased.

"As I do." He set her on the threshold, and then bent to insert a small tool into the lock, which opened the door with a quiet click.

Epione was all admiration. "How does it work? It seems a very useful thing."

Willingly, he handed it to her, and then held his hand upon hers, as he indicated how she should manipulate the tool, which was rather like a darning needle. He bent beside her as he gave instruction, his face very close to hers. "You must pull the tumblers down—can you feel? It takes a bit of practice."

She was so intent on the task that she didn't notice her landlady had approached from the other side of the door, and now opened it with some astonishment. "Mademoiselle?"

With a guilty start, Epione straightened up. "Oh—Madame Reyne. Allow me to introduce—" belatedly, she realized she didn't know her companion's name.

She needn't have worried, however, as he took the woman's hand and smiled his engaging smile. "I came to Mademoiselle's aid when she fell, and injured her ankle." Tilting his head, he pressed the hand between both of his. "Once I see her inside, I will leave her to your capable care, Madame."

The plump, middle-aged woman was no match for the full force of charm levied upon her, and stared up into his face whilst Epione arched a brow at him from behind the woman's back.

"Oh—oh I see; well, then—as long as Mademoiselle is unharmed."

"Perhaps you would be so kind as to make tea, Madame."

"Oh—oh of course; it will take but a moment." Tearing her gaze away, the woman retreated down the hallway with palpable reluctance.

Once they were upstairs in her rooms, the gentleman's manner reverted to the one with which Epione was familiar, and she watched in bemusement as he took a careful look around her rooms. She noted in a wry tone, "That is a powerful gift you have; it is almost as useful as your lock-picking tool."

He didn't pretend to misunderstand, and replied in a mild tone, "It does open doors."

She hoped he wasn't making an improper reference to his dealings with the fair sex, and was suddenly aware that she was entertaining a strange and unnamed man in her rooms. She needn't have worried, however; he made to leave, after giving careful instruction to lock the door, and go nowhere other than the shop tomorrow. "We will have someone watching you, but it is best to be careful."

Epione teased him, "Ah—I learn that there is a 'we'. I think you have given something away— you must be tired."

With his flashing smile, he said only, "*Au revoir,* Mademoiselle," and bowed his way out the door.

Chapter 7

"I will go out for a bit, Epione; you must mind the desk, if any customers come in."

"Yes, Madame." Epione looked up from her workbench, where she was bent over the Del Valle hat—which was not getting the undivided attention it deserved, unfortunately—and felt as though she were a player in a farce, although it wasn't a very amusing farce. The handsome man had been correct; when she'd arrived at work that morning, nervously turning over plausible tales in her mind, Madame had gone white about the lips and had made no inquiries whatsoever. Then, after walking around the shop with barely-concealed agitation for a half-hour, the proprietress decided to leave on an undisclosed errand. This behavior only seemed to verify her role in these mysterious events, and therefore Epione could muster no sympathy as she watched Madame hurry down the street; the wretched woman deserved the full measure of whatever anxiety she was experiencing.

Distracted, Epione pricked a finger and put it to her mouth, annoyed that Madame knew more about whatever was going forward than she did. It was no simple thing for Epione to sit at her worktable and behave as though she were not installed in a nest of traitors for purposes which were as yet unclear—*tiens*, she did not have the aptitude for this.

Out of habit, her eyes strayed once again to the doorway across the way, even though he said he'd come after the shop closed. With a sigh, she absently fingered the nearly-completed hat and listened to the clock tick in the corner, thinking over the events of the night before. I need to be firm with him tonight, she resolved, and discover who he is, and what-is-what; it does seem that his recalcitrant attitude is softening, just a little bit.

The bell rang as two matrons—regular customers—entered the shop, and Epione willingly relinquished her neglected project to greet them, and explain that Madame was currently away from the premises.

The first woman warned, "She must be careful, if she is out walking alone. They haven't caught the murderer and the latest victim was a woman—did you hear?"

"I did—it is deplorable." Epione decided she needed more information, herself; Madame wasn't very interested in discussing the murders, but no doubt these two would be all too happy to give her details—the murders were the latest *on dit,* as well they should be. "I confess I know very little of the matter—who were the other victims?"

Pleased to be the bearer of important gossip, the first woman counted off on her fingers while the other lifted a hat from its stand. "The latest was an instructress from *l'Academie.* Before that, a man in Fitzrovia who had been a retired valet to Comte—who was it?"

"Redessite," the other supplied, as she exchanged one hat for another. "The Comte himself died some years ago."

"Yes. And before that, a stabler from Portman Square, and the very first one—that they know of—was the Baron Dey."

Epione nodded, and agreed that it all seemed entirely random and unfathomable. She was aware that the Baron had been murdered; he was fairly well-known in her own circle—indeed, he'd been an occasional visitor at her mother's house. An outspoken loyalist, if she remembered correctly, and with his death, many assumed that the Napoleonites had taken a measure of revenge; passions still ran high between the competing sides, even with Napoleon now defeated. "Were all the victims loyalists?" It occurred to her that this might be a common thread.

The first matron was quick to answer, as she moved to join her companion at the display rack. "No—and that is what makes it so perplexing. At first, a political connection was assumed, but the latest—the instructress—was raised in Quebec, and had no connection to France at all."

Epione thought this over, as she lifted a capote hat from the woman's hands and invited her to sit before the gilded mirror. "How can the authorities be certain the murders *are* connected, then?"

"They were lured out-of-doors, and then their throats were cut," the woman recited with gruesome relish. "There was no robbery, so it appeared the aim was solely to kill them." As Epione pinned the handsome creation on her curls, the woman shifted her gaze from the hat to meet Epione's in the gilt mirror. "You must have a care, Mademoiselle; it appears the killer is not averse to taking a female victim." This said with the slight, superior tone of one who went home to hearth and husband.

"I will, and I thank you for your concern." Epione was to have a surfeit of warnings, it seemed, and from a variety of sources. I cannot imagine I am supposed to continue my work here, and pretend ignorance, she thought in exasperation—surely no one can expect it of me. For a moment, she entertained an impulse to flee this place, but had little doubt that the handsome man would track her down and drag her back to her post.

The bell rang again, and Epione glanced up in surprise to see Tremaine, taking off his hat and smiling at her from the entryway. "Good morning, Miss d'Amberre."

61

"Why, Mr. Tremaine—how nice to see you again." Epione felt her color rise, as the two other women exchanged amused, knowing glances. Quickly, Epione excused herself and approached him, so that their conversation would not be overhead.

He bent his head toward hers, his smile warm and his manner proprietary. "I thought we could take another walk, when you have a few moments to spare. Perhaps we could have a pastry—there is an excellent shop around the corner."

"I am afraid Madame is away on an errand, and I do not know when she will return." Epione turned to smile at the two women, who were openly observing them and whispering behind their hands. "You are going to get me in trouble," she whispered to him in an exasperated undertone. "And I do not use my old name."

"Ladies," Tremaine announced with a grin, and tossed his hat on the purchase desk. "Do you require a male opinion?"

The next half-hour was spent with Tremaine lounging against the wall, and rendering a thoughtful critique on nearly every hat in the store, while the two women laughed, preened and discarded those he deemed too 'fubsy'. In the end, Tremaine helped the women load up a dozen boxes, and then insisted that he'd earned an hour's break with Epione.

"That was masterful," Epione laughed, as she locked the shop door behind them, and turned the sign around. "And you have very good taste."

"Not at all," he disclaimed and offered his arm. "I could see which ones found favor, and allowed them to follow their own inclinations."

Smiling in agreement, she reminded herself that it was his business to be observant, and that she must be very circumspect in her dealings with him. "You'd best be careful, or Madame will hire you to come to the store and do the same, every day."

"I'd rather be persuading you."

She sighed with a small smile, and hoisted her parasol over her head. "We are back to the subject at hand, I see. I'd hoped you would ply me with pastries, first."

He shrugged his shoulders, apologetic. "I am sorry for it, but the sooner it is settled, the better."

"Who owned the land until now?" It occurred to her that this may offer a clue as to why it was so desperately sought by the various unnamed factions.

Shaking his head slightly, he steered her across the busy street. "I am not certain—I believe Napoleon bestowed the estate on a favorite, and now that he has been deposed, the true heirs are being traced. I imagine it is the same for many estates in France—it would be intolerable to allow Napoleon's supporters to retain them."

As usual, Epione did not know whether to believe this explanation, but kept her doubts to herself. "Are you certain there will be no challenge by another? What if you married me and it was all for naught?"

But he had no such doubts, and touched the hand tucked into his elbow. "Believe me; I have looked into it very thoroughly. I will inherit—there is literally no one else, on your father's side. We will battle no interlopers, when we make our claim."

She gave him an amused glance from beneath the brim of her chip bonnet. "You *do* paint a fairy tale—except that I'm making hats, rather than sweeping the hearth."

"If Salic law didn't prevent daughters from inheriting, the château would be yours," he pointed out fairly. "And—as I am repeatedly forced to confess—I am no prince. I can buy you a pastry, however."

They entered the confectioner's shop, and had a pleasant, desultory conversation on a variety of subjects whilst they shared a tart. Epione realized that she was very comfortable with him, despite the fact he was apparently some sort of spy, attempting to deceive her for purposes which were unclear. She'd never known her brother, who had been executed along with her father, but decided this must be what it felt like—this sense of easy compatibility. Until the conversation took a turn, that was.

"How many children would you like to have?" He smiled and covered her hand on the table with his own. "Assuming we marry."

"I—I hadn't thought about it," she stammered.

He moved his thumb gently over the back of her hand. "I thought every girl thought about it."

64

"Not this one," she lied. Of course she'd thought about it, but had concluded Sir Lucien probably could not have children, since he hadn't any with Marie. She suddenly remembered the handsome man's warning about seduction, and decided she should make it clear this was not in the offing. "If you don't mind, Mr. Tremaine, I should probably return to my post."

He made no demur, and withdrew his hand, saying easily, "Think about it—no more working at the shop. You can't convince me you'd miss it." He rose, and stood close to her as he escorted her out into the street again, his fingertips on the small of her back.

"I don't mind it—I like to feel useful," she admitted. "But I suppose I could find something else useful to do."

"How did you determine upon making hats, as your livelihood? It is clear you have a talent."

The romancer was now to be replaced with the flatterer—he was very adept at responding to her reactions. "I am self-taught, I suppose. There wasn't much money, when Marie and I were growing up, and it was a simple way to change the look of a well-worn *ensemble*."

"Well then; perhaps the women of Normandy are craving a new designer of hats. Come—it would be an adventure."

They strolled down the pavement, his grin infectious, and she marveled at the variety of inducements he'd presented in such a short time—a family, riches, an escape from drudgery and finally—reading her very shrewdly—an adventure. He was very good at this spying business, and she wondered why the foreign girl was so reluctant to have him.

"We are well-suited," he pronounced. "Allow me to escort you to dinner tonight, so that we may further our acquaintance."

Aside from the fact she wished to avoid any further abductions, Epione already had a clandestine meeting on her schedule, and so she politely declined. "I truly need to get my work done; your visit—as welcome as it was—has set me back."

"Let's elope, and bid a good riddance to your work." He was only half-teasing.

"If I had to elope with anyone, it would be you," she assured him. "But not just yet."

He smiled into her eyes as they paused at the shop's threshold. "Right, then—I'll try to be patient—although dangling a pretty girl and a lucrative estate in front of me is quite the distraction." He paused for a moment, then continued, "Try not to speak of it with anyone, though—the land, I mean. That fellow—the one who was speaking with you in the alley—he may approach you about it." His intent gaze watched her reaction.

Epione assumed an air of idle curiosity. "Oh? Does he seek to claim it, too?"

"No—he's a sea captain, in a manner of speaking. His name is de Gilles."

This was a revelation to Epione, who had the impression that the handsome man wasn't anything remotely resembling a sea captain. Perhaps Tremaine was mistaken.

He continued, "Just be wary, and let me know if he approaches you." He shot her another quick, assessing glance.

She smiled, teasing him. "You are asking me to repulse a tall, dark, and handsome sea captain?"

Laughing, he took her hand and bowed over it. "I can see I shouldn't have raised the subject. Until tomorrow, Miss d'Amberre."

Nom de Dieu, she thought, repeating the handsome man's oath as she retreated into the shop; heaven only knows what will happen between now and tomorrow.

Chapter 8

That night, Epione heard a tapping on the shop's front door, and stood to draw the bolt, rather surprised that the handsome man would come in through the front instead of the back door. It was dark, and the shop had closed an hour ago, but she'd stayed and waited for her appointed meeting, using the time to catch up on her projects—her recent interactions with gentlemen-who-issued-dire-warnings had put her behind schedule.

To her surprise, however, the face she saw through the glass was that of Madame Del Valle, who was accompanied by a footman. Upon coming through the door, the older woman apologized for the intrusion. "I saw your candle on my way home, Mademoiselle, and I wondered if my hat was ready. I am to attend a breakfast fête tomorrow, and it would be just the thing."

"Of course, Madame; come in, and allow me to box it up for you." Epione withheld her opinion of wearing such a hat in the daytime—one did not gainsay the customers—and went to fetch the silken confection, quietly thanking heaven she'd managed to finish it in time. As she was in the process of carefully tucking the hat into the pink-striped box, however, she was suddenly seized from behind, the footman's hand over her mouth, and his arms pinning both of hers.

Horrified, she began to struggle as he lifted her bodily from the floor, but the woman's face appeared before her, speaking out with palpable concern. "Please do not fear, Mademoiselle; you will not be harmed—my promise on it."

Wild-eyed, Epione began to furiously kick her feet, bringing her heels against her captor's shins as he shifted his hold to avoid the assault.

"Bring her," the woman directed her cohort, and they moved to the back of the shop, the footman holding the struggling Epione as he wrestled her through the narrow hallway.

"Please, Mademoiselle; you must not distress yourself—you will be shown every comfort." Sidling along the wall to avoid the kicks directed her way, Madame Del Valle opened the back door, and peered out into the alley. "Keep her quiet—*allons.*"

But as it turned out, they were not to go, because when they emerged into the back alley, the footman suddenly grunted and loosened his hold, stumbling so that Epione's feet touched the ground and she scrambled away. In the darkness, she saw the handsome man close on the footman, his arm squeezing the man's throat in a chokehold as his victim attempted to throw him off, wrenching violently from side to side and making strangled sounds.

With a smothered exclamation, Madame Del Valle turned to flee up the alley, and Epione's rescuer directed her, "Return to the shop, Mademoiselle—lock the door."

Backing up against the door, Epione frantically fumbled for the knob, and then decided that she shouldn't flee like a craven. "I have my shears," she offered, her hand closing around them as she took a tentative step toward the grappling men.

At the sound of her voice, the footman made a mighty effort to lunge toward her, a hand outstretched, and belatedly aware she shouldn't be near enough to allow him to seize her, Epione took the shears and stabbed at his arm. Unfortunately, the handsome man already had the matter well in hand, and had swung the attacker away from her with the result that the arm she stabbed was that of her protector.

"Oh—oh, I am *so* sorry—"

"No matter." Her rescuer jerked rather savagely on the other's throat, causing the man to stagger. "Inside, please."

With no further prompting, Epione flung open the door and retreated back into the shop, throwing the bolt behind her and then holding her breath, straining to listen. The door was stout, and she heard nothing to indicate what was happening without. After taking a few deep breaths, she tried to decide what was best to do, chastened by the fact she had already made a tactical mistake in her efforts to help. She could run out the front, and attempt to call the Watch, but she had a shrewd suspicion her rescuer would not wish the authorities involved; indeed, the contretemps outside was a silent one, neither side wishing to draw attention.

After a tense few minutes whilst she stood frozen behind the door, a tapping indicated the matter had been resolved. "Allow me in, *s'il vous plait*."

Cautiously, she unlocked the door and he came through, dragging the inert body of the footman as Epione hurried out of the way. "Oh—is he dead?"

"No—bring me something to bind him, if you please."

As there were materials aplenty which were suitable for such a task, Epione considered this. "Alençon lace," she decided. "It is finely-tatted, so it is very strong." She hurried to produce a length of the lace trimming, and in short order, the unconscious man was bound, gagged and laid out on the floor of the back hallway.

Her companion had removed his coat for this procedure, and a streak of blood showed red against his white sleeve. Overcome with remorse, Epione could stay silent no longer. "I am so, so

71

miserably sorry. Do you think you should see a doctor?"

He lifted his gaze to hers, amused. "No."

"Then allow me to clean it, and bind it with a handkerchief." Truly, it seemed the least she could do—she was obviously not good in a fight.

He straightened, and carefully rolled his sleeve up from where it had stuck to his forearm, the gash oozing dark blood. "A stitch or two is needed, I think. Have you needle and thread?"

Fortunately, this was something at which Epione excelled. "Yes—come to the work table, and let me fetch my packet of needles." She had never stitched a person before, but it could not be so very different from taffeta, surely.

He moved to the work table, pulling up a stool. "*Voyons*, we'll need a candle—and spirits; is there anything at hand?"

"Oh—do you need a drink?" She glanced at him with concern, as she moved the candle closer.

His lips curved. "No—to prevent festering."

"I see. I'm afraid I am at a loss, in this type of situation." Madame kept bottles of apricot cordial in the cupboard for those occasions when refreshments were offered, and Epione hurried to fetch one. Watching her, her companion removed his hat, and Epione was acutely aware that yet again, her hair was falling out of its pins and she did not appear to advantage. "Who were they— Napoleon's people?"

He shrugged slightly. "Perhaps, perhaps not."

This answer surprised her, and with a glance of alarm, she set her materials on the table. "Never say there is yet another faction plotting to abduct me—I will be tempted to flee to China."

The candle's flame flickered in his eyes. "Were you familiar with either of them—had you seen them before?"

She pulled a length of thread off the spool and decided she probably shouldn't bite it with her teeth. "Madame Del Valle is a frequent customer— I wouldn't have opened the door, otherwise." She may have no aptitude for this business, but she didn't want him to think her a complete fool.

He arranged a length of cheesecloth on the table and laid his muscular forearm upon it. "They were Napoleon's people, then."

"Who else could it possibly be?" She chose a fine needle, thinking it wouldn't be as painful, and threaded it while he watched without responding. Lowering the needle, she prompted, "Come, I should know who my enemies are—it is only fair."

Apparently he had indeed softened on his recalcitrant attitude, because he explained slowly, "It is not that you have other enemies; instead, the British may tire of waiting for you to accept their suitor."

She stared at him in astonishment. "You believe the *British* authorities may—may seize me?"

He nodded. "Much is at stake, with the Congress in session, and Napoleon rattling his saber." He met her eyes, the expression in his own thoughtful. "There was a recent report—kept very quiet—that you have been awarded your father's estate in Normandy. It appears this is of great interest to the British."

Belatedly recalled to her task, Epione lifted her needle again and leaned over his forearm. "It all makes little sense—what is to be served by giving the land to me? Especially if I am unaware of it?"

He took her hand in his own and raised it, holding it so that the needle was engulfed in the candle flame for a moment. He then poured the cordial on the wound, and blotted it with the tail of the cheesecloth. "Yes; it makes little sense. I thought perhaps the report was a false one, meant to mislead. The British, however, seem to take it very seriously."

She carefully stitched the edges of the wound together with several fine, even stitches, and glanced up at him in sympathy. "Does it hurt?"

"Yes." His eyes were amused upon hers.

"I am *so* very sorry," she repeated, mortified.

A smile played around his lips. "Next time, you will be pleased to do as I ask, yes?"

"I would rather there weren't a next time." She clipped the thread. "Although I suppose I cannot rest easy; it seems unlikely that a mere misunderstanding would inspire two abduction attempts in two days."

He leaned to scrutinize the stitches, and flex his fist. "It is not yet clear. Remember,

Napoleon's people are reacting to the British, who are reacting to the rumor."

"Then it's all a May dance?" Leaning back, she thought it over. "I don't think so; the British would not go to such lengths, based on nothing more than a rumor."

He held her gaze, and leaned forward with quiet intensity. "Yes. It does seem unlikely. So you must think very carefully, and try to guess why the British would act as they do."

The candlelight flickered in the quiet room, and Epione decided that it was past time to address that which needed to be addressed. "You don't care for the British very much, I think."

"That is true," he admitted without a qualm.

Epione continued, "I—I am not certain of your interest in all this, and why I should believe what you tell me. I am not certain that I should trust you more than I should trust the British authorities."

But he shook his head slightly. "It is the British who are trying to mislead you, Epione; not I."

She bent her head to brush at the table top, feeling her color rise at his use of her name and hoping it was not obvious in the dim light.

With his other hand, he splashed more cordial over the wound, the pungent scent of apricots filling the small room. "Did your sister tell you anything before she was killed? Give you anything to hide away for her?"

Shaking her head, Epione lifted the cheesecloth and blotted his arm with it, as he had done. "No—I had no knowledge of what was going

75

forward. I didn't know about it until she died, and then I heard the whispers." She bent her head, remembering. "It was so very terrible."

Apparently he believed her, because he leaned back, and seemed to be deep in thought.

Reminded, she lifted her head and offered, "Tonight Madame Del Valle—or whoever she was—kept saying they were not going to hurt me; she was adamant, and it seemed a little odd, considering what was going forward."

He nodded, his face in the shadows. "No; they do not wish to harm you—you would be an easy target, if that were the case. Instead, they wish something from you."

She met his gaze in all sincerity. "If I knew, I would tell you." She realized that this may not be the best course—being as he'd never really answered her question—but it was the truth.

He nodded. "*En conséquence*, I think it is best that we marry."

Chapter 9

Epione thought that perhaps she hadn't heard him aright. "What?"

He leaned forward, and rested his arms on the table, so that his face was now illuminated by the single candle. "You have no protectors, Epione. And until I discover why you have been sought out, I cannot rest easy."

"Oh." She gazed at him in the quiet darkness, unable to come up with a coherent thought.

He studied her for a moment, and then his lips curved. "There *is* someone else, yes? Shall I challenge him to a swordfight?"

The light words broke the spell, so that she teased him in return, "Any and all suitors have turned up in the past two days, and as each has suspect motivations, it is all a bit deflating."

He cocked his head. "My motivations are pure, but I am not so certain you have been honest with me."

"I think I'd be better off if I weren't so honest," she protested. "Truly."

Her companion's level gaze rested thoughtfully on her face. "If I tell you something, you must not think me vain beyond measure."

"I do not think you are vain," she assured him. "It is more as though you wear yourself like a cloak."

He raised his brows at this. "Like a cloak?"

Fearing she had offered insult, she equivocated, "Perhaps I didn't put that very well—"

He halted her with a hand over hers. "No—I understand what you meant, and it is very apt. But women are rarely indifferent to me; if they are indifferent, usually it is because they have a man."

"I am not indifferent," she protested with all sincerity. "I think you are very attractive—indeed, I thought so right from the first."

He tilted his head in skepticism. "Yet, you have not tried to attach me—even when I offer marriage. Why is this?"

The light mood vanished, and she struggled to explain, mesmerized by his gaze upon hers, and by the alarming realization that she was very much tempted to do whatever he asked. "I cannot marry anyone—after Marie—"

He rejected this excuse with a dismissive gesture. "Yours is an ancient and honorable name, *ma belle*; you could look to the greatest houses in Europe for a husband."

"Perhaps when I was born that was true, but since then, everything has changed," she protested softly. "The Revolution, the war, Marie— surely you must see that."

"Everything has changed," he agreed. "But some things remain." He was silent for a long moment, and she had the brief impression his mind was elsewhere, and the memory not a pleasant one.

After a moment's hesitation, she offered, "And in a way, you are correct. I did admire a man, but I have discovered he is unavailable."

He lifted his gaze to hers, the dark brows raised in incredulity. "He chose another?"

His reaction was a balm to her wounds, and she found that she could smile and shake her head. "No; he did not know of my regard."

"He sounds like a fool, this man."

It was so wonderful to have a champion that she found she could not resist further confession, there in the dark workroom, with the single candle flickering. "You won't tell anyone? It's rather a dreadful secret."

"No." The dark, fathomless eyes were fixed on hers.

"He was my sister's husband. Completely wrong, of course—he was Marie's *husband*, for

heaven's sake. But he was so—so loyal. And true."
She dropped her gaze and drew a soft breath.
"With everything that has happened, it is a rarity,
nowadays, to be true." She paused, and ducked
her head to contemplate her hands. "My family—
my family was horrible, and I think he regretted
marrying Marie almost immediately, but he never
faltered; he was always so courteous to her. He
paid for everything—although my mother and
Marie were contemptuous of him because he was
a baronet, and my father had been a vicomte.
And—and he was unfailingly kind to me. When
Marie was killed, my first thought—" Struggling,
she could not complete the sentence.

"That he was now free. Of course."

She made a wry mouth, and looked up at
him again, finding a warmth of sympathy in his
eyes. "I was so foolish—to yearn after him."

"And now you have discovered that he has
re-married."

She fixed her gaze upon him in dawning
amazement. "Yes, he has re-married—do you
know him, then? Oh, *grand Dieu*, I should not
have said—"

He covered her hand with his own. "No—
no, your secret is safe with me. I know of him, but
we have never met."

She hovered on the edge of asking him
what he knew of Sir Lucien's unexpected
marriage, but he leaned in to lift her chin gently
with his finger. "You must not ask me of him—it
deflates me, to think that I hold no allure; that I
have so much ground to gain."

But she shook her head in amused denial. "You don't need me to tell you that you are alluring, Monsieur—or at least you are when you wish to be. And you cannot be a credible suitor until you tell me who you are."

"I am Alexis de Gilles."

The sea captain, then. Encouraged, because she was finally getting some answers, she persisted, "And who do you represent, in this puzzle?"

He seemed amused by the very idea. "I represent no one but myself. I seek that which is best for *la belle France*."

"I imagine everyone feels the same way," she ventured. "And that is the nub of the problem."

"I must disagree—many seek only that which is best for themselves."

She nodded in concession, as this observation seemed more accurate, in light of recent events in the battered country across the channel that claimed her as a citizen, but to which she was a stranger. "Are you indeed a sea captain?"

A flash of annoyance crossed his face—so; he was not best pleased that she knew of this. "I am many things, and you must not believe what you hear from others; you must trust me, Epione."

She pointed out, "I do—I told you my terrible secret, although I confess it doesn't seem so very terrible, in light of all the other terrible secrets which seem to surround me."

There was a small pause, and when next he spoke, his tone was uncharacteristically grave.

81 .

"I will tell you a secret in turn, Epione. Under my cloak, I am not always good, and true, and honorable. Mainly, I am angry."

The words were palpably sincere, and she searched his eyes in sympathy. "I am sorry for it. You hide it very well."

"I have much experience."

At a loss, she offered, "Is there anything I can do to help?"

He smiled suddenly, the pensive moment gone. "Yes. You can marry me, and as soon as may be. But first you must show me how the hats are constructed."

Although she was aware she should scotch his rather high-handed assumption, there was no question that an awareness resonated between them, unmistakable and compelling. On the other hand, his attitude toward her was one of almost complacent intimacy—as though they were already well past a courtship. Indeed, he'd made no attempt even to kiss her, although there had been plenty of opportunities; it was only one more perplexing piece to the puzzle that was her current existence.

She cast a glance at the hats on display. "Do you think something is being smuggled in the hats?" This actually made some sense, what with the mythical Comtesse having ordered piles of them, willy-nilly.

"I do not know, but it seems a possibility. Could you show me?"

For the next twenty minutes, she explained how the hats were assembled, using some of the samples at hand, whilst he listened and asked questions, carefully inspecting her handiwork. "And you are the only one who assembles them? You know of no one else?"

"No—there are no other milliners, here." She paused. "I once suggested that another girl could be hired to make-up the straw foundations, but Madame said she was not interested in quantity, only quality."

His thoughtful gaze rested on hers for a moment. "Were you known to have made hats, before—when you lived with your family?"

On realizing what he implied, she faltered, "Yes, but surely this—this entire enterprise was not set up just for me? Why, that is *absurd*."

"Perhaps, perhaps not. But there is a reason they wish to keep you close, and whatever it is, it is very important to them."

They sat together in silence for a moment, whilst she considered this alarming suggestion. "Are you concerned that Madame Del Valle will return with reinforcements?" The thought had certainly crossed her own uneasy mind.

He rose, and carefully pulled on his coat over his wounded arm. "No—everyone seeks their own ends, but no one can afford to openly challenge the others."

This seemed to make little sense. "Why is that?"

He donned his hat. "Everyone has different interests, *ma belle*, and allegiances are constantly shifting, depending upon events. Come, I will see you home."

"Do I return to work tomorrow?" There was almost no point in asking; she was reconciled to yet another anxiety-wracked day.

He smiled at her tone, and went to fetch her pelisse off the hook. "You do. I will come to visit you, so that you are not uneasy—and I will make certain we are not caught unready again, as we were this night."

But this plan seemed fraught with peril. "Mr. Tremaine will no doubt visit tomorrow, and the two of you are on shooting terms."

But he would only say enigmatically, "You need not worry; he will not challenge me."

She eyed him doubtfully. "If you say so."

He bent his head close to hers, as he helped her into her pelisse. "You must not listen to Tremaine, Epione—he wears his own cloak."

With a wry smile, she assured him, "Oh—I do not believe him, but we are friends, I think. If he weren't trying so hard to pull the wool over my eyes, I imagine we would laugh about it together."

But this disclosure did not seem to reassure him. "*Quand même*, you mustn't tell him anything that I tell you."

"Isn't that strange?" she replied lightly, rather enjoying this very satisfactory display of jealousy. "That is exactly what he said about you."

But her companion was somber, for a moment, and met her eyes. "You must remember that you are French, Epione. Despite everything."

Matching his serious mood, she nodded, unsure of his meaning, but sensing it was important, for some reason.

He turned and indicated the back door. "Come; we go."

With his assistance, she stepped over the inert body in the hallway. "And what will happen with this one?"

"He will be gone in the morning—you need not be concerned."

But she had one last question. "Who is 'Josiah'?"

He opened the back door, and listened to the silence, for a moment, before taking her hand. "That is what I am trying to find out."

Chapter 10

"I realize the topic may be a painful one, but we must follow all potential leads."

Epione nodded, thinking that at least she should be thankful that the Bow Street investigator was not proposing marriage—although to be fair, it was still early in the conversation. She had come in to work this morning to discover two fresh crises: Madame was nowhere to be seen, and this grey-eyed Bow Street investigator was waiting on the doorstep, seeking an interview with her with respect to the recent string of murders.

They now sat together in her workroom; he'd declined her offer of tea, and Epione was doing a rapid assessment of how much she should reveal and how much she could conceal in good conscience. Her natural inclination to be helpful was tempered by the knowledge that de Gilles did not trust the British, and it seemed he had a fair point, if Tremaine's marriage proposal was all a charade. The investigator's questions had seemed innocuous thus far, focusing on her background and current situation, but now he was venturing into the family treachery, and she mentally girded her loins.

"You are aware your sister was passing information to Napoleon's supporters?"

"Yes, sir."

The grey eyes rested on her for a thoughtful moment. "Are you acquainted with Comte deFabry?"

This was unexpected, but she answered readily, "Yes—I met him a few times, at my sister's residence. I do not know him well."

"What can you tell me of him?"

She raised her brows in surprise. "Do you believe he was involved in—in what my sister was doing?"

But he was to reveal no insights. "If you would tell me your opinion of the man, please."

With a puckered brow, she brought to mind what little she knew of the Comte. "A quiet man; he kept to himself—I don't believe he attended many social events, within the *émigré* community."

"Yet he was familiar with your sister."

The statement held a hint of innuendo, and she stared at him, rather shocked. "They were—they were lovers?"

He watched her reaction, his expression unreadable. "Perhaps; it is not clear. Is it possible?"

A bit taken aback, she stammered, "I—I don't know." It seemed incomprehensible—that a woman lucky enough to be married to Sir Lucien would have an *affaire*. On the other hand, Marie had always craved attention, and when she had a bit too much wine she tended to flirt with whoever was at hand.

Her inquisitor kept his grey-eyed gaze steady upon hers. "I ask because the latest victim—the instructress—is also believed to have had a *liaison* with the Comte."

Astonished, she exclaimed, "Then you think the Comte deFabry is the murderer—can it be possible that he killed Marie?"

But her companion cautioned, "You must not leap to conclusions, Miss; we are only testing out possible connections between the victims. Do you happen to know of the Comte's political views?"

Slowly, Epione shook her head. "I've no idea." She was made uneasy by the question, though; de Gilles had intimated that the murders were connected to the various plots which were going forward with respect to the French succession, and it appeared that this investigator was in agreement with him. "I am sorry; I wish I could be more helpful."

He paused for a moment, and flipped over a page in his occurrence book. "I understand you injured yourself the other night, and that a gentleman offered you his assistance."

A small alarm went off in Epione's head; it didn't seem that her interactions with de Gilles should have anything to do with the murder investigation—unless de Gilles was a suspect, and that seemed unlikely, as he'd plenty of opportunities to murder her. Which meant—which meant that perhaps the man seated before her was yet another who was not at all what he seemed. To stall for time, she smiled. "You have been speaking with Madame Reyne, my landlady. She was smitten with the gentleman, I think."

"Can you tell me the gentleman's name?"

"He did not reveal his name to me." This was not exactly an untruth; at that time he hadn't, and as de Gilles had been kind enough to warn her about the illicit search of her rooms—perhaps conducted by this so-called investigator, himself—the courtesy should be returned. "I believe he was an *émigré*—I know he was French. He was very kind, and took a look around my rooms to make certain all was well, before he left." She added with an innocent air, "He took me up on his horse, which made me a bit nervous—I haven't much experience with horses."

"Did he mention where he stayed, or how long he would be in town?"

"He did not, I'm afraid. Is he a suspect?" She allowed a hint of skepticism to creep into her tone.

But her companion was not about to be put on the defensive, and cocked his head in a gesture of admonishment. "You may wish to be a bit more cautious in the future, if you don't mind my saying so, Miss."

"Yes—I suppose that is true." This advice was rich, coming from the illicit-searcher-of-rooms.

Bending his head, her questioner studied his notes for a moment. "You have worked at this shop for—six months, I believe."

"Yes sir."

He raised his head to give her a look of warm approval. "Quite a plum position. And you are self-taught, I believe."

There was the slightest pause. "Yes, sir, that is true." Here was confirmation beyond all doubt; this faux-investigator must have consulted with Tremaine before speaking with her. That she was self-taught was a little-known fact, as she'd allowed Madame to believe she'd trained as an apprentice in another shop. She also noted that this man used the same tactics as Tremaine—he hadn't made any headway by being firm with her, and so now he softened his approach with flattery. I am heartily tired of trying to guess what-is-what, she thought with a sudden burst of indignation, and I'm heartily sick of being surrounded by spies. She lifted her chin. "I don't suppose you can tell me what this is all about—something having to do with the pretenders to the French throne, I believe."

In the sudden silence, the grey eyes rested on hers for a long, expressionless moment. "We are merely gathering as much information as we can, Miss."

She made an impatient gesture. "Then at least tell me whether you think I am in danger." May as well solicit his opinion on this burning topic; de Gilles didn't seem to think that she was in danger, as much as she was needed for some unspecified something.

Thoughtfully, the investigator contemplated his notebook for a moment. "If there is an opportunity for you to leave the country for a time, I do not think it a bad idea."

Unable to help it, she laughed, and shook her head. "And marry Mr. Tremaine."

He frowned in puzzlement. "Miss?"

Leaning forward, she asked with all sincerity, "Can you not break your role, only for a moment? How I wish you could tell me, straight out, what is at play here."

He regarded her for a moment, impassively. "I dare not take the chance."

She could see the wisdom in this—her family did not have a good record, after all. "No, I suppose not." She leaned back again, grateful for even this small glimpse of honesty.

To the good, he'd apparently decided that he could drop his pose, and no longer take a roundabout route. "Have you noticed anything out of the ordinary, lately, at the shop? Any unusual customers?"

Almost with relief, she realized she could give him some information that might be useful without betraying de Gilles. "Yes—there was something strange that happened the other day. The Comtesse Toray is one of our best customers, but now I am not certain the woman actually exists."

His gaze was sharp upon hers. "Tell me."

91

Epione gave him an edited version of her experiences with the dressing maid, leaving out such minor details as the abduction attempt, and a rather enjoyable horse ride home—a ride which had—apparently—inspired tender feelings in her escort; enough to mention marriage as though it were already a foregone conclusion. Indeed, she'd had been unable to sleep last night, thinking about this unlooked-for turn of events. With an effort, she brought her wandering thoughts back to the so-called investigator. "The maid was rather unpleasant. She insinuated that she knew my mother, and she made a strange remark—that her mistress needed a hat to wear to a Coronation."

"Did she indeed?" This said rather grimly.

Epione ventured, "What Coronation would she mean? I didn't know that England's poor King—"

But he interrupted her in a brusque tone. "Where is this woman, now?"

"I don't know," Epione replied, skirting the truth. "She hasn't returned."

"Describe her, if you would."

Epione complied, as best she could, and concluded, "She is rather a caricature of an *aristo*'s lady's maid."

"With a mole above her eyebrow." He touched a finger to his own, indicating.

Epione decided she truly shouldn't be surprised. "Yes."

His brows drawn together, her companion thought this over. "What sort of hats does the Comtesse buy?"

"All variety—it was rather strange, but I truly don't believe anything was being smuggled in the hats. I am the only milliner, and I box them up myself." She paused, and added carefully, "You may wish to ask Madame—the shop owner—what she knows about this; I would not be at all surprised if she knows a great deal." She made bold enough to meet his eye in a significant manner.

It seemed the investigator was willing indulge her in exploring this topic, and leaned back for a moment. "What do you know of Madame?"

Epione clasped her hands in her lap, and admitted, "Very little, actually; she was not one who confided. I do know she was very preoccupied yesterday, and that she has never before been absent from the shop, at opening."

"That is indeed very troubling," he agreed in a neutral voice, his expression impassive.

There was something about his tone that made her stare at him, and she faltered, "Have you—have you any information about what has happened to her?"

"All investigations are ongoing." He closed his notebook with a small snap. "Thank you, Miss; you've been most helpful."

He rose to leave, and so Epione was compelled to rise with him, but the shocking implication that Madame had been the murderer's latest victim was enough to make her try to penetrate the mask he wore. "Please, sir; I cannot help but feel that I am the bait, in some sort of trap."

After gazing out the window for a moment, he met her eyes. "Unfortunately, I know less than I'd like. Mr. Tremaine, however, stands prepared to see to your safety."

Nonplussed, she ventured, "It seems such a drastic course."

"These are drastic times, I'm afraid." He crossed to the door, and paused for a moment. "If you will allow me to repeat myself, you are entirely too trusting, Miss d'Amberre."

She wasn't certain whether this was a veiled reference to de Gilles, but nonetheless answered in a tart tone uncharacteristic for her. "It is true that I cannot hold a candle to all the deceivers who surround me."

"Touché," he conceded with a bow, and left without another word.

Chapter 11

After the investigator had left, Epione leaned on her hands against the door for a moment and thought about what she had learned, and what she still needed to know. It seemed clear that Tremaine and the grey-eyed investigator were allied together, working for the British to fight the scheming Napoleonites. Indeed, perhaps the investigator had killed her sister himself—she thought she discerned a small but noticeable reaction, when she'd asked if the Comte had killed Marie, and he'd never answered the question.

That he was Tremaine's superior seemed evident; he had an air of authority about him. A spymaster, then; she hoped she'd said nothing to bring down further trouble—it was rather tiresome, to feel one had to weigh everything one said—and it was true she did not have the aptitude for this business, even though she was half-inclined to marry into it.

She walked over to the bow window, and, after a moment's hesitation, turned the sign over to indicate the shop was now open. The Epione from three days ago would have found the idea of marrying de Gilles absurd, but the new Epione— who was at the center of some mysterious controversy—was grateful for an ally. Besides, there was something about his understated manner that struck a responsive chord within her own breast; they were similar creatures, despite everything.

I like him very much, she thought, and I believe he likes me very much, too. And so perhaps—in light of the exigent circumstances—I should throw caution to the winds. In any event, it certainly doesn't seem to occur to him that I might refuse.

The clouds were threatening rain, and Epione watched the street for a few moments as the cart sellers and trades people hurried to their posts. The weather was not helping to alleviate her sense of foreboding, particularly now that she'd the strong sense Madame may have been added to the tally of murder victims.

Epione paused for a moment, as she was suddenly struck by the strangeness of this. Madame was a Napoleonite, and obviously had been involved in the dressing maid's abduction plot. It seemed unlikely that the murderer would want to kill her, if the murders where connected to

whatever Napoleonic plot was going forward—
Madame was on their side, after all.

It made no sense, and she wished de
Gilles would come soon, so that she could consult
with him on this development. Last night, when
they'd parted at her doorstep, she'd dawdled for a
few minutes, wondering if he would try to kiss her.
He didn't, and she had the lowering conviction that
he knew exactly what she was about, and was
amused, as he tipped his hat and left. Not much of
a suitor, certainly, despite the fact that he threw
out the subject of marriage in such a negligent
manner.

Out of the corner of her eye, she caught a
movement in the tailor's window, and saw that he
was preparing for opening. If he saw himself in
the role of a suitor, he'd best look lively—he could
not be pleased to observe someone like Tremaine
hanging about, let alone what he would think if he
saw de Gilles come to the door, in all his glory.

I am beset by a surplus of handsome
suitors, she thought in bemusement. Matters have
taken quite a turn, since last week—I should be
grateful, I suppose, and I would be, if only
someone could assure me that I am not slated to
be murdered.

With a sigh, she retreated to her workroom,
wondering if it was even worth the effort to fill
orders for clients who may or may not exist—not to
mention an employer who may no longer walk the
earth.

Almost immediately, the bell rang, and two
young women—new customers—entered and

greeted her, chatting happily with each other as they began trying on bonnets. After inquiry, they admitted to having no particular style in mind, and so Epione entertained them as best she could, judging it too early to bring out the apricot cordial—although she wouldn't have minded a fortifying glass, herself.

The bell rang, yet again—*tiens*, it was busy, for such an early hour—and Epione turned to greet a gentleman of about forty years, rather tall and lean, with a neatly trimmed goatee; his hair pulled back into a queue in the old fashion, and an impressive pearl pin resting in the folds of his cravat. Removing his hat, he bowed to Epione. "I look to purchase a gift for my sweetheart, Mademoiselle."

"Of course, sir; do you seek a formal, or a day hat?" In the sudden silence, Epione became aware that the two women behind her had ceased all conversation, and glancing their way, she saw that they were observing the newcomer like two hounds on the point. Oh, thought Epione in surprise; oh—I believe we have some sort of standoff, here.

"A formal hat, I think." The gentleman's gaze rested upon the women with a touch of amusement. "Something expensive, as I am in need of forgiveness."

Epione stepped to the display, and tried to maintain her poise even though the tension was thick in the room. "I can show you several ready-made, or if you have sufficient time, I can make one up to your specifications. Allow me to show you, Mr.—"

"Monsieur Darton," he offered with a small bow. He then stepped aside, so that she could fetch a hat from the window display, but she noted that he didn't turn his back to the other two, who'd resumed chatting, but were trying on the same hats they had previously discarded.

Epione removed a silken prie-cap from its stand, and the gentleman leaned back slightly, stroking his beard. "How does it go? Is this the front, or the back?"

"If you'd like, I can model it," Epione offered. This was often done for clueless husbands, and Madame would point out it was also a sign that a more expensive hat should be immediately put forth.

But the gentleman was not to be so manipulated, it seemed, and shook his head with regret. "*Hélas*, my sweetheart is blonde, and I am not certain I have such an imagination." His gaze shifted to the women—who'd gone silent once again—and he indicated the one who was blonde. "Perhaps if you would be so kind, Madame?"

There was a tense moment, whilst Epione could not help but admire his brazenness, and it seemed as though the blonde woman felt the same way. With a small shrug and a smile, she acquiesced, "By all means, sir."

As Epione carefully pinned the silken confection on the other's head, she noted that the woman's gaze met the gentleman's in the mirror, instead of her own. "*Très chic,*" the woman

99

pronounced in an admiring tone. "Is your sweetheart an Englishwoman?"

"From Algiers, instead," the gentleman replied softly, with a gleam.

At this, the woman's eyes narrowed in anger, and Epione hurriedly interrupted, "A jeweled pin could be placed at the base of the feather, just here—"

But the gentleman demurred, "I prefer pearls, Mademoiselle." His mocking gaze slid to the woman who was modeling the hat.

Epione said nothing, as it was evident there was an unspoken conversation going forward, and not a friendly one—not to mention one generally didn't wear pearls on a formal hat. Fortunately, she was spared having to participate any further in this rather tense sale—truly, she should never have turned the "open" sign over—because the bell rang, and with unmixed relief, she turned to greet the next customer.

This turned out to be a woman about her own age, dark-haired and attractive, and laboring under what appeared to be a strong emotion as she reviewed the other persons assembled with open disapproval. "*Peste.* This is a hat shop *très macabre.*"

"May I help you?" offered Epione, without any real conviction. Another one, she thought with resignation; and it is starting to rain, in keeping with this miserable day.

The woman's gaze rested upon her with unmitigated dismay. "*You* are Mademoiselle d'Amberre?"

"Well—yes; although I am known by another name, now—"

"You are *très jolie*," the other accused, her dark eyes flashing. "No one told me this."

This was unexpected, and Epione wondered, for a moment, if the girl's mental faculties were disordered. "May I offer cordial?" A distraction seemed needful, no matter the early hour.

"What sort of cordial?" asked Darton with interest.

But the new visitor was not to be distracted, and said to the gentleman, "You will *not* interfere."

In response, he bowed low, sweeping his hat before him with a quizzical look. "*Pardon*, Mademoiselle; are we acquainted?"

"No," the other answered shortly, and turned a shoulder to him. "I have private business with Mademoiselle d'Amberre."

The light dawned, and Epione realized why she was the object of the girl's hostility. This must be Tremaine's foreign girl—although the girl seemed French, which meant that Tremaine was *not* French, which actually came as no surprise whatsoever. "I imagine you would like to speak with Mr. Tremaine. If you would like to wait, he is expected to make a visit this morning." Let Tremaine sort through the various personnel who were present; Epione had decided she was having a glass of cordial.

In speculation, the girl's narrowed eyes rested upon the two women, who were unabashedly listening to the conversation. "My

101

Robert will come here? *Eh bien*, I will wait for him."
This said with an air of stoicism, and she began to
wander around the salon, fingering the various
wares.

Epione fetched the refreshments, half-
expecting a brawl to break out, but then
remembered what de Gilles had said—the various
factions could not antagonize each other in the
event their allegiances were suddenly required to
shift. That the two women were aligned with the
British seemed apparent; what was not apparent
was whom Monsieur Darton served—or why the
Englishwomen were so wary of him.

Lifting her wrist and nodding, Epione
politely returned Darton's elegant toast, and then
sipped on her cordial, trying not to think about the
murders, or how no one here had asked where the
shop's proprietor was. The two women no longer
made a pretense of hat-shopping, but instead held
their position, one watching out the window and
one warily watching the other two visitors.

Darton leaned negligently against the door
jamb of the workroom, but Epione noted he kept a
hand on his hip, so that his coat was brushed
back from the pistol at his side. The dark-haired,
foreign girl seemed the least concerned, and was
frowning into the mirror as she held a spray of
artificial cherries to the side of her own hat to
gauge the effect. The clock ticked, the rain
pattered on the window, and no one spoke. No
one wants to leave, thought Epione in
exasperation—save me, of course.

Into the silence, the ringing of the bell signaled yet another visitor, and Epione glanced over the rim of her glass to behold Tremaine, crossing the threshold and casting a wary eye at Darton, who bowed his head in mock-acknowledgment.

The dark-haired woman sprang to her feet. "Robert," she exclaimed in agitation. "*J'insiste*—I insist that I speak with you."

"Lisabetta," Tremaine shook out his umbrella in surprise. "What the devil are *you* doing here?"

"You must not marry this—this *banal* shop girl."

"I am not *banal*," retorted Epione, much affronted.

"Not at all," offered Darton, very gallantly. "*En effet*, I would marry her myself."

The Frenchwoman whirled upon him in a fury. "*You* will mind your own business."

"As you say," the other conceded in a meek tone, his laughing glance meeting Epione's.

Lisabetta turned upon Tremaine once again, her pretty mouth pressed into a thin line. "I will hear your explanation, Robert."

Epione listened for his reply with interest, to see how staunchly he would follow the grey-eyed man's orders when confronted with his agitated sweetheart.

But Tremaine was not about to allow himself to be so trapped. "Lisabetta—you must not embarrass Miss—" here he paused for a moment, "Miss Valois."

103

"Everyone already knows," Epione conceded. "It may as well be d'Amberre."

Lisabetta stamped a foot. "*Fah*—it doesn't matter what her name is, you must not marry her."

But an unexpected intervention was to come from Darton, who spread his hands in a Gallic gesture. "Come, Mademoiselle; if Mr. Tremaine marries Mademoiselle d'Amberre, he will be a rich man, and live an easy life. If you care for him, you must be generous."

To no one's surprise, this remark only infuriated the girl, who whirled on him, her face flushed. Tremaine placed a warning hand on her arm, and suggested, "Lisabetta, Miss d'Amberre— shall we continue this conversation in private?" With a level glance at Darton, Tremaine indicated that they should move past the other man, and into the workroom.

With a flounce of her skirts, Lisabetta turned on her heel and obeyed. Epione, who was feeling a bit *de trop*, asked Tremaine in a low tone, "Wouldn't you rather speak with her alone?"

"Lord, no," he replied fervently, and took her elbow.

Chapter 12

By the time they'd assembled in the workroom, Lisabetta had apparently taken control of her temper and addressed Epione with constrained contrition. "I am sorry I called you *banal.* I met your sister, once—she was *très courageuse."*

But this was the wrong thing to say to Epione, who lost her own temper, and retorted angrily, "She was a traitoress, and I would rather speak English."

This, in turn, infuriated Lisabetta. "Yes— English because of Robert. It does not matter; he will not marry you."

Stung, Epione countered, "He will marry me, and he will be glad to do so."

Tremaine held up his hands. "Ladies, please."

After coming to the conclusion that no good came of drinking cordial in the morning,

105

Epione held a hand to her forehead. "I beg your pardon—I am out of sorts."

"Then let's go for a walk, to clear your head," Tremaine suggested with a smile, which invoked a sound of extreme dismay from Lisabetta.

Epione lowered her hand, and eyed him in amused exasperation. "I cannot go for a walk, Mr. Tremaine. I am getting no work done, Madame is missing, and I expect a pitched battle to erupt at any moment." Not to mention it was steadily raining—the man must be desperate to get her away from the others.

But this observation did not seem to faze him. "The other two ladies will watch the shop in your absence—and we won't be gone long, I promise."

That the two women were allied with Tremaine came as no surprise, but Epione warned, "There is nothing here—there is no point in making a search."

Tremaine grinned at this plain speaking, and shrugged. "Then there can be no objection to a refreshing walk."

Darton poked his head into the doorway to the workroom, as he pulled on his gloves. "Mademoiselle, I thank you for your kind assistance."

"At the very least, you should purchase a hat, Monsieur." Epione pretended amused vexation, although in truth, she was secretly grateful that matters appeared to be de-escalating.

"Next time," the gentleman assured her with his bold smile. He nodded to Lisabetta as he donned his hat. "Mademoiselle."

The girl turned an indifferent shoulder to him, which invoked another impudent gleam toward Epione, as the visitor left through the door.

"Who is he?" asked Epione, watching him walk away through the window. That Darton had some role to play in these matters was obvious—the others all knew him—but he didn't seem to be cut from the same cloth, and apparently had no qualms about relinquishing the field to the others.

"He is *un bâtard*," pronounced Lisabetta, who scowled as she watched him walk down the street.

Tremaine turned to the young Frenchwoman, and placed a conciliatory hand on her arm. "I must speak with Miss d'Amberre, Lisabetta, but I will meet up with you later; my promise on it."

Apparently recognizing that a dignified retreat was the best that could be hoped for, Lisabetta confiscated Tremaine's umbrella and—with a final glance of feminine warning at Epione—departed out the front door, her humiliated head held high.

Interesting, thought Epione; she did not ask where she was to meet Tremaine, and he did not feel the need to inform her.

Her wary interest piqued—honestly, one needed a programme, to keep track of it all—Epione decided to venture, "If Lisabetta is working for the enemy, Mr. Tremaine, that would appear to be a significant obstacle in your path to happiness."

"And not the only one; it is clear you are very much on her mind." He seemed rather amused, as he glanced out the window.

"She seems a bit vexing." This was, of course, a politic understatement because Epione had long ago noted that men seemed to be drawn to vexing women for reasons which were unfathomable.

The smile still played around his mouth, as Tremaine faced her again. "You did not see her at her best. But let me in turn question your loyalty to Captain de Gilles."

This was said in a neutral tone, but she rushed to defend herself. "I didn't know who he was when you asked me—and he didn't strike me as a sea captain."

He allowed this rather lame explanation to pass. "What is his interest?"

She considered this, seriously, as the now-sporadic rain pattered on the window, and the two women spoke in low voices in the other room. "I think he doesn't want you to have whatever it is you want."

But Tremaine met her gaze with all sincerity. "I want to keep you safe—and that's what I'd like to speak with you about. Come, let's take our walk."

It seemed evident he had spoken to his spymaster; his former role as an earnest suitor had disappeared, to be replaced by what appeared to be the role of a trusted friend. Either way, Epione was not to be taken-in; she had been abducted too many times not to be wary of everyone—with one exception, apparently. "Why is everyone watching me, and what does it have to do with the pretenders to the French throne?"

He weighed what to say for a moment. "Some information has surfaced—although it was kept very quiet—"

"The land," Epione interrupted a bit impatiently—maddening, that no one ever spoke forthrightly. "*Desclaires* was given to me, not to you."

After a small pause, he lowered his chin and met her eyes. "You are very well informed."

"But not by you." Epione refused to be cowed. "What do you know of this?"

"What do *you* know of this?" he countered, and crossed his arms.

She shook her head, exasperated. "In truth, I have no idea what is happening, nor why."

He searched her eyes, a grave expression in his own. "No—and neither does anyone else, apparently, so that all we can do is watch, and react." There was a small pause. "Which one of the pretenders does de Gilles support?"

This question seemed rather a non sequitur, and she glanced up at him in surprise. "He has not said; why?"

"I am curious, is all. He obviously has an interest."

As this seemed a good opportunity to do some probing about her erstwhile suitor, she did not hesitate to take it. "Who is he, exactly?"

"He is—he's rather a rogue player; well-connected, politically." Tremaine chose his words carefully, as he gazed out toward the street. The rain had started up again in earnest, and it was gusting against the window. "Look, let me be frank; he is undoubtedly manipulating you—he's a good-looking devil—and his own role in these matters is not clear. You must not allow him to turn your head."

At this exhortation, she couldn't help but smile. "It would be amusing, if it weren't so alarming; he gave me the exact same advice about you."

"Don't heed him."

Epione felt she should give him fair warning. "Promise you will be civil; I expect him at any minute, and I'd rather you didn't shoot each other."

But Tremaine only shrugged a shoulder. "It is unlikely that he will make an appearance any time soon; he does not like to go about by daylight."

The words held a nuance she could not quite like, and so she was compelled to observe, "You know something to his detriment, it seems."

Her companion rested his gaze on the worktable for a moment, obviously debating, and then met her eyes and said bluntly, "I'd rather not give you the particulars, but you must trust me on this. He plies a questionable trade, and there is absolutely no chance he means right by you. Be sure to hold him at arm's length—he may seek to compromise you."

A bit taken aback, she considered this rather dire warning in the context of her dealings with de Gilles, who had been granted more than one opportunity to compromise her, and had consistently refrained—in fact, had behaved rather chivalrously, instead. She decided to turn the subject from this paradox to the more urgent matters at hand. "He seems to think there may have been some sort of misunderstanding—about the transfer of the land to me. Do you know what he meant?"

But he shook his head slightly, a frown between his eyes. "No, the land is indeed yours. But there is no doubt that something unusual is at play."

This seemed self-evident. "I don't understand; how could the land be transferred to a daughter, under Salic law?"

He glanced out the window once again. "Those who collect information believe the land in Normandy is secretly being used for some purpose, by those who would have Napoleon rise to power again."

But this seemed to make little sense—not that anything made any sense, lately. "But then—if the land is important, in some way, why would it be given to me?" Uneasily, she was reminded of what de Gilles had hinted; that the milliner's shop served no purpose other than to give her an occupation that would keep her close at hand, for purposes unknown. This theory seemed incredible; what would be the point of going to such lengths? It was on a par with the equally

111

incredible tale that *Declaires* had been suddenly transferred to her name. Why; it almost looked as though she were being rewarded—

Struck by this thought, she lifted her head. That was indeed how it appeared; small wonder the authorities had converged upon her in wary confusion. Her sister was a notorious traitoress who'd met a bad end, and suddenly Epione was the beneficiary of unexplained largesse from the enemy.

She turned to him, and protested with all sincerity, "I'm not one of Napoleon's supporters; you must believe me. I have no idea why this is happening."

He replied in a grave tone, "These people don't make mistakes, I'm afraid. Are you certain your sister gave you no information—no maps, or other articles that could be valuable?"

"Nothing," she assured him. "I barely saw her for months at a time. Indeed, I saw Sir Lucien more often."

This remark diverted her companion from the topic at hand, and he leaned against the work table. "Sir Lucien has re-married—have you heard?"

"Yes—I believe it was rather unexpected." Strange to think she was so unhappy about it, two short days ago; it seemed of little importance, now.

Tremaine made a masculine sound of appreciation. "You can hardly blame him—the new Lady Tyneburne is very beautiful."

"Oh—oh is she?" Epione paused, and then watched him from under her lashes, as she asked in a casual tone, "Do you know Sir Lucien well?"

He cocked his head, and peered up at the sky through the window, as though gauging the forecast. "I've met him. He's an importer, and spent much of the war trying to keep his shirt. War is the devil for merchant traders."

"War is the devil for everyone." She knew of what she spoke; she'd lost home, country, father, and brother. She also was made aware, by Tremaine's overly-vague answer, that Sir Lucien— of all people—must be another one of them; another agent, working for the Crown. The thought was astonishing; she'd never even heard a breath of a whisper that her brother-in-law was aligned in some way with the Home Office, but on the other hand, she was not one to be on the receiving end of vital secrets. Until now, that was.

He straightened, and met her eyes again with his own frank gaze. "Then let's try to prevent the next war. The rain's letting up—shall we continue this discussion over another pastry?"

Epione noted that the rain had not let up at all, and pointed out, "Lisabetta stole your umbrella."

He smiled his charming smile, and urged, "We can keep under the awnings along the way— it is only a short distance."

For reasons unexplained, Epione was reluctant to venture outside the shop with him, in the pouring rain and with so much to think over, but was saved from having to rebuff him outright

113

by the bell over the door, which announced yet another customer. Epione almost leapt up in her relief, and moved into the shop's salon only to be brought up short by the sight of de Gilles, shrugging out of his wet greatcoat.

Chapter 13

"Monsieur de Gilles." Epione approached to take his coat, and glanced with some surprise at the two women, who had abruptly risen to their feet and now stood in silence, their gazes fixed upon the newcomer. Why, they are surprised, or confused, or—or something, she thought, and to cover the awkward moment, she advised him with a gesture, "As you see, I have visitors." No point in pretending they were customers—even they weren't pretending, anymore.

"Mademoiselle d'Amberre." He took off his gloves, as the silence stretched out, his gaze resting for an assessing moment on the women, who'd not moved. They seemed wary, or uncertain, perhaps—it was all very strange. "Mr. Tremaine is here," she advised in an undertone.

But the gentleman's attention was already fixed upon Tremaine, who now stood in the workroom entryway and seemed every bit as uncertain as the two women. So much for the theory that de Gilles only appears at night, thought Epione; apparently, he has shocked everyone into immobility.

But on the heels of this thought, de Gilles strode swiftly across the room and drew his sword with a quick movement, the tip coming to rest against Tremaine's throat.

"Oh," exclaimed Epione, at a loss. No one else moved.

Slowly, Tremaine spread his hands in a placating gesture. "No need for this, Captain— you can't blame us for taking an interest."

The sword did not waver. "How many do you have at hand?"

"Just me."

De Gilles made a derisive sound. "Tell the others to stand down."

After a long, silent moment, Tremaine announced, "Stand down."

To Epione's astonishment, a man appeared from where he'd been hidden in the back entryway, holding his hands out to the sides, and moving slowly.

"Why, what were you about?" Epione accused Tremaine in outrage. "Honestly—"

"I wanted to take you to a safer place, Epione—"

"Mademoiselle is Miss d'Amberre, to you." De Gilles pressed the sword point into the other man's throat, for emphasis.

"Perhaps we could discuss the matter," suggested Tremaine in a reasonable tone, holding his head very still. "Miss d'Amberre is too vulnerable, here."

Epione suppressed the urge to diffuse the situation, and instead stood quietly to await events. Astonishing, to think that Tremaine's friendly visit was yet another attempt at abduction, and even more unsettling to observe this strange tableau, where even though de Gilles was clearly outnumbered, no one made any attempt to move against him.

De Gilles glanced at her thoughtfully, and then nodded. "Very well. Send them away, and we will talk."

At a word from Tremaine, the two women and the man silently slipped out the back, and as the door closed, de Gilles withdrew his sword point. "You are unharmed, Mademoiselle?"

"Yes, Monsieur. I thank you for your intervention." This with an accusing glance at Tremaine, who did not register it because his own gaze was fixed upon the Frenchman.

Tremaine slowly lowered his arms. "If you would, please tell me what your interest is in these events, Captain."

"I am afraid I must decline. Where were you planning to take her?"

Tremaine appeared to weigh his options, and then disclosed, "We thought to take her into protective custody—the Fleet Prison, if necessary. Her safety is our paramount concern."

De Gilles chided with a hint of scorn, "Nonsense. You were going to use her as bait, and risk her."

"Can you blame us?" Tremaine returned, exasperated. "Good God, man; you know what's at stake—and there's no denying she's a lynchpin of some sort."

"She knows nothing of this."

"No," Tremaine agreed. "But she's a lynchpin, nonetheless."

"I never meant to be a lynchpin," Epione ventured.

Tremaine spread his hands in a placating gesture, but then with a swift movement, lunged to grapple with de Gilles, trying to pin his sword arm.

De Gilles promptly parried by taking up the cordial bottle with his left hand, and smashing it on the edge of the work table, brandishing it in the other man's face, so that Tremaine quickly retreated, and the odor of apricots filled the room.

Watching them in openmouthed alarm, it occurred to Epione that de Gilles seemed very comfortable brandishing a broken bottle, and that perhaps she should find out a bit more about him before she plighted her troth.

"Come aside, Mademoiselle," the Frenchman said as though nothing usual was going forward. "You must not allow him to seize you."

"Look," said Tremaine, holding out a cautioning palm to de Gilles. "You must see that I cannot allow you to leave with her, and you must know that there are men posted outside. Be reasonable—we shouldn't risk her injury."

De Gilles glanced out the window, and was seen to consider this aspect. "It is not I who risk her injury, but very well; we will come with you. First, though, I will have your promise that I may accompany her, and have a voice in what is to happen. Mademoiselle d'Amberre is my *fiancée.*"

The tension in Tremaine's frame seemed to dissipate. "I see—yes; that changes things, I suppose. I've not the authority to make such a promise, but I imagine there will be no resistance; certainly your wishes will be consulted."

"Can we trust him?" Epione asked, peering out at Tremaine from behind de Gilles' shoulder. After the various threats and bottle-breakings, she was rather surprised that they were not going to battle their way out the door.

Any response, however, was curtailed by the ringing of the bell over the door. Both men immediately drew back, on either side of the doorjamb that led to the workshop, as Tremaine drew his pistol.

Into the sudden silence stepped the tailor from across the way, his boots echoing on the wooden floor. "Mademoiselle?" he ventured, and then—upon observing her—stepped closer to observe the broken glass with what Epione could only consider remarkable *sangfroid.* "I beg your pardon if I intrude—I heard a commotion. Have you need of assistance?"

Epione's companions made no effort to reveal themselves, and so she faltered, "Yes—

119

well; as you see, I've broken a bottle, but there is no need for the authorities, Monsieur Chauvelin. I very much appreciate your concern." Then, to curtail the next question, "I expect Madame at any time."

Her visitor met her eyes for a moment. "I see; I will take my leave, then."

He bowed his way out, and for a moment, Epione stood, struck; there was something about the tailor that gave her pause—he reminded her of something—

Her distraction was interrupted by Tremaine, who sheathed his pistol, and said, "Quickly, then, let us go and—"

But de Gilles interrupted the other man by reaching out to lay the candle down on the pool of cordial, which was spreading across the worktable. With a whoosh, the table was promptly set aflame.

Cursing, Tremaine grabbed a bolt of silk, and began beating at the flames as de Gilles grasped Epione's hand and pulled her on a run out the front door.

In an urgent tone, her companion advised, "Stay close to me."

"Oh—oh; I don't have my shears—"

She heard him laugh, despite the perilous circumstances, as he pulled her out into the street, the rain coming down hard as smoke began to billow out of the shop behind them. Shouts of concern could suddenly be heard, and in the chaos, Epione could see two men in work clothes, purposefully striding toward them from opposite directions, their right hands hidden beneath their coats—surely de Gilles didn't think to battle them here, in the crowded street? The situation seemed hopeless, and as Epione ducked her head against the rain, several things happened at once; a loud report to their left made the two men turn in that direction, drawing their pistols as de Gilles placed a protective arm around her. Epione then realized that a rider on a horse was bearing down on them from the opposite direction, and with a mighty heave, de Gilles tossed her aloft, to be caught around the waist by Monsieur Darton, as he thundered past.

Chapter 14

The breath having been knocked out of her, Epione gasped for air as the rider hoisted her before him on the saddle and skittered around the corner, the horse's hooves sliding on the wet cobblestones, and Epione holding the certain fear that they were going down.

They didn't, and Darton muttered in her ear, "Hold on, if you please," as they made another careening turn down an alleyway at full speed— the causeway empty, due to the rain. Mud and water splashed up as the horse dashed, pell-mell, toward the end of the alley. Yet again, an impossibly sharp turn was negotiated, but the rate of speed slowed, and Epione was able to keep herself upright, clutching the saddle with her bare hands as Darton suddenly wheeled the horse at a right angle, so that they passed into a narrow throughway, between the mews.

It seemed to Epione that they were circling back from whence they'd come, but she didn't have time to think about it, because with another burst of speed, they turned another corner and darted between two buildings where they stood for a moment, more protected from the rain, as Epione's breast heaved in unison with the horse's sides. Darton appeared to be listening, and so Epione strained to listen also, not certain whether she should be hoping for a rescue, or dreading one. All she could hear was the sound of the rain, however, until Darton made a small sound of satisfaction, and began to move forward.

Wiping her eyes with a wet palm, Epione perceived another horse approaching directly before them—indeed, it would be difficult to pass abreast, in the narrow space—and then she recognized Blue Fly, and realized the rider was no other than de Gilles, removing his coat as his horse walked quickly toward them.

When they brushed up against each other, Epione was almost unsurprised to discover she was once more to be handed over, whilst the horses paused for just a moment, shoulder to shoulder. Darton lifted her to sit behind de Gilles, who swung his coat to cover both of them as he walked away, the two men saying not a word to each other.

With a clatter of hooves, Epione heard Darton start up the mad chase again behind them, while Blue Fly stepped along without any exigency.

"Pull up your skirts under the coat, and keep your head down," de Gilles said softly. "We are almost there."

"And where is there?" Despite the coat, she was having a hard time controlling her shivering, pressed against his back.

"Hush," he warned, and they stepped out into the mews behind a row of shops, walking along as the rain came down, until he turned the horse down yet another breezeway between two buildings, where a man stood waiting for them, the rain dripping off his hat brim. After a quick glance around, de Gilles shrugged out of his coat and pulled Epione down off the horse, as the other man smoothly put a foot in the stirrup and mounted in their place, pulling on de Gilles' coat as he did so. As Blue Fly walked away, de Gilles shepherded her through a doorway in the side of the building, and quietly shut it behind them.

Once inside, he put an ear to the door, listening, whilst she tried to control her chattering teeth in the dim interior. Apparently satisfied, he turned to her and whispered, "Are you all right, *ma belle*?"

"No," she replied in all honesty. "I am not."

He seemed to find the situation amusing, however, and his teeth flashed white in the dimness as with gentle fingers, he touched a tendril of hair that had escaped her pins—she was hatless, and her hair was wet. "The rain makes your hair curl."

Unable to resist returning his smile with her own, she nonetheless shook her head. "I believe I am going to go mad, Alexis."

With his smile still in evidence, he tilted his head in a show of sympathy. "We must hide quietly for a while—they will be desperate to find you. This way." Taking her elbow, he steered her to a small storeroom, and in the dim light, she recognized men's clothing—coats hanging in rows on a rack, hats lined up on a shelf—they must be in one of the haberdashery shops, in the district. Her companion tugged a coat from a hanger and wrapped it around her, whilst she shivered mightily from a combination of reaction and cold.

"Perhaps I should allow them to find me," she ventured, as he donned another coat. "It doesn't feel right—evading the British."

But he would not hear of it, and enfolded her in his arms as he spoke over her head. "You are not British, Epione. And do not think for a moment that they would protect you over their own interests—they would regret your sacrifice, but sacrifice you they would."

Tentative footsteps could be heard coming from the shop's interior, and Epione paused, meeting her companion's gaze in alarm, but he nodded in reassurance, and looked up expectantly as he set her away from him. In the dim light, a man appeared in the doorway to the storeroom, bespectacled and in shirtsleeves, with a measuring tape draped over his shoulders. His gaze rested for the briefest moment on Epione, and then he turned respectfully to de Gilles and bowed. "Mademoiselle; Seigneur."

De Giles had taken out his pistol, and was inspecting the flint, as he spoke in French. "We must warm Mademoiselle d'Amberre; coffee or tea—with a shot of spirits, if you have it. I expect they will make a search, store to store—you will be warned when they are coming. Monsieur Darton will return once it is safe, and he will bring a visitor."

The haberdasher gravely bowed yet again. "*Oui,* Seigneur." He then turned and walked away.

De Gilles sheathed his pistol. "We wait— Monsieur Darton is laying a false trail; he will circle back when he deems it safe, and bring a priest to marry us."

He lifted a hand to stroke the damp tendril back from her temple, whilst Epione stared at him in utter bemusement, the scent of wool from the surrounding coats enveloping her. "Will he indeed? I don't recall agreeing to marry you."

He cocked his head, teasing. "You don't? Do I misremember?"

Tiens, she thought; I have no defense against this onslaught of charm, and I will be lucky to survive it, I think. "You do. And I would rather speak English."

But his expression became serious, and he continued gently in French, "You have been a refugee all your life, watching the turmoil in France from afar—and living amongst those who do not always respect her as they ought. But you are French, Epione; and from an old and worthy bloodline that has stood fast for centuries. You must learn to be French again, because you cannot ignore who you are. None of us can."

"And who—exactly—are you, Seigneur?" She placed a slight emphasis on the formal address used by the haberdasher. "Come—if I agree to marry you, I am entitled to know."

He did not immediately respond, and so she prompted, "You are no sea captain, I think. The British authorities would not be so deferential to a mere sea captain."

"*Ma belle*, you wound me; I am a sea captain *par excellence*," he protested in mock-insult.

Ignoring him, she persevered, "I wondered—I wondered if perhaps you are the Duc d'Orleans." This actually made some sense to her; the Duc d'Orleans was the pretender to the throne from the less-royal Bourbon line, and had lived most of his life wandering in exile. She would not have been at all surprised to discover that de Gilles was the reclusive Duc—and it would explain Tremaine's cryptic remark about which of the pretenders de Gilles supported; the British—who were bound and determined that Louis the Eighteenth should rule as king—would be very unhappy if the Duc d'Orleans suddenly showed up, and made a claim.

In mild reproach, he tilted his head at her. "*Le Duc* is much older than I, *ma belle*."

"Oh—oh, I suppose I am betraying my ignorance on the subject."

But he took her hand in his, and smiled. "It was a good guess, Epione. But the British

127

authorities are deferential because there are those who persist in believing that I am the Dauphin."

Epione stared, thinking that of all the nonsensical things she had been told, this seemed by far the most nonsensical. "The *Dauphin*? The Dauphin who was the heir to the throne?"

He raised a brow and nodded, as though surprised she needed this clarification. "Yes."

She gazed up at him, finding it difficult to muster a coherent thought. "The—the Dauphin who died in prison, when he was a boy?"

"Yes." He turned his head to listen for a moment, then glanced at her again, this time with a gleam of amusement.

She drew her brows together, utterly confounded. "Then—then they think you are the rightful King of France."

"Yes, they do." He lifted her hand, and kissed it. "You must marry me; you would be her rightful Queen."

He did not let go of her hand, but held it clasped in his warm one, which made it a bit difficult to concentrate. "But it *is* nonsense—isn't it?" May as well seek clarification—she was fast coming to the conclusion that nothing would ever surprise her again.

He answered readily, "Yes, it is nonsense. But there are those who persist in believing it, nevertheless."

She started to laugh, unable to help it. "I don't know whether to believe a word you say—it is all so—so *fantastic*."

"It is," he agreed. "But nonetheless, it is useful. If we are married, the British would not dare make another attempt to seize you."

"Who are you, in truth?" It occurred to her that she was indeed willing to marry this near-stranger, and she should do her best to pretend it was not an utterly mad course to take. After all, she was the surprising heiress to a wealthy estate in France, and it was probably advisable to be wary of his sudden interest. Unless he were the true King of France, of course, which would put an entirely different light on the situation.

At this point, the haberdasher came in, bearing a cup of tea which he handed to Epione. "I made only the one, Seigneur," he explained apologetically to de Gilles. "If we are searched, I did not wish to raise a suspicion."

"*Excellent.*"

Epione sipped the hot tea laced with brandy, and then offered the cup to de Gilles as a warming sensation spread through her veins—brandy was more potent than apricot cordial, it seemed.

The haberdasher continued, "With your permission, when the danger has passed I will send for my wife, who will bring the new clothes."

Merci le bon Dieu, thought Epione in relief. Her dress was sodden and muddy, and she was dripping rainwater where she stood, carefully avoiding the row of fine leather boots that lined the wall.

"Can your wife be discreet?" De Gilles fixed the man with a measuring glance, as he handed the cup back to Epione.

129

"Yes—my life on it."

De Gilles flashed his engaging smile. "It may come to that, my friend."

Unable to resist the charm of that smile, the man returned his own dry little smile. "As you say, Seigneur."

De Gilles made a gesture with his head. "Go back; I expect them soon."

The haberdasher bowed again, held out a hand for the now-empty cup, and with a measured tread, left for the storefront.

Epione gathered her coat tighter around her. "Are you certain they will come? I believe you neatly outfoxed them."

"I am—the man who commands them is no fool."

"*De vrai*—I know this." Epione was grateful to impart something useful. "He came to speak with me this morning, and pretended to be a Bow Street investigator. He asked a great many questions."

Her companion regarded her thoughtfully. "Is that so? Tell me of what he spoke."

But they were interrupted by the haberdasher's voice, calling out softly, "They come, Seigneur."

130

Chapter 15

With his hands on her elbows, de Gilles guided Epione backwards between the rows of coats, then steered her against the wall so that she was positioned behind them, instructing her to step into one of the pairs of men's boots that lined the wall. Although his manner was reassuring and almost casual, her mouth went dry as he drew his pistol and followed suit, standing against the wall behind the row of coats. Taking a breath, she closed her eyes and leaned into the material that was pressed against her face, trying to breathe as lightly as she was able.

Although the sounds were muffled by the coats, Epione could hear the entry door open with a creak, and she strained to hear what was going forward—the haberdasher was speaking to men— two men, perhaps—and his voice was raised in alarm as he stepped toward the storeroom. "—an escaped felon, you say; and in broad daylight—although the rain may have aided such an endeavor. I must make certain the back door is bolted."

"Yes, sir—could you allow us—"

"Of course, of course—"

He is good, thought Epione in admiration; just the right touch of alarm without overplaying it.

Boot steps could be heard echoing on the wooden floor in the hallway outside, and Epione held her breath whilst they paused for a moment, as though taking a careful look around, and then walked past. Snatches of further conversation could be heard near the back door, then the men retraced their steps toward the front of the shop. "If you see anything unusual—he may have a young woman with him—"

"Certainly, certainly."

The front door was heard to creak open, then shut, and silence reigned; the danger had passed.

They emerged from their cocoon of coats, Epione nearly dizzy with relief. De Gilles began piling coats on the floor in the corner. "We must stay hidden here for a time, and wait for Monsieur Darton. Come, we will make ourselves comfortable."

She nodded, and he settled them into the impromptu pallet, pulling her against his chest as he leaned against the wall with his arms around her. The shop seemed so peaceful and quiet; a far cry from the tumultuous events she'd experienced so far on this strange day. The haberdasher brought more tea laced with brandy—two cups, this time—and assured them he'd sent for his wife.

Drowsy from the brandy and bundled in the warm coat, Epione sat within de Gilles' arms in the dim storeroom, the rain pattering on the roof while the British authorities presumably scoured the area, searching for her for reasons which no one seemed to understand, including the British themselves. After a moment, her companion spoke in a level tone, his voice soft against her temple. "I am sorry to press you, but I think it best we marry, Epione—we do not have the luxury of time." Idly, he swirled the dregs of his tea. "You are a pawn to them—to the British, the French royalists, perhaps even Tallyrand himself— whoever seeks to discover why you are the object of so much interest to Napoleon's supporters. If you are married to me, you are protected—they dare not abuse you."

She thought about this for a moment. "They dare not abuse me, on the chance that you are the true pretender." She glanced up at his face, bent over beside hers. "Why would anyone think such a thing, when it is well-known that the Dauphin did not survive?"

He shrugged slightly, and she felt his chest rise and fall with a sigh. "It is part wishful thinking, and part a desire to create a controversy, so as to disrupt the Congress' plans. Many are unhappy with the idea of the Dauphin's uncle taking the throne as Louis the Eighteenth, particularly in light

133

of the rumors that he played a role in his nephew's death."

Epione was well-aware of the story, as were all the *émigrés* who'd fled the Terror. After the execution of the King and Queen, the young heir to the throne had been imprisoned and treated terribly by the Jacobins—undoubtedly in the hope he would die without their having to actually murder him. Several plots had been hatched by loyalists to rescue the ten-year-old boy, but he'd eventually died in prison, nearly twenty years ago. Rumors were rife that the Dauphin's uncle—now styled Louis the Eighteenth—had worked behind the scenes to thwart any rescue.

"And?" she prompted. De Gilles hadn't yet explained why anyone would be under the impression that he was the dead Dauphin.

Subtly, she could sense a tension in his arms, and she was once again given a glimpse of the angry man beneath the handsome cloak. "I was involved in one of the plots to rescue the Dauphin—it was called *L'ange d'Isaac*. As was your brother."

Astonished, Epione turned to stare at him. "My brother Denis?"

"Yes—we were all about the same age. The plot was to allow us to play with the Dauphin—in the guise of *sans-culottes,* of course—in an attempt to re-train the boy's mind." He paused, and Epione ran her hand along his arm in sympathy, as the topic was clearly one he was reluctant to discuss.

"One of the guards had been bribed to look the other way when a switch of the boys would be made—but then we were betrayed, and everyone involved was arrested. My nursemaid, Madame Griselde, was posing as my mother—" he paused again, and she could sense his grief, still sharp, after all the years. "She was executed, but not before she lowered me through a grate, to be rescued." Resting his cheek on her head, he continued with gentle sympathy, "Your brother was not so lucky."

Taken aback, Epione could only reply, "I—I never knew of any of this. And yet some still think that you are indeed the Dauphin? Surely, there is someone left who would know that you were not?"

"The Dauphin was held in prison for years, and few saw him. And the other boys in the rescue plot were chosen for their resemblance to him—we were brown-eyed, brown haired, and fair-skinned. And—as I mentioned—much of it is wishful thinking, by those who cannot accept the truth."

"Yes," Epione nodded slowly. "Everyone so desperately doesn't want to believe that nothing is left of the old order. I saw it every day of my life—the bitterness, the refusal to assimilate."

"Except for you." His somber mien was suddenly replaced with his usual amused one, and he tightened his arms around her. "You were not bitter, Epione. Instead, the daughter of the Vicomte d'Amberre went forth to make hats."

She smiled. "I like to make hats."

"And that is why I am going to marry you, *ma belle.*"

135

It was all so very extraordinary—but much in keeping with this extraordinary day. *L'ange d'Isaac*—Isaac's angel; the plot to swoop in, and rescue a young prince. Epione repeated in wonder, "I never knew this—never knew any of it; only that my father and my brother were executed. I suppose that explains why they stayed behind, and did not come to England with my mother—and then she was so resentful of their sacrifice that she never spoke of it."

"It was kept very quiet."

"Not quiet enough," she observed, a bit sadly. "Do you think his uncle was indeed behind the Dauphin's betrayal?"

Her companion's chest moved again in a sigh. "Impossible to know, but I confess I would not be surprised—it was whispered he worked to thwart any rescue plots because he coveted the throne for himself."

Gently, she felt obligated to point out, "On the other hand, you might have been killed, Alexis—if the plot had been successful, and you were the boy who was switched."

But this observation was no comfort to him. "It would have been well worth it. Only see what has happened to France—and see the King she will now suffer under."

Trying to sort it out, she ventured, "You support the Duc d'Orleans, then?" Those opposed to the Dauphin's uncle were making a strong push on the other pretender's behalf.

Absently, he stroked the wayward tendril back from her temple. "No one's claim is perfect—

or even very good—which means that anyone with a hereditary claim can find supporters, and the factions are splintered. It is a dangerous situation, with Napoleon waiting like a vulture, in the wings."

But a memory was stirred, and Epione knit her brow, trying to remember. "Isn't Louis Philippe—the Duc d'Orleans—related in some way to the Comte deFabry? Because the grey-eyed man—Tremaine's spymaster—asked me about the Comte deFabry."

De Gilles was suddenly alert—she could sense it, in the warm body alongside hers. "What did he ask?"

"He implied—well, he implied that Marie was having an *affaire* with the Comte deFabry."

Her companion cocked his head, thinking this over. "And was she?"

"I do not know—he was an occasional visitor, but I don't remember him very well; I think he kept mostly to himself."

There was a pause, whilst he seemed to consider this information, but in the end he shook his head slightly. "Any connection seems unlikely to me. He is—he is a bit unstable; it is why he keeps to himself."

She turned to glance up at him. "You know the Comte, then?"

"Oh, yes." He offered nothing further.

But Epione could not forget how the grey eyes were sharp upon hers, when the questions had been asked. "The British spymaster was persistent about it, Alexis, and according to you, the man is no fool."

137

"That is true," he agreed. "It is puzzling."

"Seigneur," the haberdasher called out. "My wife approaches."

"Oh," said Epione. "Shall I stand up?" It was very agreeable to sit here, warm and momentarily safe in his arms, with the brandy warming her, and the rain on the roof.

"Yes; these people risk much."

"Oh—oh, of course." Thus reminded, she allowed him to pull her upright, and tried to look as composed as she could, considering she was a muddy mess, and hiding in a haberdasher's storeroom. She needn't have worried, however; the man and his wife appeared in the doorway and the quiet, grey-haired woman took one, timid glance at de Gilles, and then carefully dropped a curtsey, her eyes on the floor. She wore a black silk gown with a fine, Chantilly lace collar— obviously her Sunday best, even though it was mid-week.

"Madame," said de Gilles, and bowed his head. "May I present Mademoiselle d'Amberre?"

"Mademoiselle." The woman gave Epione a quick nod, and then her gaze returned to de Gilles, and then to the floor. She looked as though she half expected the floor to open up and swallow her at any moment.

"My wife has brought the boy's clothes."

Boy's clothes? thought Epione, lifting her brows.

"And *le déjeuner*—pastries." In a husbandly manner, he prompted his wife by giving her a meaningful glance, which seemed to bring the woman to her senses.

"*Oui*, Seigneur. Mincemeat pastries."

"*Excellent*," said de Gilles with his wonderful smile. "If you would assist Mademoiselle d'Amberre with her clothes, it will be my pleasure to taste these pastries of yours."

"I'm to wear boy's clothes?" Epione eyed him, thinking this development rather ominous.

He turned to her, and lifted her hand to kiss it. "You are. Much remains to be done this day, maker of hats; but first, you must marry me."

Almost inaudibly, the haberdasher's wife gasped.

Chapter 16

Epione was awakened by de Gilles' mouth on hers, which was enough to awaken even the deepest sleeper. After she'd been dressed in boy's clothes—her hair ruthlessly braided and pinned—they'd shared their impromptu meal, and then he'd suggested that she try to sleep for an hour, which only confirmed that this extraordinary day was far from over. As she was indeed tired, she'd willingly lain down on the coats, and had promptly fallen asleep. Now, however, she was wide awake, as de Gilles' fingertips traced her rigid braids, and his mouth made a leisurely progress across her face.

"You do not make a very good boy, Epione," he whispered, and gently kissed her again, his breath warm against her cheek, and the stubble of his beard rough against her skin. With a causal hand, he cradled the back of her neck. "No one will be fooled."

"Not if you behave thusly," she teased, then lifted her fingers to his hair and sought out his mouth with her own. She had little experience in lovemaking, but she didn't wish him to think her a laggard—and she definitely didn't want him to stop.

He kissed her again, then his mouth moved to the side of her face as his thumb brushed her lips. "It is time to be married, Epione; you must awaken."

"You have succeeded; I am very much awake."

"Are you? I am not so certain."

He kissed her mouth again, and she twined her arms around his neck and drew him to her, willingly surrendering to the sensations evoked by the lean, masculine body pressed against hers. It was a relief to discover that he was obviously intending a true marriage—his constrained behavior had made it unclear, thus far—and she'd entertained a small qualm that he intended to tuck her away someplace dull so that he could go off sea-captaining, again. Now it seemed thankfully obvious that he was avid for her.

With a sigh of regret, he drew away. "Come; Darton will soon return with the priest."

Smiling, she teased, "I hope someone has informed him that the bride will be dressed as a boy. He may balk, and excommunicate the both of us."

With a chuckle, he propped himself on an elbow, and ran a languid hand along her hip, encased in the boy's breeches. "It is a situation *déplorable*, Epione; you should be courted—with flowers, and dancing, and settlements."

She made a wry mouth. "I am reconciled." This was surprisingly true—a mere week ago, she'd dreamed of a quiet wedding to a widower; now it seemed a lifetime ago.

Watching her, he leaned in to bestow another lingering kiss on her mouth. "We will manage well together, I think."

"Yes." It was as yet unclear where they would abide, or whether it meant more wild chases like the one today, but she knew that she would willingly follow—come what may, and however rough the road. Her comfortable existence had all been a façade, anyway, and in a strange way, she and de Gilles shared a common history; as children, their lives had been irrevocably disrupted by the failed, desperate plan to rescue a doomed prince, and nothing had been the same, ever since.

Epione had not known her father—her mother had rarely spoken of him—but she felt these latest revelations gave her new insight into the character of a man who had risked everything—his fortune, his life, and the life of his only son—in an attempt to save the French monarchy. But her mother could only see the wreckage of the failed gamble, and think of what had been lost. Perhaps if she'd let her daughters know of their father's loyalty and courage, Marie would not have been tempted to betray everything he'd stood for; perhaps she would not have been killed, and the factions that were now fighting over the carcass of post-war France would not have sought out Marie's younger sister, for reasons as yet unknown.

But Epione was not one to dwell upon useless what-ifs, and apparently the fact that she did not ponder the cruelties of fate made her attractive to this man, whose warm hands were now tracing the contours of her hips with an urgency that she did not quite understand.

"Ah—we are just in time, I think."

Darton appeared in the doorway, the haberdasher beside him, as Epione scrambled to sit up, blushing, while her companion drew himself up in a more leisurely fashion, resting his hands upon his knees and regarding the newcomer. "Well?"

Darton cocked his head. "*Mais c'est infâme;* while you dally with this beautiful girl, I have been running like a fox from the hounds. They are very unhappy with you, *mon Capitaine.*"

"I can grant them no sympathy; I am just as unhappy with them."

Darton offered his hands to Epione, and after pulling her upright, kissed both of her cheeks, with an insouciant glance at de Gilles.

143

"So, you have tamed our friend, here, Mademoiselle."

"She did stab me, once," de Gilles admitted, as he rose to his feet.

Darton was impressed, and raised his brows at her. "*C'est vrai?* Have you indeed stabbed him? I have never been given the smallest opportunity to stab him."

De Gilles obligingly pushed up his sleeve. "You see? You must never cross Mademoiselle."

"It was an accident," she laughingly protested. "I am not so menacing."

Darton shook his head. "*Au contraire,* I must respectfully disagree. You are definitely menacing to someone; I have spent a long and wet afternoon, as a result."

Epione spread her hands. "I beg your pardon—and acquit me of any knowledge of these matters, Monsieur."

De Gilles, it seemed, had tired of the topic. "Have you managed a priest?"

With a bow, Darton confirmed. "I have. We mustn't tarry, though; he has a ship to catch, which is just as well—one less to tell the tale."

"It will not be a secret," de Gilles disagreed in a mild tone, as he adjusted his cuffs. "I will marry the only remaining daughter of the House d'Amberre in plain sight of all. Let them make of it what they will."

Darton's smile flashed in the dim light, and he seemed very much amused. "You will throw the cat among the pigeons, *mon Capitaine.* They will beat their wings, in a panic."

144

"We shall see."

Epione could not quite like this characterization—as though she was but a pawn in a game of chess—but then she consoled herself with the fact that the man seemed unable to keep his hands from her, so there was that.

De Gilles offered his arm. "Mademoiselle?"

Epione took it, and allowed him to lead her to the fitting room, where the haberdasher and his wife flanked a priest, who seemed a bit taken aback to behold her disguise, but asked no questions—which was just as well, as Epione was not certain why she was dressed as a boy, herself. All in all, it seemed that the haberdasher's wife was more in need of support than the bride, as Epione was married to a man she'd met three days ago—and what she knew of him wouldn't fill a thimble.

It is less than ideal, she admitted to herself, as she listened to him speak his vows; but try as I might, I cannot muster a qualm, whether he is the true King of France or merely a sea captain with an eye on my estate. She held her bridegroom's hand and made her responses whilst wondering what was to happen next—despite the heated interlude in the storeroom, it seemed unlikely that a blissful honeymoon was in the offing.

In this she was correct. After the others offered their congratulations, Darton placed his own broad-brimmed hat on Epione, and stood back to observe the effect. "If she pulls the collar up on her coat, she'd not be easily recognizable—especially in the rain."

"Where do we go? And please tell me it does not involve the setting of more fires." Epione tilted her head back to peer at her new husband from under the brim.

"Fires?" asked the haberdasher's wife in a faint tone, and the woman's husband discreetly hustled her out of the room.

De Gilles stepped forward to hold Epione's coat as she slipped her arms into it. "There is a man in a tavern, over in Fitzrovia. I would like you to look at him through the window as we pass by, to see if you recognize him."

She looked at him with interest. "The 'Josiah', do you think?"

"We shall see."

The priest stepped forward to interrupt them, saying regretfully, "I'm afraid I must catch a ship." He bowed with a smile. "My best wishes, Madame de Gilles."

"Thank you," said Epione, who was not certain whether she should bow in response. Although she was the daughter of a vicomte, her husband may-or-may-not hold a title, and it seemed as though he did not feel it necessary to enlighten her.

As Darton escorted the priest out the back, she took the opportunity to ask de Gilles, "What does it mean—the 'Josiah', and why do you think this man in Fitzrovia may be he? Can you tell me?"

He gently pulled her to him by her lapels, and bent to kiss her, ducking his head under the broad brim. "I believe it is a reference to the Old Testament King."

146

"Oh," she replied, and decided she shouldn't betray her ignorance.

He was not fooled, however, and playfully tugged on her too-large hat so that it came down over her forehead. "He was the King of Judah, and wore a disguise so that he could participate in a battle."

Pushing the hat back, she puzzled over this. "What can it mean—how is that story connected to all this?"

He shrugged. "I am not certain. But it is the code name for an assignment given by Napoleon's spymaster—something very important, and kept very secret. I came across the name only by chance."

With a knit brow, she ventured, "One of the pretenders is disguised, perhaps? Or I suppose it could even refer to you, and the confusion over your true identity."

But he shook his head. "I do not think that is it; I have not lived in Europe for many years, and no one was expecting me to make a reappearance."

She buttoned the boy's coat, feeling its unnatural weight. "Perhaps it has to do with me; perhaps the Josiah is the one who decided to give *Desclaires* to me."

"Perhaps."

Reminded, Epione asked, "Could it refer to the murderer?"

"I do not know, but I believe there is a connection between the Josiah and your work at the millinery, Epione."

She looked at him in bewilderment. "What could the connection possibly be? Between the pretenders, and me, and Madame, and these random victims—"

"And *Desclaires*."

"—and *Declaires*. Truly, it all makes little sense."

"It makes sense to Napoleon," he replied, a bit grimly. "*Allons*, now."

No honeymoon anytime soon, she thought with a mental sigh, and hoped he would at least kiss her again, before Darton returned.

Chapter 17

Epione stood sheltered from the rain in a brick doorway, her collar pulled up, her too-large hat pulled down, and her new husband blocking her from the chance glance of any curious passersby, as he canvassed the nearly deserted street. They were standing a few doors down from *The Moor's Head* tavern, waiting for Darton to secure a position within before they would walk past the front windows.

Extreme caution had been taken in their roundabout journey here, and the two men had spoken little as they had backtracked, crossed paths and taken two different hackney cabs, their pistols at the ready and their gazes sharp on their surroundings.

The journey had given Epione an opportunity to mull over this spying business, and the various factions involved. It seemed apparent that Darton and de Gilles were aligned against Tremaine, who was aligned with the grey-eyed spymaster and Sir Lucien, her former brother-in-law—and it also seemed apparent that everyone was working toward the same end, which was to thwart Napoleon's supporters. Those supporters apparently included Lisabetta, the now-dead Marie, and the now-presumably-dead Madame.

All of them women, Epione noted thoughtfully; it made one think there was a man in the background, controlling their actions. Certainly the frivolous Marie would not have masterminded such a plot; more likely she was just a pawn to be used against her own husband, in this deadly game of secrets.

Thinking about this, she whispered a thought that had suddenly entered her mind. "Did Sir Lucien kill my sister?"

With some surprise, de Gilles glanced down at her, his face shadowed because they had taken pains to avoid the illumination of the street lanterns. "What makes you think this, *ma belle*?"

But she persisted, "If you knew, would you tell me?"

With one last glance down the street, he drew her further back into the doorway alcove, and slowly replied, "Sir Lucien is a very brave Englishman; he fought with the *guerrillas* in Spain—at a time when the odds seemed hopeless."

This non-answer told her that she'd guessed correctly, and it only made sense; if Sir Lucien was working for the Home Office, and Marie was passing information to the enemy, it took little imagination to leap to this conclusion, given that she'd been shot in her own garden, and the circumstances quickly hushed up.

Epione took a breath—truly, she'd been living in a naïve cocoon, making her hats and sheltered from these hard truths, which were now revealing themselves in what seemed like a relentless torrent. "So; Marie was betraying France, England—and her own husband, for good measure."

He lifted his head to look out over the street, and observed quietly, "Greed is a terrible driver. As we continue to see."

But she shook her head slightly, in disagreement. "No; not merely greed. Knowing Marie, it was the excitement of the scheming, and the attention it brought. That would appeal to her more than any amount of money."

With a tilt of his head, he said only, "I do not wish to criticize your sister to you."

Epione sighed a bit sadly. "No—she paid a terrible price, and I suppose nothing more need be said. I think I'm a bit shocked, is all; that he would kill her—would kill his own wife. And then he remarried so quickly."

As he watched the street, he offered, "The new wife—they have known each other a long time. It is not as sudden as it seems."

151

This was a surprise, and she stared up at him. "They were lovers?"

He turned to face her again. "I do not know. Possibly."

She made a wry mouth, and sought out his hand with her own. "You must think me foolish, not to have noticed that there were so many dark secrets, swirling around me."

He bent his head, and lifted her hand to kiss its gloved back. "No—I do not think you foolish, *ma belle.* And it saddens me that I have no choice but to pull you out into the world's ugliness."

But she shook her head slightly, in disagreement. "I am no stranger to the world's ugliness, Alexis. Indeed, I think I admired Sir Lucien mainly because I knew no one else like him; no one who was not bitter, or flawed."

"Yes. You said you thought he was true."

There was a hint of gentle irony underlying the words, and she paused, appreciating that irony—now that she knew the facts—and also appreciating that this was a delicate topic to be discussing with one's new husband. "But now I am the wiser; if he killed her, he definitely was not true."

He held her hand in his, and met her eyes. "He was true to his country, and for that he must be admired." She had the impression he regretted his implied criticism of Sir Lucien, and was trying to make amends.

"Yes, there is that." With gentle regret, she shook her head. "I shouldn't have told you—about how I carried a *tendre* for him. It makes me sound so young, and naïve."

But he drew her into a comforting embrace, still watching the street, and said over the top of her oversized hat, "You cannot be blamed, Epione, for seeking out a diversion. Your *tendre* gave you a small respite from the harsh realities of this world."

She laid her cheek on his coat front—he smelt heavenly; of undefined masculinity. "And now the harsh world has come to my doorstep, with a vengeance." She lifted her head to meet his eyes. "As have you."

"As have I," he agreed. "I was fortunate to have found my way there."

This was gratifying—she'd noted that he was not one to make tender speeches, but on the other hand, she was not one to expect them, given that they didn't know each other very well. "I kept watching you watching me, and wondered what I had done to incite such interest."

"No one yet knows why you incite such interest," he reminded her.

"No—but at least I've gained a fine husband, which more than makes up for everything else."

At this accolade, his arms tightened around her. "I will see to it you suffer no more hardships, Epione. You have asked no questions, but be assured I have the means to see that you live in comfort."

She ventured, "Will I live this comfortable existence at *Desclaires*?"

153

He tilted his head. "Perhaps. It is a fine estate."

She looked up at him for a moment. "You've been there, then?"

"Yes—when I was a boy. My family would visit, from time to time."

Epione lowered her face again to the comfort of his chest. "How is your poor arm?" In truth, she was enjoying this semi-romantic conversation, and was casting about for any additional topic that could be directed into his coat front.

"Better. Perhaps you will be kind enough to remove the stitches tomorrow." In the near distance, a door slammed, twice. "We must go," he whispered, suddenly intent. "Stay close to me."

After he adjusted the brim of her man's hat low over her face, they stepped out onto the pavement, the rain mizzling and the fog beginning to roll in. As they approached the tavern, he lowered his head to speak quietly to her. "There will be a party of gentleman seated at the table by the near window. You must see if you recognize any of them as we pass by, but do not tarry, or lift your face."

She nodded in understanding, as he slowed before the paned window which fronted the establishment, the light streaming out onto the pavement. Faintly, she could hear the sound of many voices and the clinking of dishes and cutlery—apparently the establishment was popular, despite the inclement weather.

De Gilles strode beside her, ducking his head against the rain, and lifting his hand to his hat to obscure his face, as Epione glanced into the window. There were four men seated in the midst of a meal—one of them Darton—and she quickly scanned them, but it was the man waiting on them that caught her eye. "I recognize only the British spymaster," she warned. "He is serving the table."

But this revelation did not have the expected effect, as her companion drew up so suddenly that she bumped into him. "Indeed? Show me."

Nervously wondering why they'd stopped in plain sight, Epione stammered, "He—he was serving the ale—there; now he has turned away." She could see Darton, glancing at them through the window, his brows raised in amused confusion at de Gilles' unexpected actions.

But de Gilles still did not move. "You are certain?"

"Yes—I met him just this morning." There was a pause, and then Epione pointed out the obvious, while her companion calmly stood, reviewing the interior. "It appears to be a trap, Alexis. Is Blue Fly close at hand?"

"Come with me, Epione; I would ask for an introduction."

Her mouth agape, she allowed him to take her hand, and pull her along to the entry door, hoping he knew what he was doing, and reflecting that in the end, it didn't matter, because he was her husband and this, apparently, was to be her

155

first test of marriage. She only wished she weren't wearing breeches.

With a shoulder, de Gilles pushed his way through the door, and then stood on the threshold, calmly drawing his pistol and firing; shattering the remaining tankard of ale on the spymaster's tray.

Instantly there was a wild scramble, as all the diners stood, and half the room drew on the other half, a tense silence settling over the scene.

This is a very strange sort of tavern, thought Epione, as she hovered behind her escort.

"You there," called out de Gilles. "I would have a glass of ale."

Chapter 18

Into the sudden, tense silence, the tavern-keeper pleaded from his position behind the counter, "Please, gentlemen; I've only just had the mirror replaced this week."

"Have your men stand down," de Gilles demanded of the spymaster, as he drew the hammer back on another pistol.

"I am not certain that would be wise." The other man set down the tray, the shards of broken glass skittering to the floor in the process.

"I believe we are being played, Monsieur, one against the other, by our mutual enemy."

The grey-eyed spymaster regarded him for a moment before responding. "If that is indeed the case, you would be best served by allowing me to take the girl into protective custody. You take too great an interest in these affairs for my comfort."

But de Gilles was unfazed, and his weapon did not falter. "I'm afraid I do not much care for your comfort, Monsieur, one way or the other. And the girl is now my wife."

It was not, perhaps, how Epione would have liked to announce her marriage, and she could sense the surprised reaction of those who were participating in this tense standoff, as many pairs of eyes slid to observe her. It did seem that their supporters were outnumbered, and she hoped de Gilles knew what he was doing—it was interesting that he'd decided to take the bull by the horns, so to speak, and boldly confront the British spymaster.

"I see," said the other man, and it seemed to Epione that the news of her marriage was not particularly welcome. "Nevertheless, I must insist that you cooperate with the Home Office in this matter."

"And I will insist that you cease interfering in matters which do not concern you."

The other man, however, disagreed. "These matters are of great concern; as you have pointed out, we have a mutual enemy."

Darton had stood to watch the standoff with his back to the wall, a pistol in one hand and a drawn sword in the other. "*Prenez garde, Capitaine.*"

In response to the warning, Epione turned to behold Lisabetta, dressed as a serving wench, and sidling toward them behind the counter. Upon discovery, the girl lifted a small-bore pistol to Epione, her dark eyes hard. "Do not move."

As Epione stared at the other girl in abject surprise, de Gilles addressed the spymaster. "Have her stand down. Come, Monsieur; you wage war on women?"

But the grey-eyed man would not be discomfited, and replied in an even tone, "You cannot think me so clumsy; she is not one of mine."

"Put your pistol down," Epione chided Lisabetta, instinctively aware that she should not allow anyone to separate her from de Gilles. "You are being ridiculous." Carefully, she closed a hand around one of the gin bottles which were stacked alongside the counter.

"It is you who are ridiculous," the girl hissed in response, and lifted the weapon slightly in a grim warning. Immediately, there was the sound of many pistols in the room being cocked, including the one being held on Epione.

"Gentlemen—" ventured the tavern-keeper in a put-upon tone of voice, "recall the last time—"

While they were thus diverted, Epione decided she should seize the advantage, and so with a quick movement, she flung the gin bottle at Lisabetta's head. She missed, but when the girl ducked, Darton launched himself over the counter, and placed his sword tip on Lisabetta's throat. "Drop it."

Wary, the girl straightened up, with her own weapon still trained on Epione. "No, Monsieur; it is you who will drop it."

With a flick of his wrist, Darton slashed his sword so that the lock of dark hair that had lain on

159

Lisabetta's breast was severed. With a gasp of outrage, she turned to fire upon him, but the shot went wild, because Darton had launched the cask on the counter at her. As the tavern-keeper yelped in dismay, the mirror behind the counter was shattered by the shot, and as Lisabetta leapt aside to avoid the cascading glass, she was pinioned from behind by de Gilles, who held one arm across her throat, and the other around her arms.

"*Bâtard*," spat Lisabetta at Darton, as she struggled against de Gilles. "Give me back my hair."

With an insouciant grin, Darton made a show of tucking the lock of hair into his shirt, whilst de Gilles said into the girl's ear, "I should have let you drown, Lisabetta—desist."

But the other girl jerked her chin toward Epione, her breast heaving, "Tell this one to desist—she marries you, and yet seeks to take my Robert as her lover—"

"That is not true," Epione protested hotly, acutely embarrassed that these accusations were being aired before all and sundry. "I was going to marry Robert, too."

The contretemps with Lisabetta had allowed the grey-eyed man and several of his men to advance toward the bar with their weapons drawn, surrounding them. The spymaster intervened to address de Gilles, "Come—let us come to terms. You wouldn't wish to die in a tavern brawl, I think."

In response, de Gilles held the still struggling Lisabetta and replied without rancor,

"You wouldn't wish to answer for having killed me in a tavern brawl, I think. Move aside."

Observing the standoff, Epione could see that a diversion was needful, and—having learned a useful tactic—she brushed the candlestick beside her onto the floor, where the broken cask lay in ruins. For the second time that day, the alcohol erupted into a burst of flame, and de Gilles threw Lisabetta into the grey-eyed man before grasping Epione's hand to pull her toward the back stairway.

Not one to tolerate such treatment, Lisabetta fired wildly, with the result that a window shattered with a crash, and a melee broke out amongst the assembled factions, as the tavern keeper pulled the washing tub from under the counter to douse the burgeoning fire.

Several of the combatants ran after de Gilles and Epione, drawing swords with a *schwinging* sound, and between the cacophony of curses and flashing swords, de Gilles pushed Epione up the back stairs and then turned to defend their position, his own sword slashing furiously at those who pressed toward them.

"Do not engage him," shouted the spymaster, but blood was high, and the two men who challenged de Gilles were loath to retreat, as they swung their weapons to clash against his. Having never participated in a melee, Epione stood behind him on the steps, uncertain as to what she should do to be helpful, and constrained by the memory of what had happened last time she'd tried to be helpful.

161

She hadn't long to think about it, though; from the corner of her eye she caught a movement behind her, and whirled to face another man, stepping carefully down the stairs behind them with a drawn pistol.

"*Prenez garde*, behind us," shouted Epione, imitating Darton, and frantically lifted an empty pail from the steps so as to throw it at the flank attack. The pail hit the attacker's foot just as he was stepping down, and as a result he staggered, and lost his balance. With a swift movement, de Gilles reached for the man's outstretched arm, and then yanked him headfirst down the stairs into the two attackers below, bowling them all back.

"Stand down," bellowed the spymaster again, and all the combatants paused, wary and breathing heavily, as Epione clutched the pail between her hands, wide-eyed.

"Do not stray from me," de Gilles said quietly, between breaths.

"I won't," she agreed.

As he wiped the sweat from his face with a sleeve, de Gilles addressed the spymaster. "I believe there may be a false flag operation in play, Monsieur."

The other man regarded him for a moment, then stepped forward. "I will give you assurances, if you'd like, while we parlay."

"My wife stays with me."

The spymaster blew out a breath. "As you say."

"Demand some brandy, while you are at it," called Darton from his position behind the counter. "And some punch, for the ladies." This, with a bow to the still-seething Lisabetta.

"I have no brandy." The tavern keeper spread his hands in apology, as he glanced toward the British official. "It is illegal."

With a grin, Darton reached behind the counter, and hoisted a brandy bottle atop it. "Then we'll have to make do with this cherry-juice."

Chapter 19

"What does it mean—'false flag'?" Epione was seated with de Gilles in the public room at *The Moor's Head*, which was now mostly deserted, and rather cold. The tavern-keeper was in the process of hammering boards over the broken window, casting the occasional baleful glance toward their table, while a serving-girl swept up the broken glass with the air of someone doing an all-too-familiar task. It occurred to Epione that despite the noise and commotion, the Watch hadn't made an appearance, and so she concluded that the authorities had been warned away.

De Gilles was watching as the spymaster questioned Lisabetta across the room, the girl making angry, animated gestures in response to the questions. "It means that someone is trying to divert attention from their true purpose."

Epione frowned for a moment, trying to puzzle out what was meant. "The murders?"

He tilted his head. "Perhaps. Perhaps they use this opportunity to take action, knowing it will be blamed on the unknown murderer. Or there may be something else at play—I am not certain. But the British should not have known that we were coming here tonight, and I would very much like to learn how they became aware of our movements."

Epione followed his gaze to the interrogation. "Lisabetta? I think she is more lovelorn, than capable of such a scheme. I feel a bit sorry for her."

"Do not," he warned, as he watched the defiant Frenchwoman sink back in her chair, her arms crossed in a huff. "She is ruthless, Epione."

Epione raised a brow. "Yet, you rescued her?"

His mouth thinned into a half-smile at the memory. "She was locked in the brig, on a ship which was sinking—it was little enough to pick the lock."

He seemed disinclined to expand on the topic, and almost apologetically, she ventured, "Mr. Tremaine hinted that you were involved in dark doings."

This caught his attention, and he turned to cover her hand with his own, meeting her gaze with quiet intensity. "You must not believe what he tells you, *ma belle*—it is not the truth."

"*C'est entendu,*" she agreed, then added, "And what—exactly—is the truth?" De Gilles seemed every inch an *aristo,* but other than that, she hadn't a clue.

But before he could respond, Darton approached, glancing askance at the others across the room. "Have we surrendered, *Capitaine*?" He pulled out a chair, and straddled it backwards, pouring himself a generous tot of brandy from the bottle on the table.

Tilting his head, de Gilles indicated he'd like his own refill, and replied, "We will cooperate; I believe we are all being manipulated—and it seemed only fair to let him know this."

Darton sighed, and took a drink. "You are a kind and generous man."

De Gilles stretched out his legs before him, leaning back into the chair and cradling his glass in his hand, his thoughtful gaze on the others. "Something is not right, *mon ami.*"

"The British knew we were coming here," Epione ventured. "Did the haberdasher betray us—or the priest, perhaps?" She knit her brow in doubt. "It seems so unlikely."

"Yes, it does seem unlikely," de Gilles agreed. "But no matter how they came into their knowledge, I believe the British are no more aware of what is going forward than we are."

Reminded, she told him, "Mr. Tremaine didn't seem to know about the Josiah—or at least he didn't ask me about it."

But de Gilles was not so certain, and lifted a shoulder. "He does not wish you to know what

166

he knows, Epione—you must not believe anything he tells you."

"Speaking of which, here comes another who should not be believed," Darton noted in amusement, as Lisabetta flounced over to join them, seating herself next to de Gilles with a last, defiant glare at the British spymaster.

"*Peste; mais c'est infâme*; there is no *chevalerie* in that one; he would send me to prison without the smallest regret."

But de Gilles was not willing to sympathize. "You will tell me why you are here, if you please."

With sulky reluctance, the girl said something in a language Epione didn't recognize.

"Speak French," he corrected the girl impatiently. "And I will tolerate no more threats to Madame de Gilles, Lisabetta. Heed me."

"Fah—I was not going to shoot her." Lisabetta shot a withering glance at Epione that seemed to imply she would not consider such an action worth the effort. "But you came crashing in, and I knew I would be discovered—*pour ça donc*, I needed a hostage."

"You have not yet explained to me why you are here."

With a frown, the girl rested her gaze on the spymaster, who was conferring quietly with several of his men. "I heard that the British were to be here tonight, and I wanted to see my Robert. We had a—a misunderstanding." With a resentful glance at her rival, Lisabetta crossed her arms, and made a show of ignoring Darton, who watched with an amused expression, as he took out his pipe.

Epione took this opportunity to interject, "It is a good riddance; you make Robert very unhappy."

"*Quant à ça*—he makes himself unhappy, with his foolishness." She gave Epione a look which left no doubt as to the cause of the foolishness. "And you—a married woman! For shame."

Hotly, Epione defended herself. "He is not at all foolish; he was very honorable, to offer for me, in light of—" Belatedly, she realized the brandy was making her a bit reckless.

But the other girl only tossed her head. "There is no longer a place for honorable men in this world." This, with a significant glance at de Gilles.

"Lisabetta," he rebuked mildly, "I will remind you that you owe me a favor."

Struggling with her temper, Lisabetta subsided, and then took a pull of brandy straight from the bottle, a mulish cast to her mouth. "*Peste;* I hate London," she announced, to no one in particular.

De Gilles said without sympathy, "Seek out Droughm, then; he is back in England, and Epione has not yet stolen him from you."

The Frenchwoman pressed her lips into a thin line for a moment. "Droughm has married."

De Gilles lifted his head to regard her with amused surprise. "*Droughm* has married?"

The girl shrugged her bare shoulders. "Is it so very strange? After all, you have married, and who would be less likely?"

But de Gilles continued amused, and exchanged a glance with Darton. "Tell me who has managed such a feat—she must be *une femme formidable.*"

But further discussion was curtailed as the grey-eyed spymaster approached to join them, and announced to Lisabetta without preamble, "You will be held at the magistrate's, while my people check out your tale."

"You have *no* reason to hold me," she countered hotly.

"On the contrary; you threatened the peace."

Outraged, Lisabetta made a gesture which encompassed the wreckage of the room. "What peace is this you speak of?"

But the Englishman had lost patience, and leaned his hands on the table, saying with deliberation, "You will cooperate, or it will be the worse for you." Then, to de Gilles, "I would like to have a private word with your bride."

"No," said Epione's husband.

Undeterred, the spymaster turned to Epione. "Have you indeed married this man?"

De Gilles tilted his head to indicate Epione should answer, and so she did. "I have, sir."

The other man's gaze rested on de Gilles, and his next words were imbued with irony. "A whirlwind romance."

De Gilles raised his cold gaze to meet the other's. "You will endeavor to be civil, Monsieur."

The spymaster eyed him for a moment, then indicated with a gesture that Lisabetta should be escorted out by the other men.

"Send Robert to me—I *must* speak with him," the girl insisted as she rose. With a defiant gesture, she plucked the brandy bottle from the table, and left with her escort.

Chapter 20

"What is it you would like to tell me?" The grey-eyed spymaster drew out his pipe from a vest pocket, and glanced at de Gilles from across the table. Darton sat to the side, leaning back with his boots crossed before him, and two of the British men stood at a small distance, out of earshot but—as Epione noted well—their gazes focused on de Gilles with covert curiosity. It is as though he is on display at a fair, she thought, annoyed on his behalf. How tedious it must be—to be always an object of speculation, amongst certain circles. And small wonder he stays well-away from it, doing whatever-it-was that he does, oceans away.

De Gilles began without preamble, "I believe we are being distracted, Monsieur—or manipulated. You are being fed information about my actions; I am being fed information about your actions, but each of us has little to show for it."

The other man thought about this, puffing on his pipe so that a cloud of smoke rose to mingle with Darton's, overhead. "To what end?"

De Gilles shrugged. "I know not."

"Napoleon? He acts as the puppet-master from Elba, there is no question."

De Gilles nodded. "I would agree. The situation in France is fragile, and many are unhappy—"

"Including you." The grey eyes rested on the other man.

But de Gilles did not take offense, and replied easily, "Including myself. Napoleon may attempt to take advantage of the divided factions, and return to power."

The spymaster pronounced bluntly, "There is no question he will make the attempt; it is only a question of when, and how it will happen."

Epione did her best to contain her dismay at this blunt speech—surely Napoleon would have few supporters left, after all that had been lost already? But both men seemed certain, and one would imagine they knew of which they spoke.

A shard of mirror that had clung to the frame behind the bar suddenly crashed down, making everyone startle for a moment, then settle in once more to continue the parlay, as the serving maid moved to wield her broom yet again.

The spymaster drew on his pipe, and leaned his head back to exhale. "Of course, there is little hope that Napoleon can succeed unless he obtains funding—his war chest is sadly depleted. My people have been busy, quashing various plots by his supporters."

"I am aware." De Gilles made a gesture that included Darton. "We were given information about your operation in China, and of the opportunities made available by the opium wars."

The spymaster's hand stilled for a moment. "Is that so?"

De Gilles nodded. "The gambit did not work; instead, I decided to discover why I would be encouraged to go to China. That is when I came across the information about the d'Amberre estate."

The spymaster's thoughtful gaze rested on Epione. "Given to a milliner's assistant, whose sister aided Napoleon."

His brows drawn together, de Gilles was quick to assert, "My wife knows nothing of this, Monsieur. My life on it."

"It cannot be a coincidence."

There was a small silence, in light of the undeniable truth of the words. "No," de Gilles agreed, rather gravely. "But she is no longer your concern."

Making a sound of impatience, the spymaster leaned forward slightly, his manner intent. "Come; you cannot interfere in these matters—it is not in keeping with your history. And if you do interfere, you will draw the wrath of those who were uneasy enough to divert you to China."

But Epione's husband apparently did not appreciate being chided, and for the first time a hint of steel could be heard in his voice. "I will not be played for a fool." He let the words hang in the air for a moment, leaving no doubt that he was directing them, at least in part, toward the spymaster.

Tiens, thought Epione, clenching her hands beneath the table. Another fight to break out, at any moment.

But the spymaster's manner became more conciliatory, and he leaned back into his chair with a small shrug. "What do you intend, then—will you go to France?"

With a tilt of his head, de Gilles answered with light irony, "My plans are as yet unformed." It could not be clearer that he did not trust the other man, although the words were couched in polite terms.

With a sigh, the grey-eyed man ran a hand over his face. "Then let us try to aid each other on auxiliary matters. I would like to—with all respect—have a conversation with your wife, in the hope there is something here that we are missing. In exchange, I will assure her safety—and yours—for the time being. I can arrange a safe house for your use; the East India Company owes me a favor."

There was a pause, whilst de Gilles exchanged a glance with Darton, who raised his brows in skepticism. Seeing this, the spymaster added, "I can obtain written assurances from the Home Office, if you desire. But like it or not, she is at the center of this mystery, and too much is at stake."

Waiting for her husband's decision, Epione was almost surprised when he turned to consult her. "With your permission, Madame?"

"Of course—although I don't think I can be of much use."

De Gilles asked that the tavern-keeper fetch a clean blanket, and wrapped within its warm folds, Epione answered the Englishman's questions as best she could for the next hour, while de Gilles and Darton listened without comment. She was asked to describe every visitor she'd encountered at her sister's house, the spymaster occasionally prompting her by suggesting certain names. Once again, the man mentioned the Comte deFabry.

Epione shook her head, surprised by his insistence. "I rarely saw him; but then, I was not often at her house. He was not—" she tried to articulate her thoughts. "He was not much of a *presence*, if you know what I mean. I would be very surprised to discover that my sister was—was attracted to him." She bit her lip, so as not to reveal that Marie used to decry her steady husband for not indulging her enough; or that she tended to flirt with the more dashing young *aristos,* just to annoy him.

The spymaster drew a breath, and sat thinking for a moment. "Was there ever a gentleman named Josiah?"

So—the British did know something of the Josiah, although apparently they were just as baffled as de Gilles. "Not that I was aware," she replied, and comforted herself that it was the truth, after all, and that she was not misleading anyone.

"Was there—is there anything in your residence, Madame, which came from your sister's house? Or even your mother's house?"

Epione knit her brow. "My mother's house—and everything in it—was sold to pay our debts, after my mother died. I have very little left; only my father's medal—the *Grand Croix de Saint-Louis.* And my mother's mourning brooch."

"Anything from your sister?"

"Some dresses, as well as a few of the hats I'd fashioned for her."

"Any unopened reticules?" the Englishman persisted. "Or letters, left in pockets?"

"Not that I've noticed," Epione confessed. "But on the other hand, I was not inclined to search."

The man's gaze turned to de Gilles. "It is a faint hope, but at this point I am grasping at straws."

"Come then," said de Gilles, dropping his hands to his knees. Then, to Epione, "We will visit your rooms, and allow a search. And we will retrieve your father's medal, to take it with us."

"May I change out of boy's clothes?"

He offered his hand to help her rise. "I'm afraid it would be best if you remained a boy for the time being; you remain vulnerable until we determine why you are so important to the enemy."

"Although you do not make a very good boy," Darton noted, as he tapped his pipe. "A man would have to be an idiot, to be fooled."

"I will offer no opinion on the subject," the spymaster said as he pulled on his gloves, and Epione saw her husband smile. So; a truce, of sorts, she thought with relief, as another mirror shard crashed to the floor.

Chapter 21

Upon their arrival at Epione's rooms, de Gilles opened the door with his lock-picking tool which was much appreciated, as Epione's key was still in her pelisse pocket, hanging on the hook in the milliner's shop. Once inside, the spymaster's men began a thorough search, as she stood by with de Gilles and Darton, who watched them without comment. Epione could not help but remember that morning when she had left this place—now it seemed so long ago—unaware that she was not only to be married, but that she would participate in various perilous adventures before she returned.

Secretly, she was rather proud of setting the tavern on fire, and of throwing the pail at the attacker, but she was aware that one did not boast of such things, and so only congratulated herself silently. Why, I believe I have suddenly become courageous, she thought with an inward smile; I suppose one never knows of what one is capable, until one is put to the test.

And, of course, it helped to have an incentive. She glanced at de Gilles, whose gaze remained fixed on the Englishmen, and felt a rush of affection. I am good for him, she thought; and he is good for me—how fortunate that we found each other, despite everything.

She allowed her gaze to travel around her rooms; the sparse, rented furnishings, and the window sash that had to be soaped occasionally so that it wouldn't stick. I'll not miss this, she realized without a shred of regret. He is right; I was hiding away from the world and all its hardships, and now—now, I've been pulled from my self-imposed exile with a vengeance, and in the process I've plucked up a measure of courage from somewhere—perhaps I inherited something from my father, after all.

"We form an unholy alliance, *mon ami*." Darton leaned against the settee, and spoke quietly to de Gilles. "I confess to uneasiness."

"No more than I," de Gilles answered in the same tone, watching the Englishmen as they carefully went through Epione's armoire. "But someone is manipulating our actions, and so I think it best we ally with them—in this, at least."

"Do we stay at their safe house?"

"No," de Gilles answered. "I am not such a fool as that."

179

The other offered a small smile, and nodded his head. "*Bien sûr.*"

"Where do we go?" asked Epione, hoping she would be permitted to pack a bandbox, at least. One could be courageous, and yet be better-dressed.

Her husband tilted his head in apology. "I'm afraid it is best you not know, *ma belle.*"

"Because I am not good at this—this business, I suppose," she admitted with good grace. "But I am improving, I think."

"*En effet*, Mademoiselle; you have accomplished what was once considered impossible." Darton bowed. "I stand in awe."

"Do not tease my wife," de Gilles admonished absently, as he watched the others, and Epione reflected with some sympathy that it must have come as a surprise to Darton that de Gilles—so long a bachelor—had married in such a rush. Indeed, it would not be surprising if the man was a bit resentful, but thus far he had maintained his rather insouciant good humor, for which she was grateful—she wouldn't want to come between her husband and his longtime friend.

There was a timid knock on the door, and all the men immediately drew their weapons and stepped behind door jambs and furniture, braced for battle. His own weapon drawn, de Gilles stepped to the door to lift an edge of the lace curtain with a finger. "It is the landlady, only."

"It is Madame Reyne," Epione explained to everyone, in apology. "She is rather a clinging vine."

"Answer, then," suggested the spymaster, "else she'll call the Watch." He signaled to his men to step into the bedchamber, out of sight.

Epione answered the door, and was only recalled to the fact she was dressed as a boy when the woman's eyes widened in shock, and she couldn't seem to find her voice.

"Good evening, Madame." Epione cast about for an explanation for her appearance, but found herself at a loss—she had not improved as much as she'd thought, in the thinking-on-one's-feet.

Abashed, the woman nervously clasped her hands before her. "I beg your pardon, Mademoiselle, but I heard voices and saw the light—so late—and I thought, what if it is the murderer?"

"Madame," de Gilles offered, stepping forward and taking the woman's hand. "I must assure you that I am not the murderer."

"Oh—oh, certainly not." The woman gazed into de Gilles eyes, and seemed to lose her train of thought.

Epione was suddenly aware that de Gilles' presence was not helping matters, at least in her landlady's eyes. "You must congratulate us, Madame; we were married, this day."

Astonished, the woman's rather slack mouth hung open for a moment. "Is that so, Mademoiselle? Well yes—yes, of course; my best wishes." Thinking over this unexpected development for a moment, she arrived at the inevitable conclusion. "You'll be moving out, then."

Epione found she did not wish to deceive the woman, and so admitted, "Yes. But I will make certain you are paid to the end of the month."

Assimilating this blow, her landlady paused only a moment, and then said briskly, "Ah, well; I am happy for you, Mademoiselle, indeed I am."

The woman's gaze traveled behind Epione to rest on Darton in confusion, and Epione hastened to explain, "We must—we must catch a ship, I'm afraid, and so the gentlemen are helping me pack up my things. I am so sorry if we caused you any alarm."

"Oh—no, not at all." The woman's face suddenly brightened. "I've just now baked soda bread, and you must take it for your journey—it will keep for at least a week, one would think."

"*Merci*, Madame." De Gilles glanced over at Epione, and moved his head ever so slightly toward the stairway.

Taking her cue, Epione stepped through the door, and joined the woman on the landing. "That's sounds lovely, Madame. Shall I fetch it?"

With almost palpable reluctance, the woman tore her gaze from de Gilles, and then turned to accompany Epione. "Yes. And I have a tincture powder which is helpful for seasickness— I'll put some in a packet for you. It wouldn't do to be seasick, on your honeymoon."

Epione met de Gilles' laughing glance for a brief moment before agreeing, then gently steered the woman down the stairs, whilst de Gilles stood in the doorway above, watching them.

"Such a handsome gentleman," the older woman marveled, as she led Epione through her own sitting room, and back toward her kitchen. "How did you meet?"

I should have a plausible tale, Epione realized, as this is certainly not the last time I will be asked such a question. "Our families were acquainted." This had the benefit of being true, and did not require an exposition on the perilous state of the French monarchy.

"Oh—I didn't realize you had any family, Mademoiselle."

Sidestepping an explanation, Epione gently corrected her, "It is 'Madame', now."

"Madame," the other woman pronounced with a smile, and made a gesture toward a cupboard. "The bread is there on the shelf—would you reach it for me? Then I needn't fetch the step."

Thinking that it was not very sensible to store bread out of easy reach, Epione opened the cupboard and as she did so, she was suddenly grasped from behind, a hand pressed over her mouth and a strong arm pulled tight around her, lifting her from the floor.

Struggling in horror, she clawed at the hand on her face, breathing in a sickening smell from the cloth that was wadded therein. As she was quickly carried toward the back, the last thing she remembered was Lisabetta, shaking out a blanket, and warning, "Careful; it is more than my life is worth if she is injured."

183

Chapter 22

After several unsuccessful attempts, Epione finally managed to open her eyes, aware on some level that she was not in a good place, and that it was important to fight this woolly-headed feeling.

She was in a dimly-lit room with a low, wooden ceiling which smelt of—something she should recognize. Closing her eyes to regroup, she identified the sharp, tangy scent as the river Thames. She then became aware of a slight rocking movement, and came to the conclusion that she was stowed on a ship of some sort.

Opening her eyes again, she took a tentative inventory, and her last coherent memories came flooding back as she licked her lips, which were cracked and dry. At least it appears that I am not slated to be murdered, she thought—although at long last, the enemy has managed to devise a successful abduction; practice made perfect, apparently.

There was no porthole, although it appeared to be daytime, judging from the small slivers of light that filtered in through the wooden planks. She could hear muffled men's voices outside, as she tentatively moved her arms and shifted her head, to ease her stiff neck. De Gilles was proved right; Lisabetta was playing a double game, and it would probably be best to make an immediate escape. She could leap into the Thames, as long as the shore was in sight—she wasn't a strong swimmer, but she could certainly shout for help; the wharves were always busy.

Carefully, she placed her feet over the side of the narrow bunk and stood, one hand on the upper bunk, waiting until her legs steadied themselves and her head stopped spinning. She then crept over to the cabin door, holding her breath and lifting the latch quietly. Immediately she heard a man's voice call out in French, and realized the door was locked. It would have been too easy, she thought with resignation, and headed back to sit on the bunk so as to await events. I will make a plan—I will pretend submission, and then when their guard is down, I will fling myself into the river. I am wearing breeches, so it should not be too difficult to make an escape, and surely, surely, someone will come to my aid.

Buoyed by this thought, she listened to the footsteps approaching outside the cabin door, until it was unlatched to reveal Lisabetta, who came within, accompanied by a man who secured the door after them. Epione sat docilely, and complained, "You are unkind, Lisabetta. I did not look for such a trick from you."

As the man turned to face her, Epione was astonished to recognize the priest who'd married her to de Gilles. With a leap of her heart, she carefully didn't allow a reaction, but felt much heartened; it did seem as though succor was at hand—she need only look alive for any secret instruction the man might give. That her husband was not going to take this latest piece of skullduggery in good part went without saying— she'd be rescued; she need only keep a cool head. In the meantime, she should probably learn as much as she could, so as to be useful when the inevitable rescue occurred.

"Be careful what you tell her," cautioned the priest. Although Epione tried to catch his eye, he did not seem inclined to acknowledge his hidden role, or to grant her any assurances.

"She will do as she is told," Lisabetta replied, as she assessed Epione with a critical eye. "She is not one to put up a fight."

"I threw the gin bottle at you," Epione reminded her, stung by this dismissal and thinking it very unfair. "And I believe Mr. Tremaine will be very disappointed in you, Lisabetta."

The Frenchwoman slanted her an amused look. "Robert was never my object, *imbecile*—you were. And now I have bruises that I do not thank you for."

186

Exasperated, Epione swept aside the tendrils that had escaped from her braids. "I don't understand why it is so important to abduct me—*tiens*, if Napoleon wanted *Desclaires*, there was nothing to stop him from simply seizing it."

At this observation, the priest cast an alarmed glance at Lisabetta, and Epione was reminded that she should not give away what she knew—she never seemed to learn this lesson, but honestly, it was hard to keep it all straight, when one's head hurt so.

Lisabetta lifted a flask of water, and offered it to Epione. "You will see—there is a gentleman who wishes to meet you, only.   Nothing to be concerned about."

As this seemed palpably untrue—in light of recent events—Epione could only glance at her with a healthy dose of skepticism as she lifted the flask and drank; the water was most welcome, and she felt more like herself almost immediately.

The other girl then continued in what was, for her, a remarkably placating tone. "You will be given many fine clothes—and many jewels, also. You will like this, *eh bien*?   It will be quite a change, for a shop girl like you."

But Epione could not like the implied insult. "I make some very fine hats, I'll have you know."

"And men," the other agreed with a sly glance.

"There have been no men," corrected the priest. "De Gilles dupes her, is all."

"Everyone dupes her," Lisabetta pointed out fairly. "You cannot single out de Gilles."

187

But Epione could feel the blood drain from her face as she assimilated the import of the conversation. "You—you are not truly a priest?"

"Only when the occasion warrants." The man smiled. "*Deo gratias.*"

Suddenly feeling a bit faint, Epione faltered, "You—you did not marry us? I am not married to Monsieur de Gilles?"

"*Bien sûr que non,*" confirmed Lisabetta, almost kindly. "That one—he never even takes a lover; he certainly would not take a wife."

Rather stupidly, Epione looked from one to the other. "I don't believe you—he has not duped me; he believes we are married."

"He is a slave trader," Lisabetta informed her bluntly, and removed the water flask from Epione's nerveless hands. "Whatever he tells you is not the truth." In an apparent attempt to soften this blow, she added, "You cannot be blamed for being so *stupide*—he is *très, très beau.*"

Completely shocked, Epione tried to gather her scattered wits. "*C'est pas vrai*—I don't believe you."

Lisabetta made a clucking sound with her tongue. "Fah—you are very naïve, I think. But you are better off with us, you will soon see. You are a very lucky girl—like the princess, in a fairy story."

Epione dropped her head into her hands, rubbing her eyes with her palms so as to have a moment to assess. That she'd been dealt blow upon blow could not be argued, but nonetheless, she needed to get to shore, and now she had a ready excuse to feign submission. "I feel a bit faint," she murmured from behind her hands. "What you tell me is so very shocking—please; I must lie down." If they would leave her alone, perhaps she could find something to pick the lock, in the best de Gilles tradition.

Lisabetta regarded her for a moment, then said to her companion, "Best report to him that she is awake, and ask for instruction."

"Who is 'him'?" With a show of weakness, Epione lay down, watching the faux-priest depart through the cabin door. She tried to look wan, which was not so very difficult, given the circumstances.

"Enough; you ask too many questions." Absently, the other girl lifted the flask of water.

This is probably my best chance, thought Epione, before whoever is in charge makes an appearance. Girding herself, she waited until the girl was drinking, then sprang up to shove her into the cabin wall with as much strength as she could muster. Whirling to dart through the door, she then pelted up the companionway steps two at a time, in a mad scramble to make it to the deck.

"Do not hurt her," shouted Lisabetta from below, but the startled sailors on deck needed no such instruction, because suddenly, Epione had abandoned all thought of escape. Instead, she came to a sudden halt on the open deck, and stared before her in stunned disbelief.

There were no wharves, no Thames, and no potential allies; the schooner was anchored in a cove along a stark coastline, fronted by imposing limestone cliffs. Towering above them was a massive château, the walls running along the cliffs, and the graceful towers glinting in the sunlight, as the waves crashed against the rock below. Epione had no memory of the place, but nevertheless, she recognized it immediately. "*Desclaires*," she breathed.

"Welcome back to *la belle France*," Lisabetta offered in an ironic tone.

]

Chapter 23

While Epione struggled with the realization she'd been spirited away from England, Lisabetta stepped up behind her, and offered helpfully, "You see? You no longer have any choice in the matter."

Overwhelmed with dismay—and still reeling from the disclosures about her erstwhile husband—Epione made a rapid calculation. It was evident she was in the power of some very determined people, and that she had little hope of prevailing on her own—although it was impossible to believe de Gilles was not at this very moment masterminding her rescue. Unless—unless Lisabetta was right, and he was using her for his own ends, which frankly did not bear thinking about. In the meantime, she should find out as much as she could, so as to have something to report to de Gilles when she saw him again.

I *will* see him again, she assured herself, digging deep into that well of courage she'd discovered within herself. I must believe it, or I will go mad, in this upside-down life I've been living.

To this end, she calmly faced the other girl, and asked in a practical tone, "It is past time for some answers, I believe. What is the price I must pay for holding title to this place? Come—be honest with me, Lisabetta."

But apparently, no revelations were yet to be made. "Your task is to be pretty, and stay quiet—you will see." Lisabetta shielded her eyes with a hand and gazed at the château, the sunlight reflecting off the blue-tiled roof. "You are very lucky, *sans doute.*"

"I must disagree," Epione retorted crossly. *Dieu*, her head hurt, and the bright sun did not help.

The other girl made a derisive sound, as she indicated the château with a gesture. "You are a very foolish girl, to long for your poor little rooms, and your poor little shop."

"Apparently, that was all a sham, and even if it weren't, that is not what I long for." Epione immediately wished she hadn't brought up the subject; truly, she should learn to hold her tongue.

But the other girl only shot her a surprisingly sympathetic glance. "Ah—I know you are *dévastée,* but you will have much with which to console yourself—you will see."

But before Epione could question her further, she heard footsteps approaching on the deck, and turned to behold the astonishing sight of Monsieur Chauvelin—the tailor—who strode toward her, his cape billowing out to the sides in the sea breeze. As he halted before the two girls, Epione considered the extent of the fraud that had been perpetuated upon her and wondered, with a sinking heart, why the enemy felt it was all worthwhile.

The tailor's expression was unreadable. "Mademoiselle."

Epione almost corrected him, but then realized with a small pang that she was, indeed, still a mademoiselle. For some reason, this unhappy thought engendered a spark of defiance so that she found the wherewithal to affect a chiding tone. "I am very unhappy with you, Monsieur. I thought you stood my friend."

But if she expected to hear an apology, she was to be disappointed. "You misconstrued the situation, then." The man regarded her, and she was struck by the coldness that lay behind his eyes—it reminded her of something—of someone; the wisp of a memory eluded her.

He glanced at Lisabetta. "We will go ashore as soon as possible; we are too exposed, here."

"Exposed to whom?" asked Epione with her new-found defiance. Presumably the British—it was not inconceivable that they were watching *Desclaires*, as they were already aware it was the focus of some sort of plot having to do with the pretenders to the French throne. Heartened by this thought, she allowed her gaze to scan the cliffs, but saw no signs of life.

The tailor seemed surprised that she'd made so bold as to inquire, and replied in a brusque tone, "You will ask no questions." Then, with a jerk of his head to Lisabetta, "Take her below while we lower the skiff—and do not allow her to come on deck again until I give the signal."

Annoyed at such high-handedness, it occurred to Epione that she had some leverage in the situation; they were being very careful not to hurt her—even Lisabetta—which indicated they needed her cooperation, for some reason. Lifting her chin, Epione rebuked him coldly. "You will mend your manners, Monsieur, or I will not allow you to enter my château."

Lisabetta smothered a small gasp, as the man turned to stare in outrage at Epione for a moment, obviously fighting an urge to berate her. After a visible struggle, he bowed stiffly. "Your pardon, Mademoiselle."

Ah, thought Epione, a bit surprised, despite herself; apparently I do hold sway here, and they dare not cross me.

"You will come this way, *s'il vous plait*," said Lisabetta in a forced polite tone, very unnatural for her. "We will wait below, while the men prepare to go ashore."

"You will be shown every courtesy," Chauvelin offered abruptly. "Please do as she says."

Thoughtfully, Epione accompanied Lisabetta back to the cabin below, trying to decide what was best to do so as to prepare the ground—so to speak—for an eventual escape. To this end, she decided she should not openly defy Chauvelin in the future, for fear he'd place her under lock and key; she'd little doubt that he was so inclined, but that his hand was stayed, for some reason. She'd gained the uneasy impression that he was not a man to cross, despite his guise as a tailor. "Tell me, why are you afraid of him, Lisabetta?"

The other girl took a quick glance over her shoulder and replied in a low tone, "I am afraid of no one. But you will do best to stay out of his way."

"Why is that—is he dangerous? And does he stay at *Desclaires*? Do you?"

"*Mais oui*; we will all be very merry together." This said with heavy irony, as the girl shut the cabin door behind them.

In light of the circumstances, Epione could be forgiven for voicing her exasperation. "You are of all things annoying, Lisabetta, and the British were foolish not to have you bound, hand and foot. They'll not make the same mistake twice."

Rather than respond, Lisabetta scowled and sank onto the bunk, so that Epione was left with no place to sit. "Tell me; what do you know of this—this Darton?" The name was pronounced as though it were a bitter taste in her mouth.

"He seems to be a fine swordsman." Epione leaned against the door, happy to have a chance to needle the other girl, for a change. "No doubt he keeps a collection of severed locks in his waistcoat."

Her color rising, Lisabetta raised her chin in scorn. "Such an insult is only to be expected from such a one."

"Such a one as what?"

The girl shrugged, pretending disinterest, as she smoothed her skirts. "He sails with de Gilles—*par conséquent*, he is a rogue."

This seemed a trifle harsh to Epione— especially considering that Lisabetta herself was a rogue of the first order, and so she allowed her skepticism to show. "Why do you say they are rogues? They both seem very gentlemanly to me, and not at all unmannered. Perhaps you are mistaken about—about the rumors of slave-trading."

But the girl only lifted an amused brow, and adopted the tone of a mother consoling a disappointed child. "Perhaps."

Sensing an opportunity to do some delicate probing, Epione offered, "I don't know much about Monsieur de Gilles, in truth. You said he doesn't take any lovers."

"He doesn't need to." The girl's dark eyes slid toward hers.

"I don't understand any of this," Epione confessed, biting back her impatience, "So I am not certain what you mean."

Her eyes alight with a trace of malice, the Frenchwoman explained, "I mean he trades prostitutes from Algiers—young girls."

Epione stared at her for a long, shocked moment, and then knew with complete certainty that whatever game de Gilles was playing, it was indeed a game. The idea that he was selling young girls into prostitution was so out of character with what she knew of the man that paradoxically, it was a tale too far. They may all believe that he did something unsavory to earn his living—indeed, Tremaine had hinted as much—but it was a false front, or a false flag, as these people styled it. De Gilles was true, she *knew* it; and the fact she'd been mistaken about Sir Lucien—and was a bit naïve about this whole spying business—could not shake this certain conviction. He was true, he wanted to be married to her, and he was coming; she had only to be patient.

Hiding her intense relief at this epiphany, Epione only replied, "I am certain you are mistaken, Lisabetta."

The other girl shrugged. "He needs *Desclaires* as another landing place on the coast—that is why he courts you."

Epione pointed out pragmatically, "Then—if it is true, and his purpose is to control my land—why would he dupe me with a false priest? If we aren't truly married, then he doesn't hold *Desclaires*."

"Because he wants *you* to believe you are married," she replied as though speaking to a simpleton. "But you must not blame yourself—as I said, he is *très, très beau.*" Absently, she fingered the shorn curl at her throat. "As for me, I prefer men who are not so pretty."

"Mr. Droughm?" Epione ventured, remembering the earlier conversation about this new-married man.

But Lisabetta was not to be drawn on this topic, and replied rather shortly, "Droughm is none of your business."

But Epione offered with feminine sympathy, "Believe me, I know how you feel; you wish him every happiness, but nonetheless you wish he could have been happy with you, instead."

But this tack was apparently recognized for the lure that it was, and the other girl only replied in a mocking tone, "If you have de Gilles in your bed, then you have nothing to complain about."

Swallowing a retort, Epione decided that it was of all things unfair that she hadn't, in fact, had such an opportunity, and then tried to concentrate on her new resolve to discover as much as she was able. "I am not complaining, I am simply pointing out that oftentimes things do seem to work out for the best. After all, if you had stayed with Mr. Droughm you would not have met Mr. Tremaine." Belatedly, Epione realized this was not the best subject to raise, as apparently Tremaine was yet another suitor who had thrown Lisabetta over.

But Lisabetta only laughed aloud. "*Peste*, but you are *ingénue*. Robert serves his own purposes, just as I do."

Despite having been rebuffed at every turn, Epione persevered. "I will concede that no one is who they seem. But I would be very curious to find out what all this has to do with who wears the crown of France."

On hearing this remark, the other girl's flippant attitude disappeared, and she lowered her voice, her tone very serious. "You must do as you are told, and ask no more questions, or it will be the worse for you. Do you understand?"

For a moment, Epione had the impression the girl was sincerely concerned about her safety, and so she nodded, a bit taken aback. But this rare glimpse of compassion disappeared when Lisabetta tossed her head. "If you are killed, I will be in terrible trouble."

Exasperated, Epione felt as though she were right back where she started. "Why? Why do I matter so much?"

"Because no one is what they seem," Lisabetta reminded her, and Epione was forced to be content with this cryptic comment.

Chapter 24

Her hands cold from clutching the skiff's gunwale, Epione watched the cliffs come ever closer. The small vessel plowed through the waves, and the salty spray stung Epione's eyes as the tailor and the false priest urged the rowing sailors to keep up their pace.

After a tense few minutes, Epione realized they were headed toward a grotto at the base of the cliffs which was only visible once they'd cleared the inlet. As the skiff skimmed under the low, rocky outcropping, they entered into a natural cave, and the water suddenly became still, with the sound of the oars echoing off the rock walls as they dipped into the water.

Leaning to look ahead past the oarsmen, Epione could see a wooden dock along the opposite end of the grotto, and the figures of two women standing thereon, clearly expecting them. As they drew closer, Epione was unsurprised to discover that one of them was Madame Reyne, her treacherous landlady.

As the skiff approached the dock, it suddenly occurred to Epione that she was probably returning to the same secret exit where her mother—with two small daughters—had fled from the Jacobins, over twenty years before. In this somber, echoing place, it was a simple thing to imagine her mother's fear and despair, on that long-ago occasion. My mother was a very unhappy woman, she thought; but it could not have been easy—fleeing one's home and country, and all the while knowing that you may never see your husband or son again.

The skiff bumped up against the dock, and the sailors leapt out to secure the small craft as Madame Reyne dipped a quick curtsey. "Welcome to *Desclaires*, Mademoiselle."

But Epione was having none of it, and replied with a full measure of contempt, "You should be ashamed of yourself, Madame."

But the older woman only clasped her hands before her. "You will see, Mademoiselle—it will be much the better for you, here in this fine place."

Epione met the other's gaze with open scorn. "I'd rather not have my choices taken from me." She noted that the maidservant who stood beside the woman raised her gaze for the briefest moment, before returning it to the wooden planks at her feet. The girl—a redhead, with a mass of freckles—seemed rather cowed, which was not a surprise; Epione was rather cowed herself, although she was striving mightily to disguise this unfortunate fact.

The women were handed out of the skiff, and then Chauvelin turned to the false priest. "Best be off; the ship may invite curiosity, and you are needed in Bengal."

The other nodded, and indicated to the sailors that they were to cast off again. "Good luck to both of us, then." He bowed with mock-gallantry to the women. "Ladies; *adieu.*"

As the small vessel made its silent way out of the grotto, Lisabetta turned to Madame Reyne. "*En avant,* and I am in need of a bath. How many servants have you here?"

"It is a small staff—of necessity," the woman apologized. "But Luci, here, will see to both of you—she's a bit simple, but she is very biddable."

Hearing this, the tailor made an impatient sound, as he walked down the dock toward the door that was embedded in the cave's wall. "Surely, we will have more servants for the dinner party? We cannot be seen to be lacking."

"Am I holding a dinner party?" Epione was cross and tired, and decided it was time to assert herself—she wanted a bath every bit as much as Lisabetta.

Chauvelin answered over his shoulder, "You will not ask questions, Mademoiselle; all will be revealed in time."

Epione was heartily tired of being patronized by the traitorous tailor, and forgot her resolution not to antagonize him. "I believe we have already established that you must answer to me, sir."

For whatever reason, this remark caused the man to turn on his heel, and stride angrily toward her, halting with his face only inches away from hers; his rage barely controlled. "Do not play the *aristo* with me, Mademoiselle. The old order has passed away, and will never return. You would do well to remember this."

Rather taken aback by his overreaction, Epione tempered her tone. "You forget that I am but a milliner, Monsieur. But a milliner who nonetheless holds title to this place."

For a tense moment, she could see that he struggled with an urge to make a curt rejoinder, then thought the better of it, and stepped away. "Your pardon, Mademoiselle."

Epione was not fooled—as it was apparent he would have gladly strangled her on the spot—but once again, she was made aware that she did have some sort of power, even if the reason for it was unclear. "I would have some answers," she continued in an even tone. "Now that we have arrived, surely the time for secrets has passed."

After a moment's thought, the man turned to Madame Reyne. "He is in residence?"

"He is," the woman nodded.

The tailor assessed her with his cold gaze. "Then you shall have your answers this evening, Mademoiselle."

"And who is 'he'?" Epione was understandably suspicious, but Lisabetta covertly squeezed her arm in warning, and so she subsided, and walked with the other girl to the grotto's door. Best hold her tongue and await events—whatever was going forward, it did not seem to be overly-dangerous, if it was to involve dinner parties. And she continued to hold out hope that de Gilles would come to her rescue—although how this was to be accomplished remained unclear, since she was now locked away in a fortified château. No matter; he seemed a very resourceful pretender, and she would listen and learn as much as she could, in the meantime. He *would* come, she was certain of it, and— considering the circumstances—he would need as much aid as she could provide.

Strengthened by this resolve, she followed Lisabetta up a narrow stairway, and even though it was daytime, Madame Reyne lit a candle against the dimness. They emerged through a plain and narrow door into a stillroom of some sort, and then crossed into what appeared to be the servants' hall behind the kitchen—deserted, and a bit dusty. Their footsteps echoed on the wooden floor, and Epione noted that it was very quiet—she heard only a profound silence, as Madame led them to the narrow servants' stairwell. A daunting place, she thought, suppressing a shudder; cold, and unfriendly—it was just as well that they'd escaped, long ago.

At the base of the stairwell, Chauvelin indicated he would leave them, and instructed

Lisabetta, "You will stay with Mademoiselle at all times, and I will speak with you later."

But it seemed evident that Lisabetta was chafing at her role as Epione's keeper. "You must discover how long before I can leave this place—it was not made clear."

The tailor frowned. "It is my understanding you are to stay until after the dinner party. After that time, you may leave."

With an impatient gesture, Lisabetta shrugged her shoulders. "How long is that?"

"Two days hence, I believe." He looked to Madame for verification, and she nodded in confirmation. "I will speak with you at a later time. *Au revoir.*"

Lisabetta watched him go for a moment, then signaled to Madame. "Something to eat, if you please. I am *très affamé,* from all this nonsense."

The older woman turned to the red-headed maid, and spoke to her in English, using simple words. "Go tell the cook that the ladies would like tea served in their rooms. Can you do this, Luci?"

The girl nodded eagerly, and hurried away, clearly pleased to be given a task.

Epione watched the maidservant's exit thoughtfully. If the girl was English, perhaps she could be enlisted to betray her employers. "She seems a sweet girl. Where did you find her?"

Madame Reyne looked back over her shoulder, as she lifted her skirts to mount the stairs. "Luci was hired from a service in London, and very pleased to take a trip to France. She'll not say anything she oughtn't to the wrong people, which was why she was hired."

They followed the woman up two flights of stairs until they emerged into the main living quarters, and then walked softly down the plaster-walled hallway, the wall sconces unlit; the atmosphere tomb-like. Despite her best efforts, Epione knew a moment's dread; they don't want witnesses, she realized—there is a skeleton staff, and the only maidservant does not understand what is being said.

Made uneasy by these thoughts—or at least more uneasy than she was already—she asked Lisabetta, "Tell me about the dinner party two days hence; am I to attend?"

But Lisabetta seemed preoccupied, and said only, "You will do as you are told."

Tired of hearing the same refrain, Epione retorted, "And what if I refuse? What if I refuse to play the hostess, in this charade?"

But Lisabetta was unfazed, as she followed Madame Reyne down the hall, her skirts swishing on the wooden floor. "*Je vous assure*, you do not dare refuse; it is the only thing that keeps you alive."

Chapter 25

The landlady-turned housekeeper paused before an ornately carved set of double doors, and then opened them to reveal an elaborate suite of rooms, richly appointed and flanked at the other end by long, diamond-paned windows that were framed by velvet curtains, pooling onto the thick Aubusson rug. "Your rooms," the woman announced, pleased to reveal such splendor. "I will arrange for your baths, and Luci will deliver your tea."

Bemused, Epione walked across the suite's main room, and stood beside the window, which looked out over the sparkling ocean—the view was breathtaking, but she was preoccupied by Lisabetta's ominous remark, and so could not appreciate it in full. "Who else is in residence?" she asked the housekeeper.

The woman's gaze rested doubtfully on Lisabetta for a moment, but as the other girl offered no comment, she responded, "I am sorry, Mademoiselle, but I am instructed to answer no questions." They stood for an awkward moment, and then the woman brightened and made a consolatory gesture toward the armoire which stood against the wall. "Your wardrobe has many lovely gowns—go, look at them." With a final smile, the woman nodded and withdrew, reaching to close the doors behind her with a soft click.

"Cease asking questions," Lisabetta warned, slouching onto the settee with a rustle of skirts, and kicking off her shoes with no further ado. "*Peste*, it is tedious in the extreme."

"Then I'll thank you not to make dire pronouncements." Epione crossed to the armoire, which opened to reveal a marvelous variety of gowns—evening, day, and walking dresses in an assortment of colors and styles. Utterly bemused, Epione fingered a bronze evening gown and turned its hem to examine the fine stitching and beadwork; none knew better than she the quality of the wardrobe—it was of the finest, and would have been ridiculously expensive.

Lisabetta raised her arms over her head and stretched. "Do you see? I told you; you will be treated like a *princesse*."

But Epione glanced over at the other girl. "I'd rather not be treated as a *princesse* if I'm slated to be buried in such a gown."

"Perhaps you will survive," her Job's comforter offered. "We shall see."

Absently, Epione rubbed the skirt of another silk satin evening gown—this one Pomona green—between her fingers. "Tell me where you hail from, Lisabetta—unless it another in the long list of things I am not allowed to know."

With a small smile, the girl leaned back on the settee, tucking one leg under the other. "I am from Martinique."

This was a surprise, and Epione turned to her. "Like the former Empress?" Napoleon's Josephine was from the island of Martinique.

"*Eh bien*, the very same." Lisabetta arched a brow, as though privately amused.

Epione debated how much she should ask, and then remembered she was trying to acquire information for de Gilles. "How did you come to be here, then?"

The other girl gazed out the windows at the sea. "I was found to be useful, by those who have need of usefulness."

Epione quirked her mouth. "I suppose that is a sufficiently vague description, given how you earn your keep."

The girl shrugged her shoulders, unrepentant. "It is the most explanation you will be given."

With a small sigh, Epione returned to her inventory of the armoire. "Whereas I am not mysterious in the least—everyone, it seems, knows everything about me. And I can't lay claim to being of much use."

But her companion disagreed, as she examined her fingernails. "*Au contraire, mignonne*; you have been remarkably useful, and will continue to be so."

As Epione reverently stroked the ermine cuff on a pelisse, she returned in a tart tone, "I cannot see how—unless I am required to trim a poke bonnet for the successor to the throne."

Lisabetta only clucked her tongue in a chiding fashion, as Luci the maid entered with the tea tray, the girl's brow knit in concentration as she moved carefully, so as to keep the cups from rattling. Epione came to her assistance, and together they placed the tray on the tea table. "Thank you very much, Luci—it looks delicious."

"You speak English." Luci gazed upon her in surprise, her clear green eyes wide.

"I do—I've lived in England all my life. I am Epione." She held out a friendly hand.

After a moment, the other girl took it, clearly a bit overawed, and uncertain how to react. "I am Lucrezia."

"Lucrezia—I see." Epione tried to hide her surprise that someone would give this simple girl such a bloodthirsty name. "Can you tell me—"

"Do not browbeat the help," Lisabetta interrupted in English, from her position on the settee. "I said no more questions; have you no shame?"

Her freckled brow knit, Luci looked from Lisabetta to Epione in confusion, but then took refuge in protocol. "Shall I pour out, Miss?"

"Yes, please." Epione smiled upon the maid, and took her steaming cup with gratitude. A plate of macaroons had been included, and she was grateful; the last time she'd eaten was at *The Moor's Head*, which now seemed like a thousand years ago—pausing, she was suddenly struck. "What were you doing at the tavern, Lisabetta? Were you seriously hoping to abduct me from such a place, with every eye on de Gilles?

The girl popped a macaroon in her mouth. "That is none of your business."

With a sound of exasperation, Epione quickly gathered up a few of the treats in a napkin, to prevent the other girl from eating them all. "It was certainly my business when you started shooting."

Luci stilled, and stared at Lisabetta in acute dismay. "You were—you were *shooting?*"

Lisabetta did not disclaim, but fastened a cold eye on the maidservant. "Out, before I shoot at you, too."

Hastily, the maid picked up her skirts and fled, as Epione chastised Lisabetta in a low tone, "You mustn't take advantage of her—it is cruel."

But Lisabetta only looked amused, and made no reply.

Tentatively encouraged by the fact Lisabetta had been willing to impart some scraps of information—however unuseful, Epione sipped her tea and ventured, "You are acquainted with Monsieur Chauvelin, and I have the impression you do not care for him."

The other girl contemplated the now-empty macaroon plate, and sucked on a fingertip. "It matters not whether I care for him; I do as he asks."

"He is a Jacobin, I think. He doesn't like *aristos* much."

Lisabetta leaned, and plucked a sweet from Epione's napkin. "No one likes *aristos* much."

"He needs me for a dinner party, though—which seems a bit strange, if he's a Jacobin."

"No more questions—I will not tell you again."

They sat in silence for a few minutes, until a tap on the door signaled the bath water's arrival, and a sandy-haired footman entered, carrying the steaming brass buckets. Madame Reyne directed that they be deposited by the hearth, and then looked about the room. "Why, where is Luci?"

"She left," said Lisabetta succinctly.

"She is very sensitive," the housekeeper scolded. "Please do not upset her; I need her help."

"I'll go fetch her," offered the sandy-haired footman.

"Tell her to bring me more macaroons, and much more wine," Lisabetta called after him as she began to roll off her stockings.

"I'm bathing first," Epione said firmly.

The other girl sat down again on the settee, and propped her bare feet on the serving table. "*Bien entendu, princesse.* I ask only that you leave some hot water for me."

"I'll be quick." And in short order, Epione was blessedly clean again, and sitting before the fire so that her hair could dry, while Lisabetta took her turn. As Epione had experienced a very tumultuous day, it was no surprise that she fell asleep, wrapped in the thick chenille robe, and sunk down in the upholstered silk chair. She dreamed a strange dream; of standing in the grotto to watch the tailor, as he sat on the wharf and stitched together a shroud, whilst Lisabetta quietly urged her to slip into the water, and swim for England. "I cannot," Epione whispered to her; "Alexis will come for me."

"Too late," Lisabetta whispered back; "the war will come first."

Chapter 26

Epione awoke to the sound of Madame Reyne speaking her name, and started for a moment until she remembered where she was; *Desclaires*, and apparently slated to live a cosseted life for the foreseeable future—although Lisabetta had hinted that her future may be short, and not all that foreseeable.

"You will be needed downstairs for dinner soon, Mademoiselle. I will dress your hair."

After noting that Lisabetta was no longer in evidence, Epione blinked the sleep from her eyes and asked, "What is my role here, Madame Reyne? Come, it is only fair that I am forewarned— I am the mistress, here, and I may need you as an ally."

The woman was silent for a moment as she picked up a brush. "I'm afraid I must not say, Mademoiselle."

Epione offered as a prompt, "Am I in danger? Lisabetta warned that if I'd like to remain alive, I should be pretty, and stay quiet."

The housekeeper seemed a bit shocked by this assertion, and hastened to assure her, "Oh, no, Mademoiselle—instead, you will be well looked-after." After pursing her lips, the woman unbent enough to add, "It is not such a bad bargain; much, much better than your rooms in Soho."

"That depends," said Epione slowly, "on what the bargain is."

The housekeeper twisted Epione's still-damp hair into a knot, and began to insert pins; Epione noted the woman was by no means an expert, but refrained from making suggestions and instead ventured, "And what of you, Madame? Why did you agree to this deception?"

"I'm afraid I must not say, Mademoiselle."

Epione made a wry mouth. "You don't strike me as a Napoleonite."

Stepping back to assess her handiwork, the woman replied with equanimity, "Such things matter little to me, Mademoiselle. I've had to look after myself my entire life, and I was only too happy to accept this offer, when it was made to me."

So; it seemed housekeeper would turn a benign eye to treachery in exchange for personal gain, which was a bit shocking to Epione, who had seen what such an attitude could foster firsthand, and had a dead sister to show for it. "Surely, the greater good is more important than one's own

215

comfort—you cannot want yet another war, after the misery caused by the last one."

But the woman was unrepentant, and strategically inserted a diamond pin beside the knot of curls atop Epione's head. "There's nothing any one person can do to stop a war—and both sides are the same, in the end. I'll be safe, and taken care of here, and that's all I could wish for. Up, now; I'm to deliver you downstairs at the top of the hour."

Epione stood, and allowed the woman to carefully lower the bronze satin evening gown over her head with a luxurious rustle of fabric. The elegant gown was a bit short, and some judicious tugging on the bodice only partially obscured this unfortunate fact. A necklace of very fine topazes was then strung around Epione's throat; she was to have many jewels, Lisabetta had said, as though it had some sort of significance—but Epione could not guess what that significance could be. Meeting the housekeeper's eyes in the mirror, she ventured, "Was this necklace my mother's?"

"Your mother's, Mademoiselle?" The woman paused, obviously at sea.

"My mother was the mistress of *Desclaires*, before The Terror."

Madame Reyne seemed rather surprised by this revelation. "I understood that your mother was—is no longer with us."

"That is true—she died a few months ago." Epione processed the interesting fact that the housekeeper was aware that her mother was dead, but was not aware of Epione's connection to the château. "I only mentioned it because she would often speak of her jewels—and her regret that she was forced to leave them behind, in her haste." In truth, a small casket of jewels had indeed been smuggled out and then sold, so as to set up the new widow in London. "She was very fond of topazes—that is why I asked."

"They go well with this dress." The woman stood back to admire the effect. "And there are many more in the south tower—all variety, to match the other dresses."

Turning from side to side, Epione pretended to admire her reflection in the gilt cheval mirror, and then asked casually, "Is there a village, nearby? I may need to visit a seamstress, to lower the hems a bit."

But the subterfuge was unsuccessful. "I'm afraid you mustn't leave the grounds, Mademoiselle; at least not as yet."

The housekeeper presented elbow length gloves of the finest kid, and as Epione pulled them on, she assessed her situation. It seemed clear that Madame Reyne would never be an ally, nor would Lisabetta, and she'd best find some way of fending for herself—or at least a means to aid de Gilles, when he came to rescue her.

Smiling at the housekeeper, she replied, "No matter; I can manage the hems myself—as long as you can find me a sewing kit, with shears, and a darning needle, please. And perhaps a length of lace trimming; Alençon, if it is available." May as well get the strongest lace—she may find it necessary to bind up the housekeeper, and the woman seemed rather sturdy.

"Yes, Mademoiselle; of course."

With a critical eye, the other woman stepped back to review her handiwork, and with an equally critical eye, Epione asked, "Have you any ribbons, to thread through my hair?"

"I'm afraid not, Mademoiselle; no one consulted with me, or I'd have suggested it."

"Then let us add ribbons to the list—nice, thick ones."

The housekeeper smiled with ill-concealed relief that her charge seemed to be making the best of it, unaware that her charge was in fact looking forward to trussing her up like a Christmas goose. Buoyed by this thought, Epione mentally steeled herself for whatever ordeal was to come. "Shall we go, then? I confess I am hungry."

Stepping out once again into the silent hallway, the housekeeper escorted Epione to the main staircase—a sweeping, marble-balustraded affair that reminded Epione, with every plush step, that her new silken slippers were a bit too small.

The only sound was the rustle of her skirts sweeping down the stairs; there were no servants in evidence, and no one in the vestibule that Epione could see, as she peered over the railing to gaze all the way down to the marbled first floor. This was to the good—if she were to tie up the housekeeper and attempt an escape, the fewer to raise the alarm, the better. On the other hand, if she did manage to escape, she'd hate to think that de Gilles might walk into the situation all unknowing—whatever the situation was. Presuming that he was indeed coming to rescue her, and that he was not at this very moment flirting, in his elegant way, with the next naïve milliner.

She was so busy dismissing this thought from her mind, that she almost didn't realize they'd arrived at what appeared to be the château's great hall—a high-ceilinged room, with wooden hammer beams arching overhead, and a fireplace that could roast an ox whole. She was only to have a brief impression of the cavernous room and its massive oaken table, however, before her attention was drawn to the gentleman standing before the hearth. Barely catching herself before gasping in surprise, Epione rapidly gathered her wits and sank into a respectful curtsey. "Comte deFabry." So—the grey-eyed spymaster had been proved right, and the vague and rather strange Comte deFabry—purportedly, Marie's lover—was involved in this plot, somehow.

To her immense surprise, the Comte crossed the room in swift strides to grasp her hands in his, and then press them to his chest, apparently too overcome to speak as he blinked back tears. His appearance had changed, since last she'd seen him; he was grayer around the temples, and his hair was longer, and pulled into a queue. He was also bit leaner than before—and definitely more emotional about the younger sister whom, heretofore, he'd largely ignored.

Her eyes downcast, Epione's mind raced as she resisted the urge to pull her hands away.

Was he the murderer? The latest victim of the London murders was rumored to have had a *liaison* with the Comte, and this did not bode well. It was hard to believe that such a harmless-seeming man had committed multiple murders, but perhaps his harmless appearance aided him in his evil efforts.

The Comte had not moved, and seemed deeply affected. "Epione—ah, beautiful Epione. You are taller than Marie; I had forgotten."

Feeling her way, and rather discomfited by the intensity of his gaze upon hers, she agreed, "Yes, a bit taller, Monsieur le Comte. I am so very pleased to see you again."

"Louis," he insisted with a small smile, as he gently lifted her hands to his mouth—one after the other—to kiss them. "You must call me Louis, and I will call you Epione—an apt name, for a goddess come to earth."

This was of interest, as she was fairly certain his name was Etienne, or at least that was what her mother and stepfather had called him. "Louis, then. I confess I am surprised to see you here."

"You are well?"

This, of course, was not an easy question to answer, but falling back on good manners, Epione assured him, "Very well. Although I regret to tell you that my mother has passed away; I don't know if you were aware—?"

"I am." He dropped his gaze for a moment. "And your stepfather too, leaving you quite alone, my poor Epione."

For a moment, she was tempted to recoil yet again; there was something very strange about the underlying edge of satisfaction in his tone when he made this pronouncement, and she entertained the horrifying thought that perhaps he'd killed her parents himself.

"You have no black gloves? You mustn't allow the English to make light of your sister's sacrifice—she must be properly mourned." With a solemn nod of his head, he indicated his own black gloves.

"I'm afraid I was not given an opportunity to pack." Best not to mention she hadn't worn mourning for any of them, being as she was trying to obscure her rather cloudy past.

"Are you pleased to be here? To be given back your family home?" He continued to hold her hands, his gleaming eyes searching hers.

She was fast coming to the unsettling conclusion that her companion was perhaps a bit unbalanced, and so she ventured very carefully, "It is quite lovely—extraordinarily so."

This accolade seemed to please him, and he relinquished her hands, and indicated he would sit with her at the massive table. "You will live here, then; and with every comfort imaginable. *Hélas,* I must be often away, but I insisted that you were to be installed here. I insisted most vehemently, and would not hear otherwise."

Hiding her extreme confusion, Epione once again fell back upon good manners. "You are very kind, Monsieur le Comte."

221

"Louis," he reminded her with a smile. "It may take some getting used to, I'm afraid."

"Louis," she agreed. "How kind of you to think of me." Probing carefully, she ventured, "The *émigré* community has fallen upon hard times, since last we met; there has been a spate of murders—have you heard?"

Reaching to take her hand, the Comte met her gaze, his own solemn. "Sacrifices are sometimes necessary, Epione; the benefits of the call of history are—*eh bien*—measured against the resolution of those burdened by its demands." He bent his head. "It is regrettable, but those who knew me well must bear the burden of such sacrifices." As he struggled with his emotions, tears once again glistened in his eyes. "Oh, Epione; if only your beautiful sister were here with us, to witness the triumph of her ambition. She was—ah, your sister was *une ange*; an angel come to earth."

"Yes." Epione replied in a gentle tone. Despite her increasing horror at the conclusions she was rapidly drawing, she felt a bit sorry for him. The Comte reminded her of Baron Givente, an impoverished *aristo* who'd haunted the fringes of the *émigré* community. His wife and children had been killed in The Terror, and as a result, he'd gone a bit mad, and had become a figure of sympathy. That the Comte deFabry entertained an unnatural devotion to her sister—and was now slightly unhinged as a result of her death— seemed evident. That he'd managed to convince those in power to give *Desclaires* to her and—

apparently—that he was connected in some way to the murders back in London also seemed evident. But whatever could it mean? What hold could this rather unstable man have over the factions that battled for power in Europe?

"Shall we dine, my dear? They have installed an excellent cook." The Comte smiled at her kindly.

"With pleasure." She smiled in return, and decided that the sooner she was armed with a sewing basket, the better.

Chapter 27

"Ah, my dear," the Comte said, lifting her hand to bestow a light kiss on its back. "I cannot describe my happiness at seeing you here. We will dine and speak of Marie—no one knew her as well as you did."

"I imagine not," Epione agreed, hiding her dismay, as the sandy-haired footman began to serve them. Apparently she would be required to construct some flattering depictions of her vain and unlikable sister to feed the Comte's infatuation—she was not good at subterfuge, but had best come up with a tale or two.

The great hall table featured three elaborate golden candelabras placed along its center to provide illumination, and the candlelight flickered off the planes of her host's face as he waved the footman aside, and stood to serve Epione the soup course with his own hands.

Epione absently agreed that the bisque was delicious, all the while striving mightily to puzzle out this extraordinary turn of events. Apparently, deFabry had some sort of power that allowed him to demand that his beloved Marie's sister be given a valuable estate—which made little sense, since it was hard to imagine a less likely power-broker than the man who sat across from her. She'd paid little attention to the Comte's history—her mother and Marie had been more interested in the *émigré* gossip—but as far as she knew, he was only one more in the lengthy list of impoverished noblemen who had been displaced by the French Revolution. Of course, he was cousin to Louis Philippe—one of the pretenders— but the Comte himself had no credible claim to the throne of France, and certainly in the last twenty years there'd been no indication that powerful forces were willing to support him; he'd been just another impoverished *aristo,* scratching out an existence in a foreign land.

Thinking to—delicately—explore what was expected of her, Epione smiled at him. "Are we to marry, Louis?"

This amused him, and he shook his head gently, as though denying a treat to a small child. "No, my dear; marriage would be impossible, under the circumstances. But rest assured you will want for nothing." He paused, and with a resolute expression, met her eyes. "And you have my solemn promise that your sister's killer will be brought to justice."

Rather taken aback by this reference, she thought it best to make an attempt to shield Sir Lucien. "I—I do not believe the authorities know who shot her—they cannot be certain."

"The *bâtard*," he spat out in a low voice, then tilted his head in apology. "I must beg your pardon for my language, Epione, but to think that her own husband could be so cold-blooded, so unnatural—"

In abject dismay, Epione tried to deflect his simmering rage. "Oh—Monsieur le Comte, you mustn't say such a thing; Sir Lucien—"

But her companion only clenched his fists on the table and pronounced, "I was there, Epione; I saw him. Indeed, I was lucky he did not shoot me, also."

As Epione was unable to muster a response, her companion added with emphasis, "It is well you should be shocked; you have been shielded from the truth. Sir Lucien was a foul spy, and Marie was—heroically!—attempting to stem his efforts when he cut her down, as though she was—was nothing more than *une chienne*." He paused for a moment, gazing into the fire with a lowered brow. "He will pay. I have been promised this."

Thinking that she may as well ask, Epione gently touched his hand. "By whom, Louis? Who has made you these promises?"

But the fit of fury had passed, and her companion bent his head to address the fish course. "I'm afraid I cannot tell you, my dear. And you must not ask too many questions—it is dangerous to know too much."

Pulling herself together, Epione nodded calmly in agreement. "Of course—I'd rather not be killed, along with all the others."

"Exactly." He smiled and indicated her plate. "You do not care for the sauce?"

After assuring him that it was delicious, Epione ate for a moment in silence, trying to come to grips with what she had learned. It appeared that the common thread between the murders was that the victims had been familiar with the Comte deFabry—including her mother and stepfather, although the grey-eyed spymaster was apparently unaware that her parents had been victims, too. And the only reason she'd been allowed to survive was because—for reasons only the mad Comte could explain—he wanted to honor Marie's little sister. Therefore, it behooved her to play up this angle to maximum advantage.

Rendering her best dimpled smile, she said with as much enthusiasm as she could muster, "*Desclaires* is so lovely, Louis; I am truly, truly grateful to be here."

His gaze wandered about the tapestried walls. "Yes. I intend to have Marie interred here, in the chapel." He paused for a moment, thinking about it with great satisfaction.

Epione nodded in encouragement. "I am certain she would appreciate it—we could all be together, then."

With some regret, he shook his head, and signaled for the sweetmeats tray. "I'm afraid I will be forced to spend much of my time at Versailles. It is a shame, but it cannot be helped; again, sacrifices must be made."

Epione blinked in surprise, trying to decide why the Comte would be installed at the former royal palace. "Because of your cousin? Do you believe Louis Philippe will become King of France?"

Smiling, the Comte met her eyes, his own alight with some undefined emotion. "Yes; yes— imagine it."

There was no question that her idle comment had inspired a less-than idle reaction, and so Epione probed, "Do you know him well, your cousin?"

The Comte's smile faded, and he lowered his gaze to his plate. "No; not at all. He has lived in exile for twenty years, and although for the past few years he's lived in England, he never deigned to seek me out."

There was an edge of bitterness to his tone, and so she asked with sympathy, "Was there a falling out in the family, then?" She'd known her own share of family strife, and in these turbulent times, political loyalties often were the source of deep-seated disagreements.

"He did not seek me out," he repeated. "But your sister did—thank *le bon Dieu* for her."

They were wandering back into saintly Marie territory, and so Epione valiantly sought to steer the conversation elsewhere. "It was accommodating of the British, to grant us all a refuge."

But this apparently touched a nerve, and he exclaimed with low heat, "Living in a country of inferiors—*crétins!*—was the most bitter blow of The Terror. Marie understood this as few others did."

A bit taken aback, Epione temporized, "Yes, well—I suppose it was not an easy thing, to assimilate to life in England."

"Now she abides in heaven," he pronounced firmly, "and will yet see my revenge—and my greatest glory."

Epione managed to conceal her increasing alarm. "I am certain she will. And what glory would that be, Louis?"

But his attitude changed abruptly, and he playfully shook a finger. "I'm afraid I am not to tell you yet—the others, they are concerned you will not be reconciled." He paused to take her hand, and to add with all sincerity, "But I know you will—Marie always said you were a biddable girl."

"Yes—yes, I suppose that is true." Biddable, until she had been swept up in these extraordinary events, that was; events which reeked of treason, and espionage, and—and slave-trading, and the latest exigent need to warn the unknowing Sir Lucien that he was slated to be killed. Truly; when one toted it up, it was quite overwhelming.

But succor was to come from an unlikely source, as a familiar voice could be heard from the great hall's entry way. "Etienne; pray forgive my intrusion, but there were no servants at the door."

In utter astonishment, Epione stared open-mouthed at the figure posed in the doorway; de Gilles, leaning negligently on a Malacca cane, and dressed *point de vice* in the first stare of elegance. With casual grace, he took off his gloves and bowed, sweeping his hat before him.

For a few long seconds there was absolutely no sound. "Seigneur," breathed the Comte in disbelief, as he slowly rose to his feet. "Seigneur—welcome."

Chapter 28

Apparently, the Comte was as astonished as Epione, and he stood as though transfixed, dropping his napkin on his chair and then belatedly bowing. "Seigneur—why, what brings you—"

In response to his host's bafflement, de Gilles smiled his charming smile, and flicked his gloves on the chair back. "Come, come; it is Alexis, Etienne—we will not stand on ceremony. We stole away to go eeling together at Chambord—or have you forgotten?"

Still bemused, the Comte shook his head slightly. "No—no, I have not forgotten. We were thoroughly wetted, but caught no eels, as I recall."

"And I was berated by my bear-leader, for slipping my leash."

Enrapt, the Comte nodded slowly. "Landrieu—a pinch-face; I remember. You could charm the birds from the trees, though; I had no fears for you."

There was a pause while the two men contemplated the memory; de Gilles standing at his ease, his expression benign in the firelight. Recalled to his surroundings, the Comte made a deprecatory gesture. "You—I must beg your pardon for my disarray; I confess I am astonished to behold you." He indicated Epione. "Allow me to present Mademoiselle d'Amberre—"

With an easy movement, de Gilles bowed. "I have had the pleasure of making Mademoiselle's acquaintance in London. *Comment tallez-vous*, Mademoiselle?"

"I am well, thank you." Epione responded in what she considered a remarkably level tone, all things considered. She was perfectly willing to follow his lead, if only she knew where she was being led.

"Please, please—join us, I insist." With a hurried gesture, deFabry snapped his fingers at the sandy-haired footman, who promptly moved to set another place at the table.

With a careless gesture, de Gilles handed his hat and coat to the footman, and then seated himself next to the Comte. "With pleasure, my old friend. May I beg a room for the night? My manservant can attend me; I can see you are understaffed, and I will not disrupt your household."

232

"Why—by all means," offered the Comte, with extreme gratification. He appeared to be recovering from his initial shock, as he signaled to the footman. "We will be *en famille*, then, which is much more comfortable. "How—how did you know I was in residence, if I may ask? We are staying very quietly, and made no announcement."

De Gilles sighed and lowered his voice. "I am staying quietly myself—you must not mention it to *Pere* Tallyrand."

The reference to Napoleon's former Minister caused their host to look grave for a moment, and apparently he didn't notice that his original question went unanswered. "No—no, of course not." He then added diffidently, "If you will forgive my impertinence—it may be best if you used a *nom de guerre* while you are here; there are some visitors who may be alarmed by your presence. I am assured that you will understand."

De Gilles nodded easily. "I do understand, and I thank you for the warning, Etienne. I travel as Capitaine de Gilles."

"Very good, Seigneur—"

With a smile, de Gilles tilted his head over his glass of wine. "It is Alexis, Etienne—I beg of you."

The Comte turned slightly pink, and stammered in his gratification. "Alexis. Of course."

De Gilles turned his warm gaze upon Epione. "You must forgive two old friends, Mademoiselle; we neglect you."

"Not at all," she demurred in a mild tone. "I am very much entertained, I assure you."

Thus reminded, deFabry leaned forward, and indicated Epione with a gesture of his head. "You may not be aware that I was—acquainted— with Mademoiselle's sister, while I lived in London." He then met the other's gaze for a significant moment, and Epione was given to understand the men were acknowledging a relationship that was too shocking to reveal in front of her.

"Is that so? But Marie does not visit, also?"

"No—no." The man sobered for a moment, and then with a visible effort, drew himself up. "She has—sadly—died; and as Mademoiselle d'Amberre's family has been taken from her—this regrettable business!—she is now here, and will be held safe."

"Indeed?" De Gilles allowed his gaze to rest upon Epione, a great deal of warmth in his expression. "You left London before we could further our acquaintance, Mademoiselle—I was *dévastée.*"

Epione found she was having trouble keeping her countenance, and so took refuge in sipping from her wine glass. "I am afraid I was called away unexpectedly, Monsieur." And although Epione entertained a qualm that her host would not appreciate this rather heavy-handed flirtation by his guest, it appeared the Comte could not have been more pleased to observe his visitor's interest, and he added with a meaningful arch of his brow, "In point of fact, Mademoiselle d'Amberre now holds title to this château, Alexis.

234

Perhaps she can be persuaded to give you a—a *private* tour."

De Gilles smiled his flashing white smile. "I quite look forward to such a tour. It is above all things fortunate that I am given this chance to renew our acquaintance, Mademoiselle."

But Epione could not resist throwing out a small dart. "I am not certain that fortune is to be thanked, Monsieur."

"Now, Mademoiselle—" the Comte hastily interjected, clearly alarmed that she would reveal too much of her experiences, thus far. "You are perhaps unaware that it *is* your very great fortune." He then gave her a warning look that promised edification at a later time, and Epione willingly subsided, so as to allow him to think her biddable, which was important for some unexplained reason.

As Epione and deFabry had already finished their meal, they conversed with the visitor while Luci served him, standing at the side board in attendance. For some reason, Epione had the impression that the servant girl was suddenly wary—although her rather bovine expression never changed. Perhaps she was made nervous, by having another guest to serve.

The Comte spread his hands. "I must apologize that we haven't more than two covers— the cook is new-hired—"

But his companion held up a hand with an easy grace. "You must not apologize to me, Etienne; I confess I feel as though I have been granted an unexpected boon." He allowed his gaze to flick to Epione for a quick and meaningful moment.

Epione could feel the color flood her cheeks as she pretended not to understand the byplay—it seemed evident that de Gilles was laying the groundwork to steal into her room, and it would be of all things a welcome relief, to relinquish this strange situation into hands that were far more capable than hers.

Reminded, she decided she should immediately inform de Gilles of what she'd learned, and so she smiled at the Comte. "Perhaps le Capitaine could join our dinner party, two days hence, and we can better entertain him at that time."

Clearly nonplussed by the reference, deFabry stammered, "Yes—yes, of course."

There was an awkward pause, which de Gilles smoothly filled. "I cannot stay, I'm afraid; I have pressing matters to attend, and there are those—" he paused to give the Comte a knowing look "—there are those who very much desire that I not abide in *la belle France*, just now."

"Of course; and I am sorry for it," deFabry agreed, with angry emphasis. "When I think of what has happened to our poor country—how *la racaille* holds her in their grip—"

But de Gilles interrupted, "We mustn't distress Mademoiselle d'Amberre with politics, my friend. Later, we will share a fine bottle, and rail against fortune's wheel."

Their host's brow cleared, and again, he turned a bit pink with pleasure. "I could desire nothing more, Alexis."

Reacting to the message in de Gilles' eye, Epione offered, "As I am rather weary, I will retire, then, and leave you gentlemen to your wine."

The men rose, and as her host escorted her over to the stairway, he bent down to instruct her in a low voice, "You must not—you should encourage his attentions, Epione; he is a great man."

Epione thought she should probably make a show of reluctance, which hopefully would serve the purpose of eliciting more information on this all-important subject. "Is he? I think in London it was generally understood that he is a sea captain, of some sort."

Her host hovered on the brink of revealing the truth—or at least what he thought was the truth—but drew back. "I'm afraid I cannot speak out of school; but I assure you, if you could engage his interest, you could look no higher for a benefactor."

Here was blunt speech, and Epione met it with her own. "But I thought I was slated to be *your* mistress, Louis."

He met her eyes, clearly startled. "No, oh— I beg your pardon if I have given you the wrong impression. Not that you are not lovely," he hastened to assure her. "But you are Marie's sister, and it would not be right. I doubt I will ever marry, although—" here he looked into the distance for a moment, and sighed. "Although

237

perhaps I will have little choice, and must do so, *quand même.*"

The tête-à-tête was interrupted by the appearance of Darton, playing the part of de Gilles' manservant. With a small bow which featured a knowing glance at the Comte, he offered, "I have been instructed to escort the lady to her chambers, Monsieur."

Lifting a significant brow to Epione at this obvious subterfuge to discover the location of her bedroom, the Comte took her hand, and said with some meaning, "*Bonne nuit*, Mademoiselle."

"Yes, *bonne nuit.*" Epione turned to follow the waiting Darton up the stairs, while the Comte hurried back into the dining room. When she deemed it safe, she said in a low voice, "I am very gratified to see you again, I must say."

Darton turned to her, and grinned. "It is a surprise, is it not?"

"Do you know where my rooms are?"

Shrugging in amusement, the man shook his head. "I do not."

Epione looked up the stairway, in the cavernous and silent château. "I am not certain I do, either. The third floor, I believe."

"We shall find them, *sans doute.*" With a smile, he offered his arm.

Chapter 29

"Lisabetta is here—somewhere," Epione warned Darton, as they wandered down the hallway of the third floor. "I'm afraid she escaped from the British, but I suppose they already know this."

"They do." Her escort lit a passage candle, and held it aloft as he stopped to systematically open the doors along the hallway, the candlelight flickering off the white walls, in the still and silent rooms. He kept a hand on his pistol hilt, and seemed to have little to say, as his sharp gaze swept each interior.

"She is not happy with you, and would like her lock of hair back." Although unhappy was perhaps not the best description—Epione was curious to see his reaction, and wondered if they were all as ruthless as they seemed.

Unsurprisingly, he did not give her one. "*Quelle dommage*; she will not get it." He opened a door to reveal another neglected room, the furniture shapes dimly visible under their Holland covers.

Although he seemed bent on reticence, she was equally bent on discussing this very strange situation with someone who—finally—could be considered an ally. "There is some secret plot afoot; there are very few servants, and we entered by stealth, through a sea grotto."

This seemed to catch his diverted attention, and he paused to regard her with interest. "There is a sea grotto? Where?"

Belatedly alive to the various double-crossings experienced thus far, Epione hesitated, and confessed, "I am not certain how much I should tell you."

With an amused gleam in his eye, he considered her for a moment, then said with all sincerity, "You can trust me, Mademoiselle; and you can trust *le Capitaine*."

But she remembered that it was Darton who'd brought the false priest to the haberdasher, and decided to keep her own counsel. "I'm very much inclined to trust no one, just now. You can hardly blame me, Monsieur."

With a small bow he conceded, "As you wish, Mademoiselle."

Further discussion was curtailed as they finally found her suite of rooms, illuminated by the moonlight, which dimly shone in through the windows. Wary, Darton lifted the candle and entered, his pistol drawn. Epione peered over his shoulder and offered, "I don't think anyone is here—there are very few people about."

The words were no sooner said when with a loud crack, a pistol discharged from the darkness within. Darton pushed Epione against the wall, as a musket ball lodged in the plaster over her head, and Lisabetta's voice rang out. "*Bâtard.*"

"Stand down, *vixene.*"   Mainly, Darton sounded amused, which inspired a faint hissing sound, emanating from the darkness within.

"What is your business here, *crétin*? I should kill you where you stand."

"Lisabetta—for heaven's sake, mind the plaster," cautioned Epione. This place may be an oversized tomb, but it was her oversized tomb.

Apparently the Frenchwoman's threat had little effect, because Darton stepped forward in a casual fashion to place the candle on the side table, illuminating Lisabetta's flushed face as she leaned back on the settee, glowering at him from behind her cocked pistol. With a cautionary gesture, Darton straightened again. "Stay quiet, *ma chérie*. You will bring the other one down upon us."

"I do not take direction from you, *bâtard.*"

Epione asked anxiously, "Who is 'the other one'?" All it needed was more players; she was having trouble keeping track of them as it was. "Is it Mr. Tremaine?"

"*Robert* is here?"   Lisabetta's incredulous gaze turned to Epione.

241

"I am the last person to know anything." Epione retorted, "But you are not to cause the poor man any more misery, Lisabetta."

Darton interjected in a reasonable tone, "You ask too much, Mademoiselle; this one, she deals only in misery."

With a furious gesture, Lisabetta sprang to her feet to hurl a knife, which Darton adeptly sidestepped before it lodged, with a thud, in the silk-covered wall behind him. As though it were nothing out of the ordinary, Darton pulled the protruding handle from the wall, and promptly crossed the room to return it to the Frenchwoman, presenting it over his arm, hilt first, with a small bow.

Snatching it from his hand, Lisabetta pressed the tip to his throat, her breast heaving with suppressed fury. While Epione caught her breath in alarm, Darton spread his hands to each side, and made no attempt to escape as his gaze locked on Lisabetta's. For a few seconds they stood in a tense tableau, then matters took a surprising turn, as Darton leaned in to bring his mouth down to Lisabetta's. Unresisting, the woman allowed him to grasp the wrist which held the dagger, and twist it behind her until she dropped it. Then his arm drew her body against him, and the kiss deepened until, with his mouth still on hers, Darton swung her up in his arms to carry her out of the room.

Epione stood in surprised silence for a few moments, before deciding that perhaps she should lock the door. Then, rather belatedly, she took the candle and made a careful search of the rooms, although she couldn't imagine what she would do if she found anyone within—hit them with the candle, perhaps, and start yet another diversionary blaze.

After her search, she perched on the edge of the bed to stare out the window, and think over what she had learned, as the candle stub burned down. It was rather surprising that Luci did not come to attend her, but perhaps she felt it more important that she attend the gentlemen, at their brandy. This moment of solitude was a bit strange, actually; heretofore she had been the focus of everyone's intense attention, but now that the venue had changed—or perhaps more accurately, now that the focus had changed to the Comte—apparently all interest in her had been abandoned. Except for one person's interest, that was; hopefully she had not mistaken the message in his eyes at the dinner table.

She'd been sitting alone for over an hour when she heard his tool at the lock, and then de Gilles appeared in the doorway to the bedchamber, pausing for a moment to behold her with a sound of satisfaction. "Ah, that is a very pretty dress, *ma belle. Ravissante.*"

He approached to hold out his hands and draw her up so as to review her, head to foot. "*Ravissante,*" he repeated, and bent to kiss her thoroughly, his hands moving to her waist to pull her against him.

Breathless, she twined her arms around his neck—he tasted of wine, and she was oh, so pleased to be back in his arms again. Truth to tell, she had entertained a doubt or two, despite her bravado, but he had indeed come for her, and she was more than happy to turn over all counter-scheming into his capable hands. He paused for breath, and bent to kiss her neck, which gave her an opportunity to observe, "I am beginning to believe nothing can surprise me, anymore. Do the British know you are here?"

He lifted his head to face her, and begin pulling the pins out of her hair with gentle fingers. "The British are aware of the situation, although they are guarding their plans—and in turn, we would be wise not to trust them." He framed her face with his hands. "You have not been mistreated?"

"No; quite the contrary—although I am running out of candle, and there are no others in the candle drawer."

With a chuckle, he released her to shrug out of his coat, and toss it negligently on the foot of the bed. "This place is not well-appointed, Madame de Gilles; but we will make do. And where is Monsieur Darton?"

She made a wry mouth. "I believe he and Lisabetta are—are having relations, somewhere."

He made a sound of amusement mixed with exasperation, as he undid his cravat, pulling at the long cloth and tossing it onto his coat. "Good luck to him; she'd as soon slit his throat."

"I do have her knife." She made a gesture toward it, on the side table.

"I see this." As he unbuttoned the top button of his shirt, he leaned down to kiss her again. "Well done, Madame."

As he seemed bent on disrobing, there was nothing for it, and she sighed with regret. "I'm afraid I must inform you that we are not truly wed."

Without bothering with the other buttons, he pulled his shirt over his head, and then paused to stare at her. "Why is this? Were you already married, *ma belle*?"

"No—the priest who married us was a faux-priest."

He stood for a moment, this shirt in his hands and his expression skeptical. "Who told you this?"

She was having a difficult time keeping her gaze on his face—as opposed to his impressive chest—but she persevered. "The gentleman himself, I'm afraid. He is aligned with Lisabetta and Monsieur Chauvelin, the tailor—who is another villain, and seems to be the kingpin. And the faux-priest is not here, but has instead left for Bengal."

He stared at her, frowning in surprise, and she reflected that it truly was a shame she'd confessed this to him before he'd demanded his marital rights—he did seem inclined, and frankly, so did she, after witnessing Darton sweep Lisabetta away.

Ruthlessly putting her thoughts in order, she lifted her chin. "I am not certain you weren't already aware of this."

"Epione," he remonstrated, and moved to gently pull her down beside him on the bed, and take her hands in his. "Acquit me; I would not do such a thing to you."

She trusted him, of course. She had from the start, and this left one other potential candidate in the deception. "How well do you know Monsieur Darton?"

Immediately, he understood why the question was asked, but slowly shook his head in denial. "He has sailed with me for years, and if he wished to betray me—suffice it to say he has had many opportunities."

She nodded, thinking this only made sense; someone like de Gilles, who preferred to haunt the far corners of the world so as to avoid scrutiny, would not be someone who gave his trust easily, and he was certainly no fool. "I see. It just seems an extraordinary coincidence that the nearest priest at hand was a false one, ready to aid in my abduction. And another thing; just now Darton kept referring to me as 'Mademoiselle', as though he knew I was not married."

"Did he?" He bent his head forward, absently running his thumbs over the back of her hands, but in the end he shook his head. "I cannot explain it; but I cannot believe he is aligned with anyone other than myself."

She eyed his bent head, and decided there was no time like the present. "And I am given to understand that you are aligned with slave-traders."

He lifted his head, and met her eyes very seriously. "It is not the truth, Epione. But unfortunately, I cannot deny such a thing to others—many lives are at stake."

Rather taken aback, she stared at him. "Then it is true you are smuggling young girls?"

"It is not what it appears, but more I cannot say. I am sorry, Epione."

As his tone indicated she would learn no more on this subject, she introduced a different but equally distressing one. "There is a plot afoot to murder Sir Lucien."

With a mock-rueful sigh, he bent his head again, and caressed her hands, his own very warm. "*Nom de Dieu*; this night is not going at all how I had hoped."

She couldn't help but smile. "No—I suppose it is not; it is only that I have learned so many distressing things, since last I saw you."

Her breath caught as he lifted his eyes and looked into hers, the awareness between them electric, and compelling. "Could we discuss it later, perhaps? After I have helped you out of this very pretty dress, *ma belle*?"

Here it was—the moment of truth; either she would allow this slave-trader to ruin her, or she would trust her instinct that he was indeed true—an instinct sharpened by long exposure to people who were, in fact, not true. That, and she was going to absolutely *die* if she didn't press herself against him like a wanton within the next few minutes—she was only flesh and blood, and his bare chest was a thing of beauty. "Yes, you may. And in any event, the Comte is practically pushing me into your bed, being as he believes you are the

247

true King of France, and that such a move would cover me in glory."

With gentle hands, he pushed her gown off her shoulders—an easy task, as the décolletage was so low—and leaned in to kiss the side of her neck. "Yes; that is why we must make it evident that we share a bed."

"We must?" Honestly, she didn't care; the world was upside-down anyway, and it was hard to concentrate, with his warm breath on her neck.

His mouth moved to work its magic on her shoulder. "Indeed. Then we will surprise them, by marrying in truth."

"We will?" This was welcome news, although she was fast becoming aware of why girls allowed themselves to be ruined—truly, she had no willpower to resist him, and she tilted her head to grant him access to the base of her throat.

"*Certamente.*" His nimble fingers moved to loosen her lacings. "Our enemy has gone to great lengths to ensure that I do not marry the only surviving daughter of the House d'Amberre; therefore, we must confound him."

As the sumptuous dress fell in a billowing heap on the floor, he gently pushed her back into the feather bed, and she breathlessly teased, "That is not very romantic, Alexis; that you take me to bed to confound the enemy."

His hands on either side of her, he moved, cat-like, to hover over her, as he bent his head to kiss a breast. "I have already confounded the enemy, *ma belle*. Now, I will claim my prize."

Sighing, she happily allowed the weight of the hard-muscled man to sink her into the bliss of the soft bed. "Better you, than Napoleon."

Chapter 30

An hour later, Epione lay well-content in his arms, relishing the novel sensation of his body pressed against hers, and aware on an elemental level that she'd made the right decision, to be here with him. His lovemaking had been patient, and careful— until he'd reached a point where he couldn't be patient and careful any longer, and she found she rather liked crazed and lustful much better; being careful and patient hadn't paid off very well for her, thus far. "Don't die," she said aloud.

"If you say." He tightened his arms around her.

"I worry that I'd become as mad as the Comte."

"He is a little mad," de Gilles conceded, and kissed her temple.

"He wishes to bring Marie's remains here; I wouldn't be surprised if he installed her corpse in his chambers under glass, like in the fairy tale."

He let out a breath that stirred the tendrils of her hair. "He has a weak mind, I'm afraid, and is easily led by those who use him for their own purposes."

There was an underlying significance to the words, and she frowned into the darkness—the candle had long ago guttered out. "You understand what is afoot? I confess I am at a loss."

"I can guess."

She waited for an explanation but didn't receive one, and into the ensuing silence she noted, "You are a very vexing slave-trader, my friend."

He shifted his body to so that his mouth rested in her hair, his voice muffled. "I am not a slave-trader, but you mustn't tell anyone."

"Are you the true King of France?" She was only half-joking; it was evident the Comte thought so.

He chuckled softly, the sound vibrating against her head. "No."

"Then you are very mysterious, for someone who is not the true King of France."

She felt him release a breath into her hair. "I am not accustomed to trusting anyone. I learned this lesson—as a necessity—when I was very young. I don't know, Epione, if it will ever change."

Yes; he wore himself like a cloak because beneath it all, he was an angry man. Perhaps she could help ease his anger somewhat—it had certainly seemed so, a few minutes ago. "I will not fault you for it, Alexis. I am much the same, in my own way—although I certainly have been proved too trusting in the past two days."

"You cannot be faulted, either. The enemy has gone to great lengths."

She gently pulled at the hair on his chest. "As have you, I think. Despite their best efforts, you have surfaced to openly marry a noblewoman—one whose family was involved in the *L'ange d'Isaac* plot—and raise the dreaded possibility of even more pretenders."

He covered the hand on his chest with his own. "You are as clever as you are beautiful. I am a lucky man."

She smiled, and rubbed her face against the side of his chest; it had already occurred to her that this had been his plan all along—to marry her, and thereby thwart whatever plot these carefully laid plans were advancing. In the end, she didn't much care what his motivation was; that he served the greater good seemed evident, and if it wasn't a love match on his part, it was fast becoming one on hers. She would gladly do his bidding, in the hope there were to be more nights just like this one.

They lay together for a moment in silence, and then he fingered the ends of her hair, and said quietly, "The Josiah is the Comte deFabry."

So—apparently he had decided he could trust her at least with this, and she struggled to make sense of it. "The story of the King in disguise?"

"Yes—although it is not the King who will be disguised. I was looking at it the wrong way around; instead it is the Comte who will be disguised as the King."

Surprised, she propped up on her elbows to stare at him in the darkness. "But—to what purpose? I can't imagine anyone would confuse him with Louis the Eighteenth; the Dauphin's uncle is old and stout."

"No; instead they will use him to pose as Louis Philippe, the Duc d'Orleans. He and deFabry are cousins, and very similar in appearance. The Comte will pose as the pretender, instead. "

Her brow knit, she traced a finger on the silken pillowcase and thought about this. "I suppose that explains why he has changed the way he styles his hair—and he has lost weight. She paused, struck. "And he wants me to call him 'Louis'."

"Does he? Then I suppose we are confirmed."

With a gasp of realization, she met his eyes. "Yes—yes, it does make sense. The murders in London—they've killed everyone who could recognize him, and call him out as a fake; that's the connection between the victims. My mother and my stepfather, also."

Softly, he whistled, and propped a bent arm beneath his head. "*De vrai?*"

"Yes." Blowing out a breath, she turned to sink back into the pillows. "And I remain alive only because he was infatuated with Marie, and wouldn't let them kill me."

He lifted a hand to kiss it. "Then he has my unending gratitude, despite everything."

But try as she might, Epione could not make any sense of this complicated plot. "I don't understand; what is their object, in disguising the Comte to pose as one of the pretenders? The mighty British—and the mighty Monsieur Tallyrand—are adamant that the royal Bourbon line should be re-established to rule France. As a practical matter, the Duc d'Orleans has no chance."

"Then we must suppose they are betting that the pretender will indeed become King."

He said it very matter-of-factly, but the idea was so incredible that she had trouble framing the appropriate question, and was suddenly chilled, despite the warm body next to hers. "There is— you think there is an assassination planned? They will assassinate the Dauphin's uncle?"

"I can think of no other end to these particular means, and neither can the British spymaster."

This comment was so unexpected that she turned her head, to stare at him in amused amazement. "Never say you unbent enough to collaborate with him?"

Her companion chuckled at her teasing. "He was more surprised than you are."

With a small fist, Epione gently punched at his chest. "You must tell me, Alexis; it is of all things unfair that I do not know—I am at the center of these matters, after all."

Shifting his weight, he brought both arms around her, so that his voice could be heard above her head. "I was very unhappy that you had disappeared, *ma belle.*"

She could only imagine his fury, when she had not emerged from Madame Reyne's rooms. "And?"

He sighed with mock-regret. "And I'm afraid I launched myself at the British spymaster, and pinned him to the street, with my knife at his throat. I told him if he did not tell me everything he knew, and immediately, he would bleed to death on a shabby street in Soho."

All admiration, Epione breathed, "Oh—oh, Alexis; I wish I could have seen it. And his men afraid to seize you—it does have its benefits, to be thought the true pretender."

"*Bien sûr.*" And so between us, we pieced the puzzle together—or what he was willing to reveal—and mutually decided that it would be best if I renewed my acquaintanceship with the Comte."

Epione lay in silence for a moment, digesting these revelations. It made complete sense; otherwise, there was no earthly reason why these rather ruthless people would be catering to the slightly-mad Comte, to the point of indulging his demand to give this fine château to an obscure milliner. And de Gilles was apparently betting that

255

he could be just as powerful a counter-influence on the Comte as the dead Marie, and perhaps he was right—although it remained to be seen. But there was something strange, here—something that didn't make sense. Knitting her brow for a moment, she finally realized what it was. "Why would Napoleon's people seek to put a pretender on the throne, just when Napoleon is poised to escape?"

"That," he said with a grave tone, "is what remains to be discovered."

An answer presented itself to Epione. "Perhaps they will assassinate the Comte, while he poses as Louis Philippe, so as to clear the way for Napoleon to be re-crowned as emperor. If both Louis the Eighteenth and the Duc d'Orleans are dead, France will be running out of pretenders, and the time would be ripe for Napoleon to step forward."

But her companion shook his head. "Then why go to the trouble of replacing one with the other—why not simply assassinate both men outright? I will guess that they need deFabry to perform some task for them; then he will be killed in his turn—one such as he is too great a risk, to pose as King for any length of time."

Gently, she ran her hand over his chest, feeling the wiry hair spring up beneath her palm, and wishing they were a normal couple, facing only the concerns one encountered in a normal life. "How does placing a false pretender on the throne aid Napoleon's cause? Do they think he will surrender France to Napoleon?"

"That is what I mean to find out."

Lying there in the peaceful silence, she reluctantly stated the obvious. "You are at risk. We are both at risk—we can identify the Comte as an imposter."

But he was not alarmed by this leap of logic. "Not yet, we aren't. They need his cooperation, and so dare not touch you—not until he's done whatever he is needed to do for them."

She shook her head in wonder. "How strange it is; I am still alive, due to spiteful Marie. It seems my sister did grant me a boon, even if it stemmed from an adulterous *affaire*." Reminded, she added, "Don't forget we must warn Sir Lucien."

"Yes—I will see to it."

Before any further discussion on the subject could be held, there was a soft knock on the door, and in an instant, de Gilles had sprung out of bed to approach the door from one side, his pistol held before him, as he gestured for Epione to slide down behind the bed.

"It is I," Darton's voice could be heard. "I am alone."

Chapter 31

Epione hastily scrambled back into her crumpled satin gown while de Gilles waited, and once she was more-or-less clad, he allowed Darton entry into the bedchamber.

"Mademoiselle—forgive the intrusion." The newcomer bowed apologetically to Epione.

"Madame," de Gilles corrected him easily.

"Of course—Madame." He turned to de Gilles. "I am searching for Lisabetta."

De Gilles made a gesture toward the rumpled bed. "I have not seen her here."

With a grin, Darton conceded this point. "I'm afraid she has disappeared, along with my knife."

"I have hers," Epione informed him. "We'll have to straighten it out."

"How did she manage to lift your knife, *mon ami*?" De Gilles sat on the edge of the bed and pulled on his boots, which Epione viewed with some misgiving, as it spoke of an end to her warm cocoon of silken sheets and handsome man. With a sigh, she went to hunt for her own slippers, under the bedclothes on the floor.

Darton shrugged in a self-deprecatory gesture. "*Hélas*, I am easily distracted—it is a failing of mine."

Amused, de Gilles paused, and glanced up at him. "Well?"

Again, Darton shrugged. "I could not tell."

It seemed evident they were speaking of something Darton was supposed to discover from Lisabetta, and Epione was impressed that the man had bundled the woman off to bed in such a sincere manner if, in fact, it wasn't at all sincere. "Is there something you wish to know about Lisabetta? I spent some time talking with her— could I help?"

As he stood, de Gilles exchanged a look with Darton, and then explained, "We would like to know why she is included in whatever is going forward. It is a high-level operation, and only a trusted few know of it; her role is unclear."

But Epione thought this was evident. "I think she is another spy, is she not? She was tasked with capturing me, and now she is making certain I don't escape."

But de Gilles was not convinced, and put his hands on his hips. "She was tasked with bringing you here—that much is clear. But now it

259

has been accomplished, and she is no longer needed—you have little chance of escape. The British spymaster believes she must have a further role in the plot, or she wouldn't have accompanied you to France."

Her brow knit, Epione thought about this. "I am not certain that is true; she is chafing to leave this place; and Monsieur Chavelin told her that after the dinner party, she would be allowed to go."

The two men exchanged a glance. "Perhaps she is needed to lure *le Duc* to a private place," Darton suggested.

De Gilles shrugged. "There is no need for secrecy; they could murder him on the front steps, if they wished."

They thought about it in silence for a few moments. "I will endeavor to obtain more information," Darton offered.

De Gilles grinned. "Try to ensure that she does not elicit more than you do, *mon ami;* I fear for you."

"She is from Martinique," Epione remembered. "Perhaps she wishes to return home."

"A Creole family," de Gilles affirmed. "She has a sister, Eugenie."

"The sister is trouble, also," Darton disclosed to Epione. "As blonde as this one is dark."

"I will defer to your knowledge," observed de Gilles in a dry tone, and Epione blushed, although she truly hadn't any grounds for it, considering the rumpled bed and her general state of dishevelment.

De Gilles rose to hold out his hand to her. "Come, Madame; I would like to celebrate our reunion by sharing a fine bottle of wine. Shall we search for the cellars?"

The night was well-advanced, they were in a hostile place, and surrounded by a deadly earnest enemy. "If you wish." She took his hand without a qualm, and bade farewell to the old Epione, who would have preferred hiding under the bed.

And so, ten minutes later, she found herself creeping quietly down the servants' stairs in the company of de Gilles, who in turn followed Darton, with the other man leading them with a passage candle. The light flickered off the white plastered walls, and there was no sound—only their footsteps, carefully muffled on the wooden slats as they descended the stairs. "May I speak?" she whispered near his ear.

"Of course, *ma belle*." De Gilles' voice was low, his sharp gaze on the darkness below them. "Only not too loudly, if you please."

"Why would the Comte consent to be the Josiah? Was Marie such an influence upon him that he would ally with Napoleon?" She had been puzzling over this aspect ever since the plot had been disclosed to her. It was hard to imagine any member of the *ancien régime* willingly acquiescing to such a plan, no matter how deep the devotion to a woman.

261

But her companion did not share her disbelief. "No doubt he seeks to please her, even after her death; she may have even convinced him to aid her while she lived."

"Oh—he did say he was a witness to her death, so perhaps that is so." She thought about this for a few moments, as they cautiously stepped their way down the winding stairs. "It is hard to imagine—such blind devotion. I must warn you, Alexis, that if you decide to aid Napoleon, I will not be so accommodating."

This amused him, and he paused for a moment to turn and kiss her lightly, their heads at the same level, due to the stairs. "*Quant a ca*, you have my permission to shoot me in such a case, and my eternal gratitude, besides."

"I don't know if I could bring myself to shoot you," she confessed. "I cannot imagine how Sir Lucien shot Marie, no matter the incentive."

His attitude became grave, even though she couldn't see his face, and he ran his hands lightly up her bare arms. "There are some things that transcend mere life and death, Epione. You cannot allow your affections to sway you, in such a case."

Unhappy that she'd grieved him, somehow, she teased, "Then I must learn how to shoot a pistol."

He was amused again, in his turn. "We must remedy this problem so that you may indeed shoot me, if the occasion warrants."

He turned again, and they continued their descent for a few moments, following the lurching candle beneath them.   Epione offered, "They bribed him, too—the Comte, I mean. They gave him *Desclaires*—or more correctly, gave it to me. Nonetheless, it seems almost inconceivable—that he would betray his heritage."

"Perhaps—" her companion said slowly, his low voice emanating from the darkness below her, "perhaps he felt there was nothing left to betray."

Before Epione could react to the somber timbre of this remark, Darton's voice drifted up to them. "Where do we go now?" He'd reached the ground floor, and a sweep of the candlestick disclosed only the silent servant's hallway.

Epione gestured in the direction of the stillroom. "The stairs to the grotto are through there; it was how I was brought in."

De Gilles nodded. "A likely place to put the cellars; let's continue on."

She showed them the unassuming door near the pantry, and as they passed through it, the smell of the sea was suddenly strong, and they descended the crude steps which had been carved into the limestone. It was cold, and as her dress made little effort to cover her shoulders, she began to shiver, unable to control it.

De Gilles paused to remove his coat, and tuck it around her shoulders. "A few minutes, only, and then we can return to where it is warmer."

"It's not much warmer inside," she noted, as he lifted the collar around her neck. "The whole place is a bit bleak, and well-suited for the evil plan that has been hatched."

263

"Then we must warm each other," he decided, and leaned to bestow a kiss.

Darton, who was waiting at the base of the steps, observed with amused impatience, "*Parbleu*, this is no time to be stealing kisses, *mon ami*."

Epione reminded him, "You are hardly one to make such a rebuke, Monsieur Darton."

De Gilles laughed aloud, while Darton bowed in mock apology. "*Touché*—I shall say no more."

After listening to the silence for a moment with their pistols drawn, they carefully opened the ancient oaken door, and then walked out onto the dock, their footsteps echoing unnaturally on the rough-hewn planks. As there was a half-moon, the cave was dimly illuminated through its opening, with the still water reflecting the silvery light. For a thoughtful moment, the men contemplated the area.

"They cannot offload easily here," Darton observed. "Only a small vessel can fit through the opening."

"But the fortifications are ideal—and the cargo is not large."

Epione listened to the water lapping quietly against the pilings, clutching de Gille's coat close around her. "What is the cargo?"

"Treasure," said de Gilles succinctly. "The means for war; we believe it is being gathered, and stored here."

Darton gave him a warning glance, but de Gilles shook his head slightly. "Madame de Gilles will say nothing; do not fear."

"I won't," she affirmed. "Are we speaking of the jewels?"

Both men turned to stare at her. "Where did you hear this?"

"Lisabetta. She was trying to reconcile me to my fate, by promising many jewels."

Darton looked to de Gilles. "Then the treasure must indeed be stored here—somewhere."

But Epione had even more to reveal. "Yes; it is stored in the south tower."

Darton laughed aloud, throwing his head back. "We did not think to ask Madame, my friend; we could have saved ourselves much trouble."

De Gilles took both her hands in his. "Epione, you astonish me. How did you discover this?"

"Madame Reyne told me there were plenty of jewels to match my dresses, in the south tower."

"*Bien*," said de Gilles. "It begins to fall into place." He addressed Darton with mock-exasperation. "It is just as well that we depend upon my wife, as you have learned nothing from the fair Lisabetta, and have lost your knife in the process."

Gesturing with the candle, Darton shook his head in rueful acknowledgment. "You must be patient—I've yet to mount a proper campaign."

"Coxcomb." Lisabetta's voice rang out from the darkness of the steps. "Your campaign is not much of a mount."

Epione froze in horror, but Darton turned toward the voice, and spread his hands, unfazed. "*Chérie*; you wound me. You did not seem so disappointed at the time."

"I will do more than wound you, if I do not get some answers. What is it you do here?"

"We were looking for the wine cellars," Epione offered, hoping she didn't sound nervous. "The Comte mentioned there were cellars somewhere, but he wasn't certain where."

If she'd hoped to deflect Lisabetta's interest, though, it appeared de Gilles had other plans, and he shrugged his broad shoulders. "As for me, I look for the treasure."

There was a small silence, while Epione wished they weren't so exposed, with the candle the only light in the grotto. "You are a trader," Lisabetta conceded in a generous tone. "You cannot be blamed, I suppose."

"Do you know of it, Lisabetta?"

"What, so that you can steal it? I am not quite so *stupide*."

De Gilles tilted his head. "I believe you owe me a favor."

An annoyed sound emanated from the shadows. "You will never let me forget, will you? But I am not one of your *aristos,* who thinks she is beholden by such things." With a click, the sound of a pistol cocking could be heard in the silence.

"*Chérie—*" admonished Darton.

266

"You don't dare," Epione interrupted in as calm a voice as she could muster. "Cease this foolishness, Lisabetta. You need my cooperation, and I will not hesitate to tattle to the Comte."

"She will not shoot; there would be a ricochet," de Gilles explained to Epione in a patient tone. "She is posturing, is all."

But the other woman apparently did not appreciate his dismissal, and could be heard to bristle. "Posturing, am I? I will use the ricochet to my advantage, and down the both of you with one shot."

De Gilles chuckled, and negligently leaned against the wooden dock post. "Is that so? I do not recall such fine shooting in Dover."

The other girl was instantly outraged. "That was not my fault—I am a good shot."

With a shrug, de Gilles looked to the dark stairway, and said with patent disbelief, "If you say."

"That was *not* my fault," the girl repeated. "*Peste*, but you are an annoyance beyond bearing, Capitaine."

"Shall we have a contest, then?"

Epione slid her eyes to him, wondering if she had heard him aright, but Lisabetta stepped out of the shadow of the stairwell, her pistol lowered. "Now?"

De Gilles spread his hands. "If you would rather not—"

"What would be the prize?"

"Dinner," said Darton promptly. "I haven't eaten, this night."

Lisabetta arched a brow. "Food, you mean."

"Food." The man bowed to her, and swept his hat before him. "And I have been required to exert myself to no small extent."

"We will need ammunition." De Gilles' gaze met Lisabetta's, his own with a hint of a challenge.

The girl regarded him with an unreadable expression. "*Enfin*; I will fetch ammunition, and we will meet in the ballroom."

But de Gilles was not yet finished with his demands, and indicated Epione with a nod of his head. "Epione requires a pistol—she must learn to shoot."

But this was apparently a request too far. "I am not such a fool, Capitaine."

"As you say."

With a defiant flounce, Lisabetta picked up her skirts and turned to march up the stairs.

Into the silence, Epione ventured, "Do we know where the ballroom is?"

"I imagine a shooting-match will raise the house," Darton observed, as though it mattered little to him, one way or the other.

"Yes, I imagine it will," replied de Gilles, and offered his arm to Epione.

Chapter 32

With a loud report, Darton hit the wafer that was lodged in the chandelier, the impact making the crystal strands rock against each other with a tinkling sound.

"Well done, *chérie*." Lisabetta called out. She leaned in to Epione and disclosed, "And that is not all that he does well."

Feeling that it was not appropriate to make a reply, Epione instead reflected that her current *divertissement* was not one she could have imagined in her past life, as they watched Luci dutifully lower the chandelier so as to replace the target wafers, and re-light any candles that had been damaged. She'd never witnessed a shooting-match before, and was surprised to discover that the endeavor involved drinking a great deal of champagne, which seemed rather counter-intuitive. A very surprised Madame Reyne had been roused to serve them cold meats, and Luci was enlisted to man the chandelier so as to replace the candles as needed. And in truth, it was a strange sort of contest; it didn't seem to Epione that anyone was keeping track.

"Captaine," called out Lisabetta. "It is your turn."

De Gilles stood, and approached Epione to raise her hand and kiss it with an exaggerated gesture. "*Pour la gloire.*"

"*La gloire,* Monsieur." She smiled into his eyes, and then he turned, and held the pistol at arm's length to take careful aim. The proprieties had been abandoned; both men were standing in their shirtsleeves, while Lisabetta lounged beside Epione in a gilt chair, her skirts in disarray, and her bare legs drawn up beneath her. When she'd returned with the ammunition and the servants, she'd sported a variety of impressive pearl necklaces, some of which she generously deposited around Epione's neck.

De Gilles fired, and the wafer flew. Epione was past worrying about the effect the enterprise was having on the plaster walls; it was apparent that de Gilles had some ulterior aim in mind—indeed, it seemed that Lisabetta had tacitly decided to acquiesce in his madness—and so Epione sipped her champagne and hoped to keep her wits about her for whatever was about to unfold.

"*Tiens*, he is a handsome man," Lisabetta remarked to Epione. "We can switch tonight, yes?"

"No," said Epione firmly.

The girl shrugged, and continued her scrutiny of de Gilles, observing him from behind her wine glass. "What is his aim, do you suppose? Why does he court you?"

Epione could not quite like the tenor of the question. "I suppose it is because he admires me."

Lisabetta laughed aloud, spilling her champagne on her skirts.

Before Epione could make a retort, they were interrupted by a voice, coming from the elaborate double doorway. "Why—what is this?" The Comte stood in his dressing gown, holding a candelabra aloft, and the picture of dismayed disbelief. "A shooting-match, and I was not invited?"

De Gilles bowed low. "It is unpardonable, indeed; a thousand apologies, *mon ami*. Tempers were high, and immediate retribution was demanded."

"Ah; I understand completely. Say no more." With a knowing look, the older man's glance encompassed the women.

De Gilles smiled his engaging smile. "Come; you must take your turn."

"I have no pistol," their host confessed.

"Then take one of mine, please." De Gilles promptly handed one over.

The Comte held it reverently, his cheeks flushed with pleasure. "No—no, I couldn't, Seigneur. "

"It is Alexis, Etienne." With a graceful wrist, de Gilles tapped his glass against the other man's. "You have forgotten we are old friends. And—" here he leaned in, and slid his gaze over to Epione, "I have much to be thankful for."

While Epione blushed at such plain-speaking, their host sketched a self-satisfied bow. "A beautiful girl."

"Ah—the most beautiful girl. I believe I am compelled to marry her." With a causal hand on his hip, de Gilles raised his glass to Epione.

The Comte had the look of a man who could not believe his good fortune. "*Marry* her? You are serious?"

"I am. Will you have me, Mademoiselle d'Amberre?"

"I will," Epione replied, trying to match his light manner, and wondering what he was about.

"Why—why, this is extraordinary news, Seigneur—Alexis—"

"It is past time I am wed, I think. It is only a shame that her sister is not here to support her. You will miss her support, will you not, Mademoiselle?"

"I will indeed," said Epione, taking her cue. "I will miss her acutely."

Overcome, the Comte bowed his head, blinking away tears. "Yes, yes—if only she could have known of your triumph—"

Firmly, Epione assured him, "She abides in heaven, Monsieur le Comte, and I am certain she smiles upon me, even now."

Inspired, the other man strode over to take both her hands in his. "Yes—yes; she is a saint in heaven, and surely, *surely* has her hand upon you."

De Gilles raised his glass in tribute. "We can expect more blessings, then. Perhaps we should arrange to have Marie interred here, Mademoiselle. You can pray at her monument, as can anyone who seeks her blessing."

"*Perfection*," breathed the Comte, battling his emotions, and nearly overcome; "*Très marveleuse.*"

As though the matter were a mere trifle, de Gilles turned to the Comte. "Is there a chapel on the grounds? I've a mind to be married quietly, and quickly." He bestowed a speaking glance upon the other. "An heir may be on his way, as we speak."

The Comte clipped his heels together, and bowed. "There is indeed a chapel—rather neglected, unfortunately."

"No matter. I would ask that you stand as my supporter, Etienne; I insist, and would have no other."

The other man bowed his head in silent acquiescence, as it was apparent he was too overcome with emotion to speak.

"Can we arrange for it, say—two days hence? I am afraid I cannot linger."

273

Faced with his dilemma, the Comte could be seen to hesitate. "I am expecting some guests for a dinner party, two days hence; would it be possible—"

De Gilles immediately spread his hands in contrition. "Ah; a thousand pardons, *mon ami*—I had forgotten. It is lamentable that I should impose myself upon you in this way; please do not think of it again, I beg of you. We will be married elsewhere."

But the other man could not countenance such a thought, and drew himself up. "No, no— unthinkable. It shall be done; it *must* be done. I haven't the staff, as you see, so it will of necessity be a quiet affair."

With a small smile, de Gilles observed, "*Enfin*; it must be a quiet affair—there are those who would be very unhappy, to witness such an alliance. Indeed, my very presence in the country—"

"Say no more; I completely understand. The affair will be kept very quiet, and you may rely upon me." Having come to his decision, the Comte was all smiles, and turned to Luci. "I'll need a glass—I must lead a toast."

"As you wish, Monsieur le Comte," said the girl, who then exchanged a covert glance with the sandy-haired footman.

She is unhappy about this turn of events, thought Epione; and who can blame her—she is the only maidservant, here, with too much to do. And I was mistaken; obviously she does speak French, if she was able to follow the conversation.

As the glasses were re-filled, Epione glanced over at Darton with a smile. "It seems you must wish me happy yet again, Monsieur."

"With the greatest pleasure." The man took her hand and bowed, but it seemed to Epione that he was also preoccupied—or perhaps she was being too sensitive, after having been exposed to so many cross-currents, and double-dealings. Thinking to test him, Epione added, "The last wedding didn't count, you see, as the priest was a false one."

Her tone caught his attention, and he met her gaze with rueful honesty, "The Capitaine informed me of this—forgive me; I wasn't certain what to say to you, and I am mortified that I participated in the man's imposture."

This was plausible, and rang true; Darton would be embarrassed to raise the matter, now that she'd spent a blissful night abed with de Gilles—although the night had unfortunately been cut short, so as to look for treasure and shoot at chandeliers. She looked up to catch her betrothed's eye, but he was too busy discussing the finer points of his pistol with his host.

Lisabetta seemed to find it all very amusing, and approached to lay a light hand on Darton's arm. "I cannot bear to be a bridesmaid, *chéri*; perhaps we should make it a double wedding."

The other man grinned, and lifted her hand to kiss it. "I would live the remainder of my days looking under my bed for your lovers; I think not."

With a philosophical shrug, Lisabetta took the rejection in good part. "Fah—I have yet to find a man who cares not for the proprieties." To emphasize this point, she casually fired at the chandelier out of turn, knocking one of the candles from its perch.

Laughing, de Gilles called out, "Toss the bottle up."

Lisabetta launched the champagne bottle toward the ceiling, while Darton, de Gilles and the Comte all fired upon it, shattering it into a thousand pieces which fell in a cascade, and skittered across the wooden floor while Epione covered her head with her arms.

"Well done," applauded the Comte, pink with pleasure. "We must find the armory, and try our hand at duck hunting, tomorrow."

"Oh? Is there an armory?" asked de Gilles in a casual tone.

But he was not to get an answer, because another voice could be heard from the entry doors.

"*What* is the meaning of this?" They all turned to behold Monsieur Chauvelin, taking in the scene with barely-concealed incredulity.

The Comte spread his hands with an amused, conspiratorial glance over at de Gilles. "A shooting-match, Monsieur; an affair of honor."

The other man's gaze rested on de Gilles, and his color could be seen to rise. "You!"

"Monsieur." Gracefully, de Gilles made a sweeping bow.

Chapter 33

"You will not insult my guests, Monsieur Chauvelin." The Comte turned to de Gilles, and tilted his head in apology. "I beg your pardon, Seigneur. Pray do not regard him; he is *irréfléchi*."

"Not at all; we are already acquainted."

Surprised, Epione glanced at him, but he did not expound on the nature of the acquaintanceship, and instead only stood at his ease, sighting down the barrel of his pistol with a practiced eye.

"Might I have a word with you, Monsieur le Comte?" Chauvelin's words were clipped.

"You may not." The Comte drew himself up, and regarded the other man with barely concealed distaste. "You must not interrupt your betters, Monsieur."

At the rebuke, the other man's face became mottled with fury, but the situation was defused as de Gilles backed away with a deprecatory gesture. "Pray do not regard me, gentlemen; I must step away, to give Mademoiselle d'Amberre instruction."

Lisabetta promptly twined her arm around his. "But you neglect me, Capitaine—I will be happy to obey any instruction you may give." This, with a great deal of meaning.

Chuckling, the Comte shook a playful finger at the Frenchwoman. "For shame, Mademoiselle; you are not to interfere with the Seigneur and his affianced bride."

With Lisabetta clinging to one arm, de Gilles gallantly offered the other to Epione, and as he escorted both women away, he remarked over his shoulder, "A gentleman must never disappoint an importuning lady, Etienne."

His amused host nodded in masculine approval, then reluctantly turned to confer with the tailor, who drew the Comte into a corner of the room, and began speaking in low, urgent tones.

"Save me from tedious men," remarked Lisabetta, to no one in particular.

De Gilles paused at a small distance from the damaged chandelier. "Acquit me of tedium, Lisabetta."

The girl rested her amused gaze upon her escort. "No—you are never tedious, Capitaine. Perhaps we should sail away together; I've a mind to see Algiers."

"You will not be rude to Epione, Lisabetta, and I do not have fond memories of sailing with you."

Annoyed, the other girl shot Epione a resentful glare. "I will be as rude as I wish; she has thieved my knife."

With a quick, practiced gesture, he bent to pull the knife from his boot. "I will trade it for the loan of your pistol to Epione."

Lisabetta promptly lifted her skirts to insert the knife in her garter, exposing a great deal of leg as she did so. "*Peste*; she is in more danger with a pistol than without one, I think."

Epione watched this byplay in confusion, but held her tongue; it seemed evident de Gilles and Lisabetta were fencing with one another, and she should not interfere—hopefully her betrothed would resist the girl's half-hearted attempt at seduction, which seemed a bit strange, considering she'd already been with his friend Darton this same night. It was equally puzzling that de Gilles seemed so complacent, despite the ominous, low-voiced argument between the two men who stood in the corner of the room. I feel as though I am a player in a play, she thought, but I do not know my lines. I suppose I should watch for my cues from de Gilles, and improvise as best I can.

"Come, Epione; I will show you how to shoot my pistol, instead." Standing behind her, he drew her close against his chest, and bent his head next to hers as he positioned the weapon in her hands. "Close this eye, and focus on the sight—just so; do you see it is aligned?"

"Oh yes; I see. Shall I try to fire it?"

"Not yet," he murmured into her ear. "I may have need of it."

"Oh," she replied, and tamped down a flare of alarm. She realized that Darton stood at a small distance, a hand on his hip and apparently at his ease, but with the Comte and the tailor within his line of sight.

De Gilles straightened, and motioned for Luci to re-position the wafers, but he had to ask twice, as Luci was daydreaming, her blank gaze resting on the two men in the corner.

Epione's listened to de Gille's voice, as he explained how the firing mechanism worked, and congratulated herself for staying calm, considering it was unclear if crossfire was about to erupt at any moment.

Apparently her apprehensions were unfounded, because Chauvelin approached the group, with the Comte following behind him, the older man's hands clasped behind his back in an attitude of satisfaction. The tailor paused before de Gilles, and bowed his head in a curt gesture. "I must beg your pardon, Monsieur; I was taken by surprise, to behold you here."

"I was equally surprised to behold you," de Gilles assured him.

"I understand there is to be a wedding," the man continued with a strained smile. My congratulations."

De Gilles inclined his head toward Epione in gracious acknowledgment. "Mademoiselle d'Amberre has agreed to make me the happiest of men."

The tailor turned and bowed. "My best wishes, Mademoiselle."

She nodded with good grace. "*Merci,* Monsieur."

The Comte made an apologetic gesture. "I'm afraid I must ask if it is possible to advance Mademoiselle d'Amberre's wedding from two days hence to tomorrow evening, instead, so that our attentions will be wholehearted, with no other distractions."

De Gilles deferred to Epione. "Is this acceptable, *ma belle*? You will have less time to change your mind."

"It is indeed acceptable," she agreed, not certain if she should or shouldn't.

The Comte beamed, pleased to have resolved the scheduling issue. "Then it is settled; we will hold the wedding tomorrow evening, at the chapel." He paused, and then shrugged elegantly in apology. "I'm afraid it will of necessity be a small affair."

"Exactly to my liking," de Gilles assured him. "I am not one for ceremony."

"You must give me away, Monsieur le Comte—I would be so very honored." Epione thought to flatter the man, so as to aid de Gilles in his campaign, but found her betrothed had other ideas, as he turned upon her in mock-outrage.

"He is to stand up with me, Mademoiselle; he cannot do both."

His eyes alight with pleasure, their host held up his hands. "You must decide—I cannot risk expressing a preference."

Taking her cue, Epione conceded with a smile. "Then I will defer to your long-standing friendship." Apparently, de Gilles wished to stay within arm's length of the Comte, which seemed an ominous sign. She could only hope there would be a real priest, this time, and no abductions—although truly, she didn't have high hopes.

"Then it is settled; an evening wedding, with a late supper to follow."

"*Excellent.*" De Gilles seized a bottle of champagne from the serving table. "Come, Mademoiselle; we will celebrate in our rooms."

Taking his leave, he lifted Lisabetta's hand and kissed it, as the girl fell into a deep and ironic curtsey, and then he led Epione to bid good night to their host, who took both her hands in his and gazed upon her with deep emotion. "I am of two minds," he pronounced in a low voice. "If only your beloved sister were here, to witness the great honor bestowed upon her family."

"We will light a candle to her memory, during the ceremony," de Gilles pronounced in a serious tone. "It is only fitting."

Overcome, the man ducked his head and waved them away, so de Gilles took the opportunity to grasp Epione's hand, and lead her out into the silent hallway

Chapter 34

"I forgot my slippers." Epione realized a bit belatedly. "I took them off because they pinched."

"Up on me, then." De Gilles handed her the bottle, then hoisted her onto his back, so that she wrapped her legs around him, and clasped her arms around his neck, giggling. Despite these uncertain events, she was very happy to be thus with him, and pleased that he wished to be alone with her again. She shifted the pearl necklaces to the side, so they did not press against her, and then squeezed his neck in affection.

The silent, dark château stretched above them as her escort began to mount the sweeping stairway. Epione asked a bit dubiously, "Can you see where we are going? Do we need a candle?"

Faint moonlight was the only illumination, and she wasn't certain how steady he was, after the excesses of the evening.

"I can see well enough, *ma belle*. The maidservant did not offer to accompany us, did you notice?"

"She's a bit simple, Alexis. She may not have realized that she should." Surprising that he was not aware of the poor girl's failings; Luci did the best she could, and in any event, it was clear that she'd been hired because of those very failings.

He said nothing, and she had the impression that his thoughts were rather serious, as he ascended the stairs. She ventured, "Did you learn whatever it was you wished to learn?" It seemed evident to her that the shooting match was a pretext, of sorts.

He did not attempt to disclaim, which she thought a rare compliment. "I did. Do you think you could shoot a person, if the need arose, *ma belle*?"

The question was sobering to the point that as she considered it, she lifted the bottle and took a drink—apparently, the reason he wanted to be alone with her was to discuss battle strategy. "I—I suppose, if it is necessary. Is that why we held a shooting match, so that you could show me how?"

"We held a shooting match to discover who is on the premises—to draw them out."

"I see. Very few, it appears." With a gesture, she offered the bottle and he nodded,

then paused to lean his head back, so that she
could tilt it up to his mouth, and let him swallow.

"Yes; very few. Although there is a cook,
who was not at all curious about the noise."

"Oh—now that you mention it, it does seem
a bit strange."

He squeezed her legs against him, gently,
and began climbing the stairs again. "Can you
swim?"

They'd arrived at the next landing. "I can,
but not very well, I'm afraid. Are we to be driven
into the sea?"

"I confess I do not know—not as yet." He
paused to share another pull from the bottle, and
she wondered if perhaps they should have taken
two bottles, instead of the just the one.

Thinking there was no time like the present,
she leaned her cheek against his head and
offered, "At least you have a counter-plan—you've
swayed the Comte's loyalty, I think. Do you think
you can tell me what you are about, Alexis? I
promise I will help you, but I think I would be of
better use if I knew your aim."

He cocked his head, and ran a thumb over
her calf, where it was exposed beneath her
ruched-up skirts. "My aim is clear, is it not? I will
marry you, and in the process, wean the Comte
away from the enemy. He is the only one who can
pose as Louis Philippe, and the Josiah plot—
whatever its aim—will be in ruins."

But Epione ventured, "I think that you are
deliberately trying to provoke, with this talk of
marriage to me, and of—of new pretenders, which

may already be on the way. Is it Lisabetta, you are baiting? Or Monsieur Chauvelin, perhaps? He was not best pleased to see you—and you claim a prior acquaintanceship."

Rather than answer, he tilted his head to rest it against hers. "Tell me what you know of him, if you please."

She shifted the bottle to her other hand, as the first was getting cold. "He was the tailor from the shop next door, and very much kept to himself. We never spoke, although I rather thought he admired me, because he always seemed to be watching my comings and goings. Now I am humbled to realize he was only monitoring me for the purposes of this plot."

This realization compelled her to take another fortifying sip, although she leaned so far back she lost her balance, and had to clutch at his shoulders, making his lose his own balance, and stagger.

"Yes. They have gone to great lengths— although we still do not know their aim, in having the Comte take the throne."

She sighed into the side of his face, as she tilted the bottle for him—now almost empty. "It is like blind man's bluff, with neither side certain what the other knows."

"Very similar." Again, he stroked a thumb across her calf where he held it; it seemed he could not resist touching her—for all his *sangfroid*—and she hid a smile at this hint of pleasures to come. Blind man's bluff rather described her relationship with this man; as events unfolded, she was coming to the rather unsettling conclusion that his true motives—at least when it came to her—were unclear.

With this in mind—and fortified by the champagne—she continued to press him gently. "You sought me out to discover how I was connected to the mysterious Josiah; I understand this. But what is your purpose now, in making it apparent that you mean to marry me and that we have already—we have already shared a bed? Can you tell me? If it is a ruse, I would like to know my part."

He was surprised, and lifted his head. "It is no ruse. My purpose is to marry you, Epione, and abide with you all my days."

She could swear he was sincere—although she was not very adept at discerning the truth, as late events had thoroughly demonstrated.

He tilted his head, to press his cheek against hers as they headed down the hallway. "Will you have me?"

"I will. I think we are well-suited—although unlike you, it appears I am far too trusting."

He chuckled, the sound reverberating in a very pleasing way against her breast, and she chuckled in response. She'd wanted him to be aware that if she was merely a pawn in this battle of shadows, then she was a willing pawn, and he needn't worry about her feelings. Apparently, however, she was truly to be a bride—the bride of the true pretender, which was going to make for a very interesting life. If they survived this first week, that was.

His voice broke into her thoughts. "I have discovered that I would very much like to have children—I had never thought to, before."

"As an act of defiance?" she teased.

"As an act of faith."

"Then we should have a dozen, Alexis; after all that has happened to us, it would be a fine thing to have an overabundance of faith." She dropped the empty bottle down, and found the idea very agreeable; she had never thought to have children, either.

They arrived at the entry to her suite in the silent hall, and he swung her down to the floor, steadying her when she staggered a bit from an excess of champagne. He drew his pistol, and carefully opened the door, listening. When he deemed it clear, they entered the darkened suite, and he took a quick look around as she began to pull at the lacings of the much-abused dinner dress. "I will need your help with these when you have a moment, Alexis."

"Ah—willingly." He walked over and began kissing her neck, as he pulled at the strings.

She leaned back into him with a sigh, wanting nothing more than to feel his weight upon her again and forget, for a few moments, the miserable succession to the miserable throne of France. "I hope Darton does not intrude again," she teased breathlessly.

"No—Darton is concerned with other things." He shrugged off his coat, and began unbuttoning his buttons with her help, all the while leaning in to plant lingering kisses on her mouth.

Once the shirt was off, she was soon beneath him with the bed to her back, and his warm body against hers. She used her hands with more confidence, this time—he was beautiful, but she knew instinctively that she shouldn't remark upon it; she felt as though she was beginning to penetrate his formidable defenses, and his appearance was only another aspect of the cloak he wore.

Hard on this thought, he murmured into her throat, "You are so beautiful, Epione," which made her smile as she gave in to the mindless pleasure with more enthusiasm this time, now that she knew how it all went.

Afterward, she lay with her face against his chest and breathed in his scent, thinking that—despite the grim talk of gunplay, and escape by ocean—she was finally alive, and it was an improvement over her past life in every conceivable way.

His voice broke into her thoughts. "Tomorrow I must spend some time with the Comte. I may decide to pick a quarrel with you, Epione. Do you think you could feign heartbreak?"

"Easily; I will think of Sir Lucien," she teased.

But this, apparently, was the wrong thing to say, and her companion was distracted from whatever instructions he was going to give, as he shifted his head to meet her eyes. "Tell me the truth, Epione; if he were free, and stood before you now, offering his hand, would you take him?"

She pretended to consider this question. "Is he is the true King of England?"

With heavy irony, he replied, "I think not."

"Then no, I would not have him."

He shook his head slightly, smiling, but she knew he was not best pleased, so she pressed her fingers against his chest in contrition. "Please, Alexis; I told you that I had a foolish *tendre* because he was—oh, he was kind to me. And I thought him heroic—until I discovered that he'd murdered his wife."

He covered the hand on his chest with his own. "Then you should have me; I will not murder you, Epione, my promise on it."

She raised herself on her elbows to look into his face—so compelling, in the moonlight—and said with all sincerity, "I have already married you, if you will remember. Indeed, if it was necessary to have a wedding once a week for the rest of our lives, I will continue to have you—my own promise on it."

This assurance earned her a heart-felt embrace, which soon developed into another heated session of lovemaking—apparently, the process could be repeated multiple times, which was a very pleasant surprise.

Finally, the mixture of satiation, champagne, and lack of sleep caught up to her, and she lay in his arms, drowsy and fading. Unfortunately, it seemed that her companion was not yet ready to concede, and squeezed her slightly. "Are you awake, *ma belle*?"

"Barely." *Again?* she thought.

But his thoughts were apparently not of a carnal nature. "I may desire to be alone with the Comte; if this is the case, I will touch my nose."

Epione knit her sleepy brow, trying to keep up. "Is this after we quarrel?"

"We may not quarrel; I will gauge which I think will be more effective. Follow my lead, if you will."

She nodded. "Will you have enough time to sway him, do you think?"

He sighed. "There is little choice—we have no time left. And I act in his own interests; I imagine he will not be allowed to live very long, once their object is obtained." He paused. "If it does not go well, Epione, you will be smuggled out to the British."

It was not a surprise that the British were lurking somewhere without; after all, de Gilles had collaborated in this plan with the spymaster. "I'd rather stay with you," she protested.

"You will do as I ask, Epione."

She had forgotten that she was no match for him in authoritative tone, and found she could muster no further protest.

Chapter 35

"Higher, Luci—hold your fingers here, while I pin." Madame Reyne was attempting to adjust the décolletage of the gown that was to serve as Epione's wedding dress, as the bodice was a bit too tight. Epione had decided on the blue silk brocade, which seemed most appropriate of all the gowns, with its gossamer silver overlay.

Luci's assistance was making Epione nervous, since the servant tended to put her fingertips in harm's way. So—as to prevent potential bloodstains—Epione suggested, "If we pick out the seam at the waist—where the darting crosses it—it will save a great deal of trouble, and no one will notice because it will lie beneath the sash. It is a common trick, when time is short. Please; allow me to show you."

Madame Reyne's hands stilled, but she nevertheless demurred with no real conviction, "You should not have to sew your own wedding dress, Mademoiselle."

"Have her make a hat, instead; it is only fitting." Lisabetta was in a sour mood as she reclined on the settee, eating almonds and watching the proceedings.

Gently, Epione put a hand on Luci's to stay her before further damage was done. "I truly would not mind—and as I am more accustomed, it will go that much faster. You have other tasks to perform, after all."

With a relieved expression, the housekeeper relinquished the sewing basket and signaled to Luci. "As you wish, Mademoiselle." The two then escaped out the door without a backward glance.

Epione concealed her own relief as she carefully stepped out of the dress; neither the housekeeper nor Luci had anything more than rudimentary skill, and it had been difficult to stand patiently by. That, and she was finally armed with her sewing basket, complete with shears and good, strong lace—although her potential victim was now Lisabetta, who seemed as though she'd be more of a challenge than the housekeeper.

Eying her sullen companion, Epione began ripping the bodice seam with quick, precise movements. "Tell me why you are out of sorts, Lisabetta."

With a languid gesture, the girl popped another almond in her mouth. "I am weary of this place."

Epione glanced up, as she bit off a thread. "Oh? Is Darton not enslaved?"

Lisabetta shrugged. "Darton amuses himself, as do I."

It seemed evident that her companion was not inclined to converse, so instead Epione speculated aloud, "I wonder if Monsieur Darton will want to remain here, at *Desclaires*." She had not considered this aspect before, but thought it may well be the case, since the other man had traveled with de Gilles for so long—assuming they all survived the Josiah plot, of course. All in all, it was just as well that Lisabetta was not smitten; Epione could not look with favor on the possibility that she'd be constantly underfoot.

But apparently Lisabetta's mind was not on Darton, as she lifted her head to regard Epione with a frown. "I think *le Capitaine* truly means to marry you."

Epione smiled as she plied her needle. "Yes, I believe he does." It had certainly seemed so, sunk into the soft bed last night.

The other girl leaned forward with a hint of exasperation. "But why? Why would he do something so provoking?"

Thoughtfully, Epione sewed another stitch, and debated how much to relate to the other girl, who had—after all—abducted her so as to bring this wretched plot to fruition. "I think that is the point; he is looking to provoke."

Lisabetta eyed her thoughtfully, then sank back to pick up a ribbon from the basket, and draw it through her fingers. "He is reckless, then. Who will sell the slaves, if he is killed?"

Epione did not react to the barb, and instead suggested, "You, perhaps? I imagine you'd make a formidable pirate, Lisabetta."

"*C'est vrai;* I would make a good pirate." The girl nodded, as though this was a shrewd insight. "But I am too busy, just now."

"Busy doing what? Causing trouble for the British?" Epione casually tied off a thread, and hoped she'd hear something she could report to de Gilles, although it seemed unlikely—Lisabetta was not one to give anything away.

"I am not the trouble-causer," the girl replied, brushing crumbs from her skirts. "*Le Capitaine* is the trouble-causer."

"I suppose it depends upon one's point of view." Epione paused, and then decided she may as well ask. "Are you a danger to him, Lisabetta?" It had occurred to Epione—as the undercurrents had swirled around her in the ballroom last night—that Lisabetta's invitation to run away to Algiers may have been an attempt to draw de Gilles away; or a warning, perhaps.

"Fah; I am a danger to no one." The girl examined her nails.

Epione could not allow such an out-and-out falsehood to stand, and replied with heavy irony, "I beg to disagree."

But the girl only threw her a superior look. "You are ungrateful, then."

295

This seemed a provocative remark, as it seemed clear that de Gilles was correct, and they would all be killed as soon as the Comte outlived his usefulness. Unless—unless Lisabetta was not what she seemed; after all, de Gilles had hinted that the British would smuggle her out, if his campaign was a failure.

Eying the girl, Epione ventured, "Are you working with the British, Lisabetta?"

Thoroughly affronted, Lisabetta viewed her with all scorn. "*Peste*; bite your tongue."

They were interrupted by a cursory knock on the door before it was flung open to reveal de Gilles, followed by the Comte deFabry, both gentlemen dressed in their outdoor clothes.

"*Les bonhommes—milles mercis*," exclaimed Lisabetta with relief. "I am sick of playing the nursemaid."

"Come, Mademoiselle d'Amberre." De Gilles rested a boot on Epione's footstool, and leaned in on his knee. "We will go shooting."

Epione laughingly stated the obvious. "I am dressed in my shift, Monsieur."

"Come as you are," suggested the Comte, with a gleam at de Gilles. "We will not demur."

"Take me, instead," suggested Lisabetta with heavy innuendo, the request directed to the Comte.

"*Hélas*, I am—for all intents and purposes—a celibate," the man disclaimed with a small bow that nonetheless expressed his appreciation. "Many regrets, *belle* Mademoiselle."

But de Gilles was impatient with the flirtation, and said with finality, "You are not invited, Lisabetta. Mademoiselle; if you please."

As he hadn't attempted to signal by touching his nose, Epione willingly stood, and allowed de Gilles to take the blue dress from her hands, and then negligently lay it over the back of the settee. "You mustn't see my wedding dress," she warned. "It is bad luck."

"Yes, of all things, we must avoid the bad luck," Lisabetta groused.

De Gilles ignored the other girl, and lifted Epione's day dress from the armoire. "I will not look, then—although the blue is *très belle*, Mademoiselle."

"You must be patient, Seigneur; you will see your bride—in all her adornment—this very evening," pronounced the Comte, his voice rich with suppressed emotion. "*Merci le bon Dieu*; I can scarce believe it."

"It looks to rain," Lisabetta offered sourly.

"Come, now," the Comte rallied her, "Your turn will come, Mademoiselle." With an arch look, he teased, "Monsieur Chauvelin is unattached, I believe."

As de Gilles helped Epione into her day dress, he threw a laughing glance at Lisabetta. "*Eh bien*; you could do much worse, I think. You could be his helpmeet, and hand him his tailoring tools."

"Fah; I'll not touch his tools." This said with heavy innuendo, and the Comte threw back his head and laughed aloud.

297

"Shall we go?" de Gilles held out his arm, and Epione took it, hoping that de Gilles' plan—whatever it was—was a good one.

Chapter 36

Epione stood, holding her hat against the sea breeze, and soberly considered the view from the main terrace. The grounds stretched out before them, and beyond the distant walls lay the churning sea. Although the prospect was impressive, the grounds themselves were overgrown, with a rather forlorn pall of neglect hanging over them. The near acre was laid out for a formal garden, but the pathways were overgrown, and the weeds outnumbered the flowers in their beds so that it was almost impossible to see the geometric design. "It is very impressive," she offered.

"Your rightful legacy." The Comte stood resolute, apparently unaware of her own lack of enthusiasm, as he looked toward the distant vineyards with his hands clasped behind his back. "I was adamant that it be returned to you, Mademoiselle."

"I thank you." It remained to be seen, of course, whether she would ever act as chatelaine for *Desclaires*. Unless de Gilles' plan was successful, none of them would be allowed to survive—which was a sobering thought, here in the cool breeze, and Epione fervently hoped that the combined wiles of de Gilles and the British would prevail over Napoleon's supporters. And Lisabetta was right; it did look as though it was going to rain, which was very much in keeping with this rather foreboding place.

"Perhaps we should seek a lady's weapon from the armory, for Mademoiselle to use." De Gilles made a casual gesture toward the inner bailey, behind them. "It is in the south tower, I believe."

Epione threw him a glance, but his mild gaze was fixed on the Comte, who apparently thought this an excellent idea. "Indeed; a lady should always be armed." Then, in an open aside to her, "Essential for a happy marriage, I think."

She laughed as though this was a witty remark, thinking that he obviously wasn't thinking of Marie, or he wouldn't have said it.

De Gilles took Epione's elbow, and began to steer her toward the bailey. "I hope it is well-stocked; I have need of more ammunition, myself, after the excesses of last night."

"Then you shall have it. It may be locked, though—and I confess that I am not certain who holds the key."

"The Jacobin, perhaps?" De Gilles' tone was faintly scornful.

Startled, deFabry looked up in dismay. "Why—whoever do you mean?"

His jaw set, de Gilles considered the path ahead for a moment, as they made their way toward the bailey. "Monsieur Chauvelin is an ardent Jacobin, *mon ami*. I cannot cavil, because I do not choose your guests for you." He paused, and then added fairly, "And as I am an uninvited guest, myself, it would be very bad manners."

But the Comte was aghast, and begged his companion to reconsider. "You—you are mistaken, Seigneur; I would not allow such a–a *cretin* on the premises, I assure you. Monsieur Chauvelin is a Napoleonite, instead." He paused. "He must be tolerated for that reason; I owe it to Marie—to the cause for which she gave her life."

For the first time, de Gilles' casual elegance was replaced by a certain stiffness—a hint of distance. "It is you who are mistaken, Monsieur le Comte; I have known him for many years, *je vous assure*."

Struggling for words, the other man forgot himself so much as to step in front of Epione, the better to opportune de Gilles. "Yes—I agree he is a scoundrel, but it cannot be true—"

Pausing in apparent dismay, de Gilles turned to the other man, and placed a conciliatory hand on his arm. "*Mille pardons,* Etienne; I am thoughtless to raise such a subject, when you have been all that is hospitable. Forgive me, *mon ami;* you must think me a sorry guest."

With obvious relief, the Comte shook his head. "There is nothing to forgive; I am mortified, if this is indeed true."

"We will not speak of it again; instead tell me what you know of this place."

Epione trailed behind them, listening as the men discussed the layout of the château's ancient fortifications, and speculated as to the age of each addition. It seemed evident that de Gilles was laying the groundwork to make the Comte come out from under the grip of the tailor, who held power, here, for undisclosed reasons—although the man had certainly capitulated to de Gilles' presence last night, despite his barely-controlled rage. It was a strange state of affairs; the conspirators dared not cross the Comte, and the Comte seemed to consider himself de Gilles' *courtier.* It was almost absurd, that the fate of France hung on the caprices of a slightly mad nobleman.

They approached the inner bailey, the ancient walls rising up before them; foursquare, thick and impregnable. The Comte paused before the scarred oaken door, and pulled on the iron ring with no success. With a flourish, de Gilles produced his lock-picking tool, and bent to apply it, while the Comte watched with unfettered admiration. "*Parbleu*, there is a talent."

"It has served me well, my friend." With a conspiratorial look, he raised his eyes to the

Comte as the door clicked open, and Epione thought it interesting that de Gilles always seemed to make a reference to female conquests when he was with the Comte, even though it seemed apparent that the Comte had never been much in the petticoat line—and the man's inexperience had no doubt been exploited by Marie. But the Comte always seemed well-pleased to be included in de Gille's ribald remarks, and she could only admire her betrothed's shrewd reading of their companion.

They passed through the thick entry door, and entered the armory; the arrow slits in the venerable stone walls the only source of light. Arrayed along the tower's interior walls were wooden racks which supported only a few weapons, and even to Epione's unpracticed eye, they seemed old, and outdated.

"Not much to see." The Comte reviewed the offerings, and made a clucking sound. "It was too much to be hoped for, that we would find something worthwhile." He turned to Epione in apology. "I see no lady's weapon, *chère* Mademoiselle."

De Gilles lifted a blunderbuss from the rack, and examined it. "Who held this place, after it was seized by the Jacobins?"

"I understand it was a *biens nationaux*—held by the state. I am not certain who resided here."

De Gilles nodded, and returned the heavy weapon to its rack. "And who will hold it after

303

Mademoiselle d'Amberre? Not Monsieur Chauvelin, surely?"

Once again, the Comte was seen to be acutely dismayed. "Why—why, no; this I swear to you! Mademoiselle will hold the title as long as she lives—and you, Seigneur, as her husband."

De Gilles lifted another weapon from the rack, and tilted his head in mild disagreement. "Come, my friend. Napoleon would never allow this place to be held by one such as me."

But the other man was passionately adamant, and made a slashing gesture with his fist. "I will insist upon it—I have insisted upon it, and I have received assurances."

Epione thought it prudent to add, "I do hope you are right, Monsieur le Comte. If Marie is to be interred here; who will care for her grave, otherwise?"

The Comte faced her, trying with little success to hide his dismay at the turn the conversation had taken. "You will hold *Desclaires* forever—my promise on it." But a hint of uncertainty had crept into his voice.

"As long as the Jacobin does not." De Gilles casually opened a cupboard, and examined several silken bags of black powder, perched haphazardly along the shelves.

The Comte was silent for a moment, struggling with his emotions. "I confess your concerns alarm me; I hadn't thought of the reaction by—I mean to say—"

"Yes; my presence makes the situation most awkward." De Gilles smiled at Epione with mock-chagrin. "My Epione has chosen the wrong husband, perhaps."

At this remark, the Comte drew himself up, resolute. "All will be well, and I beg you not to think of it again—I have been given the most solemn assurances."

De Gilles glanced at him sidelong, an ironic smile on his lips. "By whom?"

The Comte declared, "I have a document, under the seal of Napoleon, himself."

As he returned to his inspection of the ammunition, de Gilles made a small sound which indicated his skepticism of such an assurance. "You and I have both seen what lawless men can do, *mon ami*—and that one is more lawless than most."

Unable to argue, the Comte bowed his head. "Indeed."

De Gilles lifted a leather ammunition satchel, and began loading it with musket balls and black powder. "What is on the next floor?"

"I know not," said the other man, relieved at the change in subject. "Shall we see?"

De Gilles and Epione followed the Comte up the narrow, winding stairwell, Epione holding her skirts up to keep them off the crude flooring. The second level was similar to the first in terms of layout, but instead of weapons, there were a variety of new-looking wooden caskets, stacked against the wall.

De Gilles leaned down, and with a negligent gesture, lifted a lid to reveal a luminous tangle of pearls. "Now, here is an inheritance, Mademoiselle."

"Ah, yes—the pearls." The Comte nodded, stepping over to take a look. "I am given to understand there will be more to come—although they are not slated to remain here, you understand. Merely temporary storage, until they can be moved to Paris."

"The other caskets contain jewels?" asked Epione, remembering Lisabetta's comment.

"Many jewels—indeed, a fortune," the Comte assured them placidly, clasping his hands behind his back. "All is in train, to honor Marie's dreams."

De Gilles arched a brow. "Who is donating such an honor?"

The Comte shrugged with benign disinterest. "Why—I am not certain, but I am given to understand the treasure will be transferred to Paris, within the next month."

De Gille's hands stilled for a moment, then he slowly lowered the lid on the pearls casket. "Ah. I see."

Epione found the reference confusing. "But why—"

Moving with casual grace toward the stairwell, de Gilles interrupted her. "There are unsuspecting ducks awaiting us, *ma belle*. Since we can find no lady's weapon, I will gladly lend you my pistol."

"I don't think the ducks have much to fear from me," Epione confessed. "But I will be happy to assist you gentlemen, with your hunting."

306

The Comte offered his hand to Epione, as he stood beneath her on the stairwell. "Your assistance will be much appreciated, my dear, but where is your manservant, Seigneur?"

De Gilles' voiced echoed off the narrow walls. "I would not be surprised if he was assisting *la belle* Lisabetta."

The Comte laughed aloud, as they rounded the final twist of the stairwell, only to behold Monsieur Chauvelin, standing in the entry door, and observing their approach with stone-faced incredulity. "*What* is the meaning of this?"

"We take a tour." De Gilles pulled the brim of his hat in a mock-salute. "Mademoiselle d'Amberre is counting her strongboxes."

The man's expression did not change, but a dull red flush spread up his face. "You will leave this place, Monsieur, and immediately."

"Fie—you do not hold sway here." The Comte's tone was cold, and it was clear de Gilles' earlier remarks had made an impression. "You will mind your manners, Monsieur."

With ill-concealed displeasure, the newcomer met the Comte's gaze for a long moment, and then made a visible effort to control himself. "Your pardon." Bowing his head, he stepped aside to allow them to pass.

Epione, however, stood rooted to the spot; the tailor's expression—coldly furious—had pricked her memory, so that she now knew why he seemed so familiar. His face—so rigid with suppressed rage—was the image of her mother's.

"Why is he so dangerous? Why is he here?" The tailor was not an imposing man, yet the others definitely seemed wary of him. She lifted her head, struck with a thought. "Why, *he* should be the true heir to *Desclaires*."

Her companion tilted his head, and gently corrected her. "If there hadn't been a Revolution, perhaps. There is no longer an heir to *Desclaires*; you hold title because Napoleon is indulging the Comte."

She glanced up at him, holding the brim of her hat against the persistent breeze. "Yes—have you determined why this is? Does the Josiah plot have something to do with the jewels in the tower?"

He glanced around, to be certain they were quite alone. "I can guess. We know the Comte is needed to impersonate Louis Philippe; I believe he will placed on the throne, and then he will willingly abdicate to Napoleon. He swear allegiance, and then surrender the contents of the Royal Treasury."

Epione stared at him in wonder. "They plan to *steal* from the Treasury?"

But he corrected, "There is little to steal— except that the Congress of Vienna has been infusing funds, so as to keep France in operation. But the Emperor will need a formidable treasury to aid his efforts—there are bribes to be paid, and generals to be rewarded."

Epione shook her head in amazement. *"Grand Dieu*, but it is a diabolical plot—they plan to murder two of the pretenders, and then steal the throne from their own imposter."

311

"It is extraordinary," he agreed. "But then again, we live in extraordinary times."

The breadth of this nefarious plot led Epione to one, ominous, conclusion. "Denis must be the murderer—he is the killer; that is why he makes everyone nervous."

Facing her, he held her elbows and said gently, "It is rumored that he was used by the Emperor for years, as an assassin. I am sorry, Epione."

Bleakly, she stared up into his sympathetic gaze for a moment, considering the poor, remaining wreckage of what was once a proud family, and—incongruously—how it didn't seem to matter as much as it should. "Thank *le bon Dieu* for you."

He drew her into his warm, reassuring embrace. "I will say the same."

She sank into the comfort of his arms for a moment, then drew a steadying breath, and asked, "What now?" It went without saying that their own lives would be forfeit, if they were not able to thwart the evildoers.

"I will go shooting with the Comte. I will ask that you return to your chambers, and stay there until the wedding."

"It looks to rain," she warned. "Don't be caught out-of-doors."

"All the better; I would spend some time with him alone."

Hard on this thought, the Comte could be heard to hail them. "Ah—behold the fond lovers. Shall I leave you to it?"

312

Epione stepped away from de Gilles, and smiled at him in apology. "I've decided I must bow out of the shooting expedition, Monsieur le Comte. If it rains, my poor hair will be a disaster for the wedding."

"Of course." The Comte took her hand, and raised it to his lips. "*Eh bien*, it is a very special day." He indicated Luci, who attended him, bearing a claret jug. "The girl will accompany you back to the house, Mademoiselle; we can see to the claret, ourselves."

But Luci seemed dismayed. "Oh—are you certain? I will be very quiet."

Again, Epione noted that the girl seemed conversant in French. "The gentlemen wish to be alone, Luci; if you would, please come with me."

"*D'accord.*" De Gilles took up the jug, and nodded to the Comte. "Come, *mon ami*, we shall see who strikes first."

Chapter 38

Once back in her chambers, Epione patiently altered the seams on the wedding gown's bodice, deciding to do a more thorough job, now that she had the time, and then wiggled the gown over her head to assess her progress in the mirror. Luci seemed disinterested, and had instead taken the opportunity to stand at the window, silently looking outward over the sea.

Thinking that there may be more to the girl than had first appeared, Epione attempted to draw her out, and offered in a friendly fashion, "How do you find France, Luci?"

The girl did not turn, but remained facing out the window as she replied absently, "I've spent plenty of time in France, Miss. And I can't say I've enjoyed it much."

This seemed a surprise, but before Epione could frame the next question, the chamber doors banged opened to reveal Madame Reyne, who paused on the entry, her bosom heaving with palpable agitation. Epione turned to her in alarm. "What is it, Madame? Is anything amiss?"

The woman did not answer, but instead fixed her gaze upon Luci, as she closed the door behind her. "Who are you? Tell me now, or it will be the worse for you. "

Upon the housekeeper's dramatic entry, Luci had whirled to face her, and now stood with a blank expression, her jaw slack—the picture of befuddled confusion. "Ma'am?"

The woman approached Luci slowly, viewing her with abject suspicion. "Who is it that you signal to? Don't lie to me—I saw you from the kitchen garden. Tell me, Luci."

Epione looked between the two in surprise. "Please, Madame Reyne; you are frightening her."

"I—I have a mirror," Luci confessed, dropping her head in embarrassment. "I was shining it on the water." Turning over her hand, she revealed a small, round mirror in her palm.

But the housekeeper remained wary, and confronted the girl with barely-concealed alarm. "What were you about? It looked like a signal, of some sort."

"Perhaps she has a beau." Epione remembered what she thought was a certain awareness between the girl and the sandy-haired footman—she'd been worried that the man might take advantage of the simple-minded maid.

315

But the housekeeper shook her head. "No—she was signaling over the water to someone, and Monsieur Chauvelin must be told immediately." With resolution, the woman stepped forward to seize the other girl roughly. "He will get the truth from you; come with me."

Her face crumpling, Luci pulled back, and then cast a nervous glance out the window. Seeing this, the housekeeper quickly stepped forward, craning her head to see what it was the girl had seen, but suddenly, with an abrupt and practiced movement, Luci heaved on the woman's arm with both hands, propelling her headlong through the diamond-paned window with a horrendous crash. Before Epione's horrified gaze, the housekeeper fell from sight, as the cold ocean breeze blew the curtains back from the remaining jagged edges of the window.

While Epione gaped in shock, Luci leaned over the sill to observe the results of her handiwork. "Stupid cow."

Somehow, Epione managed to find her voice. "Luci—oh, *mon Dieu*—"

"You will say nothing of this, my fine miss." With a jerk, Luci drew the curtains across the broken window, and Epione noted that she now spoke in a completely different tone. "I'm half-wishing that you'd disappear as well—you and that Captain o' yours—so don't be tempting me."

This seemed an alarming observation, and Epione scrambled to grasp the shears out of the sewing basket, and then brandish them before her. "Do not come near."

This defensive action seemed only to amuse the girl, who stood and regarded Epione with a smile, her hands on her hips. "Aye, that's the spirit—take no prisoners."

Irish, thought Epione in surprise; the maid spoke with an Irish accent. "Who are you—or I suppose more properly, who are you allied with?"

But it appeared that no answers were to be divulged, as the girl lifted her mirror from the plush carpet where she'd dropped it, and then polished it absently on her skirts as she crossed the room. "Lord, nothing is going according to plan. You know nothing—not that I'm expecting anyone to be asking—and you're to stay here, right and tight."

Epione stared in bemusement. "I cannot stay here; I'm to be married."

"No, you're not; the visitors are due at any minute, and you're to stay well out of it." As the maid closed the doors, she boldly winked.

Epione stood in center of the now-quiet room as thunder could be heard in the distance through the open window. Perhaps the girl worked for the British—which seemed likely, considering she was Irish, and she'd dispatched poor Madame Reyne without a moment's hesitation—but Epione decided she should make no assumptions. The maid's comment about the visitors seemed ominous, as it indicated Louis Philippe was to arrive sooner than expected, and above all things, de Gilles must be warned that all plots and counter-plots had to be advanced immediately, before the man was murdered.

Straightening her shoulders, Epione hesitated for a moment, then pushed the sewing shears up into a beribboned silk sleeve, so as to have some sort of weapon—her history with shears was not a good one, but perhaps one got better with practice. It did seem as though she was growing more competent by the hour, mainly out of necessity.

Striding over to the doors, she pulled on the handles only to be met with resistance; Luci had locked her in. After thinking for a moment, she turned and rummaged through the sewing basket for the darning needle, and then bent to manipulate the keyhole as de Gilles had shown her. Unfortunately, either she was not as facile as he, or it was not the same sort of lock. With acute frustration, she continued to jimmy it for the next ten minutes, crouching in the dim light as the sound of the rolling thunder moved closer.

The door handles suddenly rattled in her face, and Epione leapt back in alarm. The rattling was followed by knocking, and Lisabetta's voice. "*Allez,* the door is locked."

Epione never thought she'd be relieved to hear Lisabetta's voice, but matters had definitely taken a turn. "I know; I'm locked in. Can you pick the lock, Lisabetta? I have a darning needle I can push under the door."

There was a pause. "Who locked you in the room?"

"Luci," Epione replied, thinking rapidly. "I think she didn't mean to. And it's cold, because the window's broken, so please hurry."

"Stand back," said Lisabetta.

This seemed alarming. "What are you going to do?"

"I am going to shoot the lock off, *imbecile*."

Epione was certain the door was hand-carved. "Is that truly necessary? Can't you pick the lock?"

"Stand back or I will shoot you, too."

Epione shrank back, and covered her ears as Lisabetta suited deed to word—although it took two rounds and a great deal of muttering between, to splinter off the lock.

With the acrid smell of gunpowder floating in the air, the other girl entered and took a measuring look at Epione, before she casually began to reload her pistol. "Where is Madame Reyne?"

Epione decided it would be prudent to follow Luci's advice, particularly because Lisabetta was allied with the newly-deceased, and may not take the news well. "I don't know. Where is Monsieur Darton?" If Epione could entrust a message to him, he could probably deliver it to de Gilles more quickly than she could.

But Lisabetta, as was her wont, paid little attention to Epione, and crossed into the room, her thoughtful gaze on the billowing curtains. "*Peste,* I am hungry. Do you have anything to eat?"

"The almonds, or what is left of them." Impatiently, Epione indicated the dish on the side table. "I must speak with Monsieur de Gilles, so I will go."

319

"What is so important?" Lisabetta's sharp, speculative gaze met Epione's. "It rains."

Belatedly, Epione realized she shouldn't raise suspicion, and so tried to backtrack. "I am having second thoughts, and I am not certain we should marry. I hardly know him, and if he is a slave-trader, as you say—"

But Lisabetta was very much amused, and arched an insolent brow. "Yes? You believe you could do better, perhaps?"

"I must speak with him, and soon," Epione repeated firmly. "Perhaps I could send Monsieur Darton to fetch him—wasn't he with you?"

Lisabetta popped an almond into her mouth. "I will not tell you, because you will undoubtedly say the wrong thing to Monsieur Darton, and ruin all my plans. You have a gift, I think."

This seemed an odd thing to say, and Epione paused mid-stride. "Never say you are making plans to stay with Monsieur Darton?" Once again, the specter of having Lisabetta constantly underfoot raised its alarming head.

Amused, Lisabetta sank down upon the settee, resting an out-flung arm across the top as she tilted her head back to pour some more almonds from her fist into her mouth. "*En effet*, I should; he is very appreciative in the bed, which is always, in turn, much appreciated."

Barely holding on to her temper, Epione continued with a firm step toward the broken door. "If you will excuse me, I must speak with Monsieur de Gilles."

Although Epione was braced for resistance, the other girl shrugged and brushed off her hands. "Suit yourself. *Adieu,* then."

Chapter 39

The finality of Lisabetta's farewell seemed rather ominous, but Epione decided there was nothing for it, she had to find de Gilles and warn him that the Duc d'Orleans was arriving early, and that his plan must be put forward—hopefully he'd had enough time to turn the Comte, although there may be another enemy on the horizon, depending upon to whom Luci was signaling. It seemed almost certain it was the British—de Gilles had hinted they were positioned close by, probably watching as events unfolded. But there was no question he was uneasy about his alliance with them, and had warned her not to trust them. With this in mind, Epione hastened her steps, in her hurried progress down the sweeping stairway. If the British shouldn't be trusted, all the more reason to inform him immediately that Luci was the sort of person who threw people out of windows without a second thought.

As she rounded the final landing, she wished she'd thought to bring a cloak; her wedding dress would be ruined, if she went out in the rain—although apparently there was not to be a wedding, unless Luci was lying. It was all very fatiguing, truly—but with any luck, her resourceful betrothed could sort it all out.

There was no one about, and the only sounds were her gasping breaths as she raced, soft-footed, down the final level of the stairway; the cavernous great hall swathed in shadows, due to the storm. Lifting her skirts, she flew across to the massive entry doors, thinking that it would be best to get outside as quickly as possible—away from the vulnerability of the shadowy chateau—and then once outside, she could search for the hunting party. She recalled that there was a large pond on the western side of the grounds—

"Mademoiselle."

Her hand on the door handle, Epione froze, then turned with as much composure as she could manage to bow to Monsieur Chauvelin, who stood framed in the entryway to the great hall. "Monsieur." She found that she could think of nothing to say, and so said nothing.

His hands clasped behind his back, he stepped toward her. "You are upset, perhaps? Might I be of assistance?"

No point in pretending otherwise—she was running out into the storm in her wedding dress. The lightning cracked overhead, and she replied as calmly as she was able, "It is—I'm afraid it is a private matter, Monsieur. I have heard some unsettling reports about my fiancé." Let him think she had unearthed the rumors of slave-trading. To add credence, she dabbed at her eyes with a knuckle, feigning distress.

His expression impassive, Chauvelin glanced up the stairs. "Is Madame Reyne about?"

"I—I am not certain of her whereabouts, Monsieur." This was—strictly speaking—true.

He regarded her for a moment, his expression unreadable, and she had the distinct impression he was not certain he believed her. "You should not go out alone, Mademoiselle. Allow me to accompany you."

She met his gaze—so like her mother's, now that she recognized it—and found that she was compelled to say, "As you wish. I believe we have much to say to each other."

There was a moment's profound silence, and then he began to circle her, his own gaze cold and impenetrable. My only remaining blood kin, she thought with her heart in her mouth, and I am very much afraid of him.

He cocked his head at her, and she had the impression he was much enjoying the fact that she was afraid of him. "You are mistaken, Mademoiselle; we have nothing in common."

Perhaps it was his attitude—barely concealed menace; or perhaps it was the incongruity of standing thus, with her long-lost brother, but in any event, Epione suddenly decided she was not going to allow him to intimidate her. De Gilles said there were some things that transcend mere life and death, and one would think that family was one of them. He is my brother, she thought, squaring her shoulders; I should make an effort—an effort to connect to him. He has had it so much harder than I.

"I would like to hear of my father." Their mother had rarely discussed him, and then only with venom; his heroics for King and country had only served to deprive her of his support, and she was not one to care for anything but her own comfort.

The question evoked a strong reaction— just not the one she sought. He leaned slightly toward her, the unveiled hatred in his gaze making her step back a half-step. "He was an *aristo* who lived only to oppress those who lived beneath his heel."

Epione stood her ground, even though his breath was hot on her face; that she had evoked such a strong reaction surely must mean that he was not as coldly indifferent as he seemed. "What did he look like?"

His features twisted into a sneer. "That depends, Mademoiselle; before or after he was torn apart by the mob?"

Without conscious thought, she slapped his jeering face with all her strength, and he caught her arm in a rough grasp, just as the door banged open, and the thunder rolled.

"Mademoiselle?" De Gilles strode over to stand between Epione and Chauvelin, so close that his greatcoat dripped rain onto her skirts. "Do you require assistance?" He spoke to her, but his gaze was level with Chauvelin's, his manner holding its own hint of menace.

Seeing that the Comte stood aghast in the doorway, the other man stepped away. "Nothing of moment; the lady is seeking private conversation with you."

Reminded, Epione said in a stiff tone, "If you have a moment, Monsieur de Gilles."

The Comte observed the interaction with a worried eye, clearly distressed that emotions were running high. "Now, Mademoiselle—I have kept the Seigneur from your side, and you must take issue with me, instead."

Unwilling to lead the poor man to think she was having second thoughts about the wedding, Epione managed a small smile, and assured him, "It will take but a moment, Monsieur le Comte, and then I will be most willing to seek out your company."

"Of course; of course." Clearly relieved, the Comte hastily gestured to Chauvelin. "Come, Monsieur; let us leave the lovers to themselves."

But at this juncture, the sandy-haired footman signaled to Chauvelin from the great hall, and the tailor immediately stepped over to hold a whispered conversation with the servant. Epione decided this was a fortuitous development; if Chauvelin was informed that Louis Philippe approached, the distraction should allow her to confer with de Gilles without fear of interruption.

This proved to be true; the tailor straightened for a moment in obvious surprise, and then signaled to the Comte to follow, as he brusquely excused himself.

De Gilles watched them all exit, his expression unreadable. "Did he offer you violence, *ma belle*?"

Epione had the impression he was looking for an excuse to draw his pistol and pursue the tailor, so she put a reassuring hand on his arm. "No—no, Alexis; nothing like that." Best not to mention the bruises that would surely form on her arm by the morrow.

He turned to face her, his gaze probing. "You struck him, though. He had a mark on his face."

But she had other concerns, and informed him in a low voice, "Never mind that; Luci killed Madame Reyne, and the Duc d'Orleans will arrive ahead of time—I believe the footman just informed Monsieur Chauvelin of this fact."

As she said the words, lightning struck again outside the window, making her jump, but he only knit his brows slightly, and regarded her for a moment. "How is it you know this, *ma belle*?"

"Which one?"

"Any."

She marshaled her thoughts, and recited, "Luci is Irish; she is working with one of the factions—she didn't say who—and she had no problem hurling Madame Reyne out the window when the woman caught her signaling to someone."

"*De vrai*?"

Rather than being surprised, he seemed a bit amused, which reminded her that he'd lived in ruthless Algiers, after all, and so could not be expected to have the same reaction to these events as she did. "Luci is the one who said the visitors are coming early—I think it was part of the message that was signaled to her."

"That is of interest," de Gilles acknowledged. "Come, let us find Monsieur Darton."

He took her hand, and she followed him through the great hall, wishing her petticoats weren't quite so heavy—a dress such as this one was not made to run to and fro, but instead, for its wearer to stand and be admired. "Do you think Luci is allied with the British? It seems likely."

But he did not see this as a boon. "If she is, it is not reassuring to me, *ma belle*."

"Because they didn't tell you."

"Yes, because they didn't tell me." He stood at the foot of the stairway and whistled, sharp and loud, then lowered his head to hers, thinking over this development.

She ventured, "I imagine the British would not truly mind if the Duc d'Orleans is assassinated by the Josiah plotters—it would mean one less pretender, and thus would boost their own candidate. Perhaps they have no interest in moving quickly to thwart the plot."

Raising his head, he met her gaze. "We cannot know, and therefore we must work to thwart it from both ends. We must warn the visitors of what is planned before they enter the gates, and we must gain control of the Comte. I will send Darton to warn *le Duc*, and in the meantime, we must marry, and lead the Comte to believe that a child is soon coming; I have already hinted as much to him."

Blushing, she stared in confusion. "Wouldn't—wouldn't such a thing be impossible to know, so soon?"

Patiently, he explained, "I told him that when we first met in London, I made my way into your bed. It is why I pursued you here; I was *bouleversé.*" He paused, letting her assimilate this. "The idea of a child should weigh heavily in our favor."

Darton suddenly appeared on the landing above them, his gaze sharp upon de Gilles as he quickly descended the stairs. "Yes? What has happened?"

"You must put down the fair Lisabetta for a few minutes; Louis Philippe and his party approach."

The other man raised his brows in surprise. "So soon?"

"Unfortunately so." He nodded toward Epione. "Mademoiselle d'Amberre tells me that she believes Luci was signaling to the British."

Darton's expression turned grave. "The maidservant? Why weren't we informed of this?"

De Gilles cocked his head. "Perhaps they do not share our aims. I think it best that you slip away to warn the approaching party on the road, and I will convince the Comte to put the marriage forward also; I have explained to him that it is a

329

marriage of necessity, as Mademoiselle is *enceinte*."

The other man turned to Epione in surprise. "*De vrai?*"

Epione blushed, and de Gilles continued, "Enough; you must warn them, and quickly. With the British watching the front gates, it may be best to slip away by the grotto, and then take the skiff to shore."

With a confident nod, Darton agreed. "*D'accord.*"

"You will attempt to row ashore in the storm?" Epione ventured doubtfully.

But as they strode toward the servant's hall, de Gilles assured her, "Monsieur Darton has seen seas worse than this, *ma belle*. Come, we will cast him off."

Chapter 40

Walking quickly, they followed Darton as he passed through the small pantry door, and then down the rock-hewn steps to the grotto. The cold air rushed to meet her, as Epione gathered her wide skirts before her, the silver netting getting caught on the rough walls. Once they'd passed through the wooden door, they entered the grotto, the atmosphere eerie in the subdued light, and the rain making a hissing sound on the ocean's surface, outside the cave's entrance.

"I may not be able to send word," Darton warned as his footsteps echoed on the dock. "I will reconnoiter, to determine whether the British are also lying in wait—"

"*Bien*," de Gilles replied. "And stay wary; as soon as it is clear the plot has been thwarted, no doubt the British will move in."

Darton knelt beside the dock post, and attempted to untie the knots that bound the small boat to the wharf, as the lightening illuminated the interior briefly. Making a sound of amused frustration, he held out his hand. "This knot is not that of a sailor; your sword, *Capitaine*." De Gilles tossed it to him, and with an exaggerated swing, Darton raised it over his head to cut the rope. Unfortunately, his actions cost him his balance, and as he stumbled back to regain it, the sword flew out of his hand, and splashed into the still water.

Epione gasped in dismay, and Darton swore in contrition. "I will find it, *Capitaine*—it is quite shallow here." He began to remove his greatcoat, but de Gilles stopped him with a gesture. "Rest easy; I will retrieve it, *mon ami*—you should not be wet to go out in the storm, and you must hurry." With an easy movement, he discarded his own greatcoat, and then leaned on the post to remove his boots.

But to Epione's astonishment, Darton drew his own pistol, and aimed it squarely at de Gilles, as he swept up the discarded greatcoat, and stepped away. "Forgive me, *Capitaine*. I'm afraid the time has come to part ways."

There was a moment of stunned silence, and then de Gilles slowly straightened, taking Epione by the arm, and drawing her behind him.

"Surely there is no need for this, *mon ami*. Go; and we will say no more."

Darton's manner was, for once, quite grave. "I'm afraid there is every need, and I must beg your pardon."

Aghast, Epione was so horrified she couldn't find words, but de Gilles continued to speak in a reasonable tone. "Then allow Mademoiselle to leave us. She will return to obscurity, and breathe not a word of any of this, won't you Mademoiselle?"

"Yes," she managed to agree in a small voice, silently vowing to pursue Darton to the ends of the earth if necessary, to make him pay for such a betrayal.

His expression sympathetic, Darton shook his head. "She knows too much, to my deep regret."

"*Quand même*," said de Gilles, with an urgent edge to his voice, "you cannot kill her. Instead, report that she has disappeared; you can be assured she will not emerge again."

With a show of sympathy, Darton only shrugged slightly. "Even now, she may carry another pretender. The chance cannot be taken."

"A bastard, only," de Gilles pointed out. "No threat to any."

"Nonetheless, the chance cannot be taken."

Clinging to his back, Epione carefully drew the sewing shears from her sleeve, and laid them in his hand, while he continued, "Send her away, then—on a ship to China, where it would take months for her to return."

"I cannot," the other man said with real regret, as he raised the pistol. "My sincerest apologies."

Epione could feel the muscles beneath her hands tense in anticipation, even as de Gilles continued to speak in a reasonable tone. "A last favor, for me; for all we have been through together—"

But he didn't complete the sentence, as he lunged toward the other man, slashing the shears in an arc before him. Darton was no fool, however, and leapt beyond de Gilles's reach, as the loud report of the pistol echoed off the rock walls. Epione frantically launched herself at Darton, thinking to prevent a second shot, and hoping the first one hadn't been fatal.

Her intention, however, was thwarted by de Gilles himself, who didn't fall as she'd expected, but instead closed with Darton, seizing the wrist that held the pistol just as the other man unexpectedly collapsed to the ground.

As the smoke cleared away, Epione could only stare in astonishment at Lisabetta, who was revealed to have been standing at the foot of the stairway, behind Darton. As the lightning flashed outside the grotto, the girl lowered her pistol. "There, *aristo*. Now I owe you nothing."

"*Mille mercis*." De Gilles pulled Epione to him for a moment, and squeezed her so that it was difficult to catch her breath—or more difficult, as she was already having trouble breathing, and felt a bit light-headed. "Whose was he, Lisabetta?"

The girl approached to observe the dead Darton, crumpled in a heap upon the dock. "Tallyrand's; and now I have spoiled my own assignment."

De Gilles bent to take the pistol from the dead man's hand. "Napoleon asked you to shadow Darton?"

"Yes; he is aware that Tallyrand had him shadowing you, and *l'Emperor* knows Tallyrand cannot be trusted." Casually, the girl checked her pistol. "It is all very fatiguing."

"Everyone is shadowing me," Epione pointed out, finding her voice again, and nearly giddy with relief. "I am the one who should be fatigued."

"Then you should sleep alone tonight, and I will entertain this man, who has had a very difficult day." But it was clear the offer was made only as a matter of form, as Lisabetta bent to relieve the corpse of his gold watch.

De Gilles looked up to the other woman. "Should he disappear?"

Lisabetta sighed. "Yes; let us sink him in the sea, and profess no knowledge of him. *Pere* Tallyrand will be in the dark for a few days, which will serve him exactly right, *si vous voulez mon avis.*"

They secured the corpse with rope, and affixed it to the skiff's anchor, Epione noting that both Lisabetta and de Gilles seemed to be proficient at this task. As she straightened to shake out her skirts, Lisabetta addressed de Gilles, a speculative look in her dark eyes. "And why, *Capitaine*, do you suppose Tallyrand would have paid this man to be your shadow for all these years?"

De Gilles took a final jerk at the knots which bound the dead man's body to the anchor. "It is not such a puzzle; Tallyrand hedges his bets. If the British put the Bourbon on the throne, he becomes France's Prime Minister; if his former master Napoleon returns to power, he returns to power, also. I am a problem for him, because I could disrupt either plan."

But Lisabetta was not satisfied with his answer, and watched him thoughtfully for a few moments, as he pushed up his shirt sleeves to drag the corpse to the edge of the wharf. "The British spymaster believes you are the true King of France."

"Then he is mistaken." De Gilles said it in the tone of one who has disclaimed this point often.

Lisabetta narrowed her eyes. "I don't think he is mistaken very often."

"He is mistaken, this time."

Darton's body hit the water with a splash, and de Gilles rose to look upon Lisabetta. "These are difficult times, Lisabetta. If you ever need a refuge, you will always have one with us. I owe you a debt I can never repay."

But Lisabetta tossed her head. "I will find my own refuge, *aristo*."

336

De Gilles nodded as though he'd expected nothing less, and then sat on the edge of the wharf to pull off his boots, placing them beside him, one by one. As he pulled his shirt over his head, he slanted her a glance. "Yes, you are a very resourceful girl. It was surprising that you managed to escape from the British, so easily."

Astonished, Epione stared at the girl. "You are working for the *British*, as well as for Napoleon?"

Lisabetta shrugged a shoulder. "The British are concerned about *Pere* Tallyrand's doings— and small blame to them. Since this concern is shared by *l'Emperor,* I deigned to offer my assistance to both sides."

"The British paid you to keep their part quiet," de Gilles concluded with amused cynicism, as he slid into the water with a small splash.

"They did indeed. Handsomely."

He grinned up at the Frenchwoman. "Then I will pay you also; it is the least I can do, since I have spoiled all your assignments."

Lisabetta bowed her head. "I will gladly accept your money."

Bemused, Epione watched as he ducked his chin to peer into the dark water. "Do you see it? I hope you can recover your sword, Monsieur."

"I must," he replied. "It does not belong to me."

He disappeared beneath the surface of the still water, and Epione turned to the other girl with a rush of gratitude. "*Thank you*—oh, Lisabetta—"

337

Lisabetta only lifted a shoulder. "Do not think we are friends—if I can take this man from you, I will. *Dieu*, but he has a fine chest."

"You can't—no one can," replied Epione, and knew that it was true. She turned to contemplate the surface of the water, knowing that de Gilles's loyalty to her arose—at least in part—from her family's involvement in the *L'ange d'Isaac* plot, and the terrible sacrifices made. She knew, down to her bones, that he did not give his loyalty easily, but once given, it was unshakable. Hard on this thought, she remembered this betrayer, whose corpse now lay in the cold water beneath the wharf, and wished she had helped to kick it over the edge when she had the opportunity

After a few moments, de Gilles re-surfaced, and lunged up to deposit the wet sword on the wharf, shaking the water from his hair.

Epione smiled in delight. "Well done, Monsieur."

"I thank you." Placing his palms on the dock, he hoisted himself out of the water, and kissed her in the process, making her laugh, and draw back. He is upset, she realized; he is very angry, beneath his cloak.

"I go," announced Lisabetta, who had seen enough. "Say nothing to the British of this, or they may not pay me."

"*D'accord.*" He approached Lisabetta, and casually lifted the hem of her shawl to dry his face and arms. "But I confess I thirst—can we not toast our victory over *Pere* Tallyrand?" Lifting his boots with a hand, he motioned for Epione to precede him up the stairs. "We have time, I think, before the next skirmish—and I'd like to keep the Comte close to hand. Shall we call for champagne, and shoot again?"

"I do like champagne," Lisabetta acknowledged. "And I think it would be prudent to re-load."

As she came to the top of the steps, Epione looked up to see the door ajar, and Luci framed in the doorway, her blank gaze looking beyond to Lisabetta, and de Gilles. "Is anything amiss, Miss?" she asked Epione in careful English, as though their last meeting hadn't involved murder and mayhem.

With an expansive gesture, de Gilles indicated Lisabetta, coming up behind him. "We must celebrate, Mademoiselle. Please fetch me—" But before he finished the command, with his free hand he yanked Luci into Lisabetta, so that both girls tumbled down the narrow stairs. He then quickly slammed the door shut behind them, and slid the bolt into place with a decisive movement.

Chapter 41

"Oh," said Epione, startled by this unlooked-for development. "I suppose we cannot trust them."

"No. And since Lisabetta no longer has a reason to serve the British, she may now decide to help with the Josiah plot. She is never to be trusted, Epione."

Taking her hand in his, he led her away, through the dimly-lit kitchens. The thunderstorm had quieted, and the only sound was the steady rain against the window panes, and a faint but persistent pounding, coming from the pantry door. Epione ventured, "Do you suppose Luci will kill her?" It seemed unkind to leave Lisabetta to the tender mercies of the redhead, considering the French girl had just saved their lives.

"No; Luci serves the British, and knows that Lisabetta is an ally."

"Oh—of course."

He steered her toward the kitchen door that exited out into the back garden, and she wondered if he intended to venture out into the rain; with Darton dead, the counter-plan became much more complicated. The approaching party must be warned, but at the same time, the Comte must be kept from taking his part in the deception—and all the while, the British may be working against them.

Softly, she offered, "I am so sorry, Alexis. To think Darton was a vile Judas, all this time."

In a level tone, he replied, "I should have been more wary, when the priest was shown to be false. But I was certain Darton did not serve Napoleon—nor did he serve the British; he had too many opportunities to betray me, and did not take advantage. I would have done better to remember that there are many enemies in this age, and not all of them the obvious ones."

Epione shook her head in wonder. "No one is who they seem. Except me, I suppose."

Pausing at the door, he flashed his ready smile at her. "I beg to remind you that you were posing as a milliner's assistant, and using a false name. It was no easy thing, to find you."

"Oh, she said, much struck. "I suppose that's true."

He took her hands in his. "Now, you must go upstairs to your bedchamber, lock the door, and if anyone knocks, you must lead them to believe that I am within, with you. I must keep watch at the entry gate; the visitors must be warned, and we have no allies, within."

He pulled his hat down low over his brow, and quietly opened the garden door to take a long look outside, where the rain fell steadily. "*Bien*; go now, and open the door to no one but me, *ma belle.*"

Be brave, she urged herself; don't make him think you are incapable of such a simple task. "*Bonne chance, mon cher.*"

As the door quietly closed behind him, she took a steadying breath, and turned on her heel, gathering up the now sadly crushed skirts of her wedding dress. Hurrying over to the servant's stairway, she tried to quash the growing sense that there was every chance she may never see de Gilles again—he had feigned confidence, but she knew he was deeply uneasy, and wanted her locked in her bedroom to keep her safe from whatever was going to happen. The British were playing a double game—which was ominous in itself—and made even more ominous by the sure knowledge they were just as unhappy as Tallyrand to have de Gilles insert himself in these matters; he could easily disrupt all the careful negotiations that were taking place in Vienna. We have no allies, he had said, and it was true.

She paused, suddenly, with her foot on the stair. But they did indeed have an ally—truly, the only one that mattered. The Comte was the Josiah, and he was the key to this foul plot. She hesitated, trying to decide what to do. On the one hand, de Gilles wanted her to lock herself safely away, and perhaps she should follow his instruction, so as not to cause him any worry. On the other hand, she was the pawn in this miserable affair, and with good reason. Perhaps her time could be better spent seeking out the Comte. She could prevail upon him to support de Gilles, and abandon the conspirators—somehow convince him that Marie would wish him to act thusly.

Turning, she began to walk slowly toward the servant's dining room. This seemed a daunting task, as Marie was a Napoleon supporter, herself, and would probably approve wholeheartedly of the Josiah plot—especially the part about amassing all the jewels.

Coming to a decision, she began to move more quickly, out toward the great hall. Here was another way she could be useful; she could raid the jewels in the south tower, and try to secret them away somewhere, or even toss them into the ocean—anything to thwart these evildoers. De Gilles had picked the tower's lock, and hopefully no one had attempted entry since then.

With renewed determination, she hurried through the great hall, trying to decide whether she should first seek out the Comte, or attempt to hide the treasure—although perhaps she could enlist him to help her, and accomplish both tasks at once. Her slippers made soft slapping sounds on the marble floors, and the thunder rolled once again in the distance, as she made her way to the solar, hoping to find her host there. I can't imagine ever trying to live here, she thought with a shudder—presuming we survive this day. It is such a desolate, miserable place, and now there is a corpse in the grotto.

"Mademoiselle?"

The sandy-haired footman suddenly appeared in the shadows before her, coming out from under the minstrel's balcony. "Might I be of assistance?"

"I am searching for the Comte." Epione was well-aware she shouldn't trust anyone, least of all this servant, who had brought whispered messages to Chauvelin. "Monsieur de Gilles is upstairs, preparing for our wedding, and I have crept away to ask a private boon of the Comte—a surprise gift, for my bridegroom." She was rather proud of herself for thinking of this plausible tale on the spot, as it were.

The footman regarded her for a long moment, his face expressionless. "I see. I believe the Comte is closeted with Monsieur Chauvelin, in the library."

Calmly, Epione put her shoulders back, and tried to pretend she didn't look like a disheveled mess, instead of a radiant bride. "If you would escort me there, *s'il vous plait.*"

He bowed his head. "*Certamente,* Mademoiselle. This way, if you please.

The footman led her to the library doors, and after a deferential tapping, opened them to announce her. The Comte and Chauvelin were within, and looked up in surprise, both men's expressions rather serious. Despite the heavy air of interrupted intrigue, Epione rendered a bright smile. "May I borrow you for just a moment, Monsieur le Comte? I have a favor to ask, and I cannot be denied on my wedding day."

The man's face softened, as he drew himself up to bow. "Of course, Mademoiselle."

"Where is your companion?" interrupted Chauvelin with barely-concealed irritation. "She is charged with keeping you upstairs."

With a show of embarrassment, Epione confessed. "Lisabetta is locked away with Monsieur Darton, I believe." This being the truth, more or less. Remembering her subterfuge, she added, "I have only a short time while Monsieur de Gilles readies himself upstairs, and I must beg you for a boon."

With a last, meaningful glance at Chauvelin, the Comte took Epione's arm, and led her away. "*Je suis votre très dévoué serviteur*, Mademoiselle."

Lowering her voice, she leaned in with a conspiratorial smile. "I would ask a favor; to honor Marie, perhaps I could beg a few strings of pearls—there are so many, after all—and wear them, on this historic occasion. Then we can donate them to—to the children orphaned by the war, which was Marie's favorite charity."

The Comte stared at her for a moment, too overcome to speak, as his eyes misted over. "Ah—a most excellent idea, Mademoiselle—so worthy! Let me inform—"

"Oh, you must not tell anyone, Louis." Epione pulled urgently at his arm. "It must be our secret—I so wish to surprise the Seigneur, and I do not think Monsieur Chauvelin would approve."

With a twinkle, the Comte drew her hand into his arm. "Very good. Let us go and purloin some pearls, then—but quickly."

Chapter 42

With predictable gallantry, the Comte held his own hat over Epione's head, as they hurried along the cobblestone walkway that wound around to the south tower. The rain had lightened a bit, but the dark clouds overhead portended more stormy weather. Once at the tower, she discovered with relief that the heavy door was indeed unlocked, and the Comte heaved it open enough to allow them to pass through.

The musty scent of the ancient stones greeted her as they entered, the only illumination coming from the archery slits in the walls. It was cold and damp, and Epione shivered in her silk dress, a bit daunted by the enormity of the task ahead—her life had consisted mainly of avoiding confrontations, but there was no one else who could perform this task, and so much was at stake. If she had any powers of persuasion, it was time to test them; after all, she'd observed de Gilles first hand, and he was a master.

"The pearls are upstairs," the Comte reminded her, making a gesture toward the narrow, winding stairs. Shall I go first, Mademoiselle?"

It was now or never, and Epione gently drew him over to one of the vertical openings in the wall, so as to see his face more clearly. "I confess I am concerned, Louis. I fear there will be more bloodshed today, and surely we have seen more than our share, you and I."

He did not seem at all surprised that she broached matters treasonous, and instead looked upon her with indulgence. "You could not understand," he replied kindly, patting her hand. "Pray do not worry about these matters—you must leave such decisions to the men."

"I must intervene," she insisted. "Marie would wish it."

Gently, he shook a finger at her. "I fear you did not know your sister as well as I did, my dear Epione. She was a—a soldier, to her cause. Such courage! Such principle!" His eyes held a far-away look as he sighed, the sound heartfelt, and bittersweet.

It was past time to be blunt; someone would no doubt wonder at their absence soon, and she was making no headway. "No, Monsieur le Comte, they are going to cruelly murder your poor cousin when he arrives here, and then they will use you to seize whatever national treasures are left in the Treasury, and turn over our poor country to Napoleon. *Surely* you cannot wish for such a thing to happen to *la belle France*."

But the Comte remained unmoved by her plea, and regarded her with patient sympathy. "It is important, my dear, to understand that sacrifices must be made. Your sister understood this better—ah, better than anyone."

If Epione was previously not certain as to whether the Comte was fully aware of the extent of this plot, this hope died aborning. Since she would be unable to convince him that Marie would have disapproved, she tried a different tack. "But it is not right, Monsieur—after all, the Crown Jewels rightfully belong to the Seigneur."

Frowning, the man slowly lifted his chin to gaze at the ceiling, considering this.

Pressing her advantage, Epione continued in an urgent tone, "*Tiens*—what of the Crown of Charlemagne? It is the Seigneur's rightful inheritance, and we cannot think to break such a chain of ownership, no matter how noble the cause."

Apparently troubled, her companion lowered his chin, and frowned. "I confess I hadn't considered this aspect. But of course, I hadn't known that the Seigneur would appear—hale, and big as life—at my table."

His brow cleared, and he lifted his gaze to meet hers, a fanatical light in his eyes. "Imagine it—he calls me by my Christian name, and

349

condescends to joke and laugh with me—me! As though I am a boon companion."

"He is not one to make friends easily," she said honestly. "You have touched a chord with him, I think."

He nodded eagerly, his lips quivering slightly with emotion. "Yes; yes, I remind him of—of the old days. Of the times that are no more." His mien became melancholy, as he once again contemplated the floor. "It is all so *very* hard to bear. Your sister—" here he lifted his gaze to hers again. "Your sister made the unbearable bearable—she was so clever, and so alive. And now she is dead."

"We will all be dead, if this plan succeeds, Monsieur."

At this he looked at her in surprise. "No, no—you mistake; I will be living in Versailles—I have been promised. And you will live here." He smiled. "You and the Seigneur; I shall visit often, if I may."

No point in arguing; if he was unable to see what kind of people he was dealing with—who had already murdered everyone who could possibly identify him—she would not be able to convince him otherwise. Instead, she pronounced in grave tones, "They cannot allow the Seigneur to live, Monsieur. Surely, you must see this."

At this, his mouth gaped slightly, and he gazed at her in alarm. "No—no; surely—" he paused, and she said nothing, so as to allow him to come to grips with this undeniable fact. After a moment, he straightened his shoulders. "I shall insist that he be allowed to live here with you—*sub rosa*. No one need know." He nodded in emphasis, "I shall insist."

"He is the true pretender," she said quietly. "If this plot succeeds, Napoleon dare not let him live." She could see that he was shaken, and so she emphasized, "He will be vilely murdered, Louis—probably in such a way that we will never even know of it, but of a certainty, it will happen."

She waited, the issue hanging in the balance, as her companion thought it over in silence. Finally, he admitted, "I fear you speak the truth." He paused, his jaw working. "He must flee, then—take to the seas, again."

Ruthlessly, Epione did not allow him an out. "He will not flee, Monsieur—he is too honorable. He bears no love for Napoleon, and hopes to dissuade you from your course."

"Yes," the other man admitted somberly. "He has already attempted to dissuade me from my course."

"Of course he has; his life will be forfeit, else." With cautious hope, she could see that she'd made an impression, and so she added firmly, "We can't allow Monsieur Chauvelin to murder the Duc d'Orleans this night, or all is lost."

After a moment's reflection, the Comte lifted his eyes to hers, and with acute relief, she could see that he was now resolved to aid her. "You are a very brave girl. You are worthy of him."

"And my sister," she added, touching his hand, and hoping to encourage this fragile change of heart. "I must honor her memory."

Diplomatically, she didn't try to explain how thwarting Napoleon's plot would honor her traitorous sister.

With a firm step, he moved over to grasp the old blunderbuss from the rack and check the barrel. Encouraged by this show of action, she ventured, "Should I take one, also? Can you load one for me?" She didn't know the first thing about firing such a weapon, but surely she could create the appearance of competence—if she could lift it, that was.

As he tamped the powder in the barrel, he replied without looking at her, "Better to go upstairs, Mademoiselle, and choose the pearls for your wedding raiment."

He was not right in his mind, of course, to be thinking about the wedding in the same breath as an attack on Chauvelin, but she would humor him by any means she could, and so gathered up her heavy skirts to hurry up the winding stair to the upper floor. Once in the storeroom, she reckoned that one of the archery slits faced the front gate, and so dragged a wooden casket beneath the opening, stepping atop it so as to peer out; perhaps she could spot de Gilles—although there would be little point in letting him know of the Comte's change of heart, it was more important that he warn the visitors away.

She could not see much through the narrow opening, and after a moment, stepped down so as to open the casket. The exposed pearls lay in a jumble, gleaming even in the dimness, and unable to resist, she buried her hands in them up to her forearms for a moment, feeling the luster of a fortune against her fingers. They are indeed beautiful, she thought; small wonder everyone covets them.

Suddenly, there was a tremendous blast beneath her, painfully loud as it echoed off the walls of the stone tower. Her heart in her throat, she stumbled toward the stairs, fearing that they were under attack—they should have barred the door—fool!—why didn't she think of it—

But instead, she froze in horror as she rounded the stairs down to the first floor. Through the drifting smoke, she was met with the gruesome sight of the Comte's body, lying on the stone floor with the remains of his head spattered over the wall. In a last act of devotion to his Seigneur, the Comte had put a halt to the plot.

Chapter 43

Time seemed to stand still for a moment, until Epione heard alarmed voices in the near distance. For a wild moment, she feared the others would believe that she'd killed the Comte, but then realized that it didn't matter either way; with the death of the Comte, not only was the plot thwarted, but there was no longer any reason to keep any of them alive.

Whirling, she frantically pushed at the heavy wooden door and managed to move it into place, then yanked with all her strength to bring the cross bar down with a thud, just as she heard running steps approaching the tower from the outside. Gathering up her skirts yet again, she pelted up the stairs to the upper storeroom, and frantically looked around her, as she heard

Chauvelin pounding on the wooden door downstairs, and shouting for the Comte.

Looking up, she gauged the width of the archery slit, and decided she had little choice. Dropping to her knees before the casket, she began clipping the pearl necklaces end to end, so as to create a makeshift rope, willing her hands to stop shaking. Would it hold her weight? The pearls were each knotted securely onto their strings, but she had no idea of the strength of the strands. To reinforce them, she twisted several strands together, but had no more time; they were pounding the door below with something heavy, so that she could hear the sound of splintering wood.

After securing one end of her rope to the casket handle, she climbed atop the wooden box just as she heard the door burst open downstairs. After tossing the pearl rope through the slit, she clambered up, and managed to barely wriggle sideways through the opening, scraping her cheek against the rough stone in the process.

With the wind whipping at her, Epione wrapped the rope of pearls around her hands, praying that it would hold, and carefully lowered herself, hand-over-hand, to the very end of its length as she braced her feet against the tower. She would have to jump the remainder of the distance to the roof, but had no idea how far it was, and was afraid to look, for fear she would lose her nerve. With the rain making it difficult to see, she gritted her teeth, and let go, falling about four feet to land hard on the steeply-pitched roof.

She lost her footing almost immediately, and so flung herself forward to cling with hands and feet to the slippery blue tiles for a moment, gathering her courage as the wind blew, and shouts were heard coming from the tower above her. She then began to scramble along the tiles toward the front of the château, trying not to think of what would happen if the wind grew any stronger, and she couldn't keep her footing.

With her head kept low, she tried to stay away from the area under the tower's archery slit, so as not to afford an easy target. But in this she held a vain hope, as she heard a report behind her, and with a ping, a musket ball ricocheted off the tile a few feet away from her head. Immediately, she altered her course, so as to slide over the roof's crest and down into the adjacent valley, protected from any more shots by the crest of the roof, even though it was not the route she wished to take.

"*Au secours*!" She shouted into the wind. "Alexis—"

She heard another shot behind her, and started, losing her footing for a moment so that she skittered and slid for a few feet before regaining her balance. Above all, she needed to warn de Gilles that the Comte was dead, and their own lives were now at risk. The best course, it seemed, was to hide behind a chimney pot—so as to be protected from the tailor—and try to signal, somehow, to de Gilles. With this in mind, she scrambled to the nearest chimney pot, working hard to maintain a foothold on the slick tiles, and then paused to carefully pull herself up, so that she could peer over the crest of the roof.

To her horror, a musket ball pinged off the tile to the right of her—someone was shooting from the west tower, also, and she was utterly exposed to the crossfire. She tensed, terrified and waiting for another shot, but none came. With little hope, she looked up to the west tower, to see the sandy-haired footman, leaning as far as he was able out an archery slit and shouting something. As he hadn't taken this opportunity to kill her, Epione thought perhaps he was an ally, trying to gain her attention, and so she strained in the wind and rain to hear what it was he said. Faintly, she thought she heard, "Where is Luci?"

Unaware of his allegiances, she debated what to say. Without hesitation, he aimed his weapon squarely at her, and his shouts could be heard faintly yet again. "Where—is—Luci?"

She licked her dry lips, and pantomimed to him that Luci was below, and a door locked. Hopefully, he would leave to find the girl, and indeed, it seemed that this was the case, as he immediately disappeared from the window.

There seemed little chance that de Gilles could hear her, and so she gathered up her courage and stood upright, balancing so as to heave upward on one of the tiles that shielded the top of the chimney pot. The action exposed her to the south tower, and she heard another musket ball whiz past her head as she managed to push the tile off the chimney, so that it skittered down the roof, and then fell to the courtyard below, landing with a satisfying crash that even she could hear.

Crouching to pant for a few moments, she repeated the action, and rose to push another tile after the first, nearly losing her balance in the process. Within moments, she was gratified to see de Gilles run out into the courtyard, his raised face pale against the rain-darkened courtyard. "The Comte is dead," she shouted, but she could see he could not hear her, and he gestured for her to stay still.

"I cannot," she shouted, and then ducked, as the ricochet of a musket ball pinged off the chimney pot. Crouching down, she looked down along the peak to see that Chauvelin was now on the roof, a pistol in his hand, making his way along the slippery, precarious footing in her direction. Her only hope was to reverse course, and stay alive until de Gilles could intervene.

Her painful breaths coming in gasps, she ducked and scrambled along the traverse peak, toward the west tower. She strained to hear the pursuit, but it was impossible, with the wind howling, and the rain barraging her. As she clawed frantically along, she glanced back, and could see that Chauvelin was steadily gaining ground—she was encumbered by her skirts, and was no match for him. He would soon have an easy shot unless she circled behind the tower, and so with this in mind, she scrambled to the lee side, where it was a bit quieter because the wind was blocked.

Panting to regain her breath, she thought she heard a shout from ahead, along the north-west traverse. She lifted a hand to shield her eyes from the rain, and saw de Gilles, standing astride the roof's peak ahead of her, as he brandished his pistol and motioned for her to lie flat so that he could shoot at her pursuer.

She obeyed instinctively, dropping down to the tiles as she heard his shot pass over her head. Cautiously she lifted up to look behind her, and was met with the sight of her furious brother, bleeding from his shoulder, but only a few feet away. Afraid to leap up, for fear that de Gilles would shoot again, she could only frantically kick at her attacker as he closed in on her, grasping her legs as she pounded with a fist at his bloody, wounded shoulder and struggled to get away.

"Cease," he hissed at her, and jerked her upright against his chest to hold a long, thin blade to her throat. "We will await our exalted guest."

Her breast heaving, she clawed at the arm across her waist, but her captor only shook her roughly, and pressed the point of the knife in a meaningful way. She subsided, standing as still as she was able, while de Gilles cautiously approached, his hands held out to his sides.

The wind swirled, and the rain bounced off the tiles, sluicing down the sides. "Drop your weapons," Chauvelin shouted.

"Denis," de Gilles replied, his manner deferential. "We will both lay down our weapons, and come to terms."

359

"There is no coming to terms. You are less than a dust mote in a whirlwind." He pressed the knife against Epione's throat while she tried to communicate with her eyes that she was prepared to move, if de Gilles wanted to try to take a shot. "Come no closer."

De Gilles promptly halted, his hands still held where they could be seen. "Come, Monsieur—your only surviving sister; she serves no purpose in this."

With cold satisfaction, Chauvelin ground out, "Indeed she does; you will watch me cut her throat."

De Gilles didn't flinch. "Your people need money; I have money."

"From selling whores," the other man jeered.

De Gilles repeated, "I have a great deal of money."

"Too late; you will watch her die."

To Epione, it seemed that the cold-as-ice Chauvelin was showing glimpses of a white-hot fury—almost deranged in its intensity—and she struggled to maintain her calm, as her brother taunted the other man. "You will dance on a string for me—how does it feel, to be helpless? I was helpless, once, and I swore I would never be helpless again. Shall I tell you how I was made to watch them all die? Griselde went first, because they were so furious with her."

Almost imperceptibly, de Gilles' flinched. His nursemaid, Epione remembered; the one who'd saved his life.

Seeing the reaction, Chauvelin warmed to his cruel subject. "Yes—I saw her meet Madame Guillotine. She held together until the very last, but then she broke down, keening like a little girl—"

"Stop it," Epione shouted in horror, watching de Gille's face.

"She was still wailing when her head fell into the bloody basket—"

It was unbearable, to think that de Gilles was at the mercy of this fiend, who was going to taunt him and then cruelly slay her, before his eyes. In that instant, Epione decided that indeed, some things did transcend mere life and death, and if the Comte was willing to die to save de Gilles, she could do no less. Planting her feet, she shoved Chauvelin backward with her body as hard as she could, so that they would both fly out from the roof's peak, to be dashed on the flagstones, far below.

As she began to fall through the air, however, she was jerked, hard, and then landed with a thud on the roof tiles, with Chauvelin's momentum causing him to tumble over her head toward the roof's edge. Frantically, the tailor clutched at her as he slid down the steep slope, seizing her arm, and clawing at the wet tiles with his free hand in a futile attempt to halt his slippery progress.

With a literal death grip on her out flung arm, he slid over the edge of the roof, and then dangled, suspended over the courtyard below, as the heavy weight on her arm make Epione cry out in agony.

Without grim determination, she reached to claw savagely at his hand, and managed to pry his fingers loose, one by one. His face a mask of rage, he fell to the courtyard below, twisting frantically, and then landing with a sickening thud.

Epione lay for a moment, her breast heaving, and then she carefully propped herself up on her elbows to look over her shoulder, behind her. On the slant of the steep roof, de Gilles lay, spread eagle, one fist clutching a handful of her petticoats, with the other grasping the grip of his sword, which he'd hooked on the chimney pot at the crest of the roof.

"*Merci le bon Dieu*," she panted, turning to rest her cheek on the wet gutter tiles.

"*Merci le bon Dieu* for Alençon lace," he replied.

She found this exceeding amusing, although her voice was so hoarse that she could only manage a chuckle. What a beautiful day it is, she thought; with the clouds so dramatic above, and the vineyards stretching out in the distance, in their symmetrical rows. Faintly, she could hear the waves crashing on the cliffs.

"Careful, *ma belle*. Come back toward me." Inch by inch, she obeyed by moving backward, on knees and elbows whilst he gathered up more of her petticoat in his hands until finally he grasped her waist, and set her beside him on the roof's crest, his arms coming around her.

She clung to him, her words tumbling over each other. "I love you. I think I have loved you

362

from the moment I saw you, but I didn't want to say—I was afraid to hope—"

"Hush, *ma belle*."

"I shall abide with you all my days," she declared, and managed to take a steadying breath. "I can scarce believe it."

The timbre of the voice above her head was deep and sincere. "Not as yet, Epione; I cannot encourage another to put a knife to your throat—not with so many, vying for power. We must part, for a time, and I will return to the sea until Napoleon is put down, and a new King is safely established. But I will return to you; this I swear."

"Yes—yes, I understand, Alexis." It made sense, unfortunately; she had no desire to repeat this experience and she could be patient—she could wait until the succession was more firmly established. After all, she'd been waiting for him all her life.

With a deep breath, she looked out over the neglected estate, as the light rain continued to fall. "I will wait for you here—I love this place; I love every corner. It needs but one thing; children. More pretenders, to plague Tallyrand, and Louis the Eighteenth."

"And the British," he added. "A few extra, to plague the British."

"*D'accord*," she agreed.

They sat, embracing on the roof in the rain; the future uncertain, and Epione happier than she had ever been.

Chapter 44

"You were never a mark—a target," the sandy-haired footman explained yet again. "You have nothing to fear from us."

But de Gilles continued to hold his pistol on him. "Allow me to be skeptical."

They were seated around the table in the great hall, de Gilles the only one with a weapon, because he had demanded that the footman, Luci and Lisabetta relinquish theirs. That they had done so without demur led Epione to believe that they were not in any danger from them, and it seemed that de Gilles was of the same mind, as he leaned back in a casual pose, with his boots crossed before him. They'd been seated thus for over an hour, waiting for the Duc d'Orleans and his party to make their anticipated arrival.

While the footman seemed slightly exasperated, Luci had instead chosen to be amused, and now addressed Epione. "It seems you're a feisty one, my lass—now, there's a surprise. And you've spoiled my assignment, for which I canno' thank you."

"You may take full credit for killing Monsieur Chauvelin," Epione offered. "I do not mind at all."

"No, lass—we wanted information from him, and now only the devil will be hearing what he has to say."

"They spoiled my assignment, also," Lisabetta offered in a huff. "They kill people without any consideration."

Epione noted that de Gilles did not correct this falsehood, and concluded she should also pretend that de Gilles had killed Darton, if anyone asked—although no one had mentioned the man's disappearance, which seemed a little strange.

Crossly, Lisabetta rearranged her skirts. "Fah—I am weary of waiting. Who wishes champagne? There is plenty to be had."

The girl glanced at de Gilles, and it seemed to Epione that a message passed between them. "I will have champagne," he said with a nod. "Many thanks."

Happy to have a task, Epione rose to help, and the two girls made their way into the servant's hall. Vaguely, Lisabetta gestured toward the bottles in the wine pantry. "Take two bottles; I will go to the kitchen to fetch the glasses."

Once in the pantry, Epione hesitated, and then decided to take an extra bottle, as she suspected two would not last very long, with this group. Clutching the bottles, she carried them back into the great hall, to set them down on the massive table. "Oh—has Lisabetta not returned with the glasses?"

"Not as yet," said de Gilles easily. He produced a knife, and began to untwist the wires that held a cork in place.

"You're making a mistake," pronounced Luci, who held out a hand for the first bottle. "Mark me."

"Perhaps," was all de Gilles replied, as he jimmied the cork loose with his knife, and then handed the bottle to her.

Realization dawned, and Epione faltered, "Lisabetta—Lisabetta has flown?"

"She won't get paid," the footman noted with satisfaction, as he took a long drink from Luci's bottle.

"I would be very much surprised if she has not already seen to her payment," de Gilles replied, and offered his own bottle to Epione. Remembering the pearl necklaces from the shooting match, Epione was inclined to agree with him, as she took a sip of the champagne. Reminded, she asked, "What happens to the jewels, now?"

"We will see to them," said the footman immediately.

"I believe the jewels belong to Mademoiselle d'Amberre." De Gilles lifted his gaze to the footman.

There was a tense silence. *Tiens*, Epione thought; here we go, yet again.

But the footman only raised his bottle to her. "You are a wealthy woman, then. My congratulations."

Epione was spared a flustered response, when the knocker on the entry doors sounded. De Gilles raised his pistol on the other two. "Would you answer the door, Mademoiselle?"

Epione made a cursory attempt to smooth her hair, but decided there was little hope for it, as she approached the entry door. "Who is without?" she asked, just to be safe—at this point she wouldn't have been surprised if Napoleon himself was on the stoop.

"We are expected," was the response, and so she opened the door. Four men stood and regarded her in confusion for a long moment, two gentlemen, and two servants. One of the gentlemen indeed resembled the late Comte, but Epione was distracted by one of the servants, who was regarding her without a twinge of recognition. "Why, Mr. Tremaine," she exclaimed politely. "How good it is to see you again." So; the reason the pretender's party came early was because it wasn't the pretender's party at all, but the wily British, hoping to achieve whatever aims they sought. Hopefully, there'd be no more shoot-outs on the roof, but she was past being surprised.

She could see Tremaine's wary gaze quickly assess the interior behind her. "Are there no servants to see to the door, Mademoiselle?"

"I'm afraid your compatriots have been found out, and are under watch." She gestured for the visitors to enter, and as they stepped within, she took a closer look at Louis Philippe, and noted he had grey eyes. She said in English, "Your arrival is anticlimactic, sir. Monsieur Chauvelin is dead, as is the Comte."

The British spymaster did not attempt to disclaim his identity, but only reviewed her disheveled state with a thoughtful air. "You have been very busy, it seems."

Epione smiled with her new-found confidence. "You don't know the half of it; it is difficult to know whom to trust—no thanks to you."

But the man was unrepentant, and bowed his head slightly. "I do what I think best for England, Miss."

As there was no point to arguing, she led them into the great hall and announced, "A faux Duc d'Orleans, Monsieur—lately of *The Moor's Head* tavern."

De Gilles cocked his head, his pistol still held negligently on the two servants. "I would have appreciated a bit more honesty, Monsieur."

"Forgive me," the spymaster replied as he tossed his hat on the table, and removed his gloves. "I could not foresee that these two would be so clumsy." He cast an eye toward Luci and the footman. "I believe you have a ship to catch."

Rather than appear abashed at being thus reprimanded, the two stood with alacrity, the sandy-haired footman grabbing a champagne bottle as they made for the door.

"Where is Lisabetta?" asked Tremaine, pulling out a chair to sit.

De Gilles replied, "I believe she has departed, to deliver some unfortunate news to *Pere* Tallyrand."

The words were said in an even tone, but the undercurrent made Epione tense, and look at de Gilles for a moment, hoping the swords were not to break out again.

But the grey-eyed man hastened to explain, "I could not be certain of Darton's allegiances, or I would have told you of him."

De Gilles' level gaze did not waver. "You played me for a dupe, Monsieur."

"No," the other man protested rather forcefully. "No," he repeated, in a quieter tone. "I allowed Lisabetta her freedom, when she told me of her assignment. I wanted to see to your safety."

"You let her seize Mademoiselle d'Ambere, and you knew Darton would betray me."

"No," the man said again, his gaze holding the other's. "I did not know for certain, in either case."

De Gilles considered this, and Epione had no idea what he was thinking—it seemed fairly clear that the spymaster hadn't taken any pains to aid them, but on the other hand, he'd other priorities to think about.

De Gilles finally addressed the spymaster, "I would speak with you privately, if I may."

With a nod, the others were dismissed, and Epione stood to follow them, planning to collapse into a comfortable chair, somewhere, but de Gilles touched her arm, and asked her to stay. "This involves you, Mademoiselle."

Rather than pulling out a chair to seat her, de Gilles drew her onto his lap, so that she leaned back against his broad chest. Gratefully, she rested her head on this shoulder; she was dead on her feet, and hoped she wouldn't disgrace herself by falling asleep, while the fate of the world was being discussed.

De Gilles started without preamble, "I cannot stay; it was a mistake to insert myself in these matters."

The other man nodded gravely, offering no protest.

"I will go back to the Mediterranean, and return here when matters are less volatile."

The spymaster assured him, "A year—two at the very most, I would venture."

"*Eh bien.* I will marry Mademoiselle before I leave, but it would be best if few know of it."

This was of interest, and Epione plucked up as the spymaster assured him, "None will hear of it from me."

"I will not leave her unprotected." This said with a significance which was lost on Epione.

"I would not expect you to."

Apparently satisfied, de Gilles added, "And she will keep the jewels in the south tower."

But the spymaster leaned forward, his gaze intent. "Please reconsider; the funds are desperately needed."

De Gilles cocked his head, contemplating him. "As bad as that?"

With abrupt honesty, the other explained, "We continue to be bedeviled by schemes to siphon off riches, for the benefit of the enemy. It's been a close-run thing."

Epione decided it was time she spoke up. "Then I would like to render aid to my adopted country, if I may, Monsieur. England took us in, and my sister betrayed her. It is the least I can do."

De Gilles leaned down to meet her eyes in protest. "The English have used you ill, *ma belle.*"

She smiled. "*Everyone* has used me ill; I can harbor no grudges."

The spymaster offered, "I will see to it that she keeps a goodly amount—enough to restore this place, and keep her in comfort."

De Gilles nodded. "*Enfin*, it is Mademoiselle's fortune to do with as she wishes; I cannot gainsay her in this."

They sat in silence for a few moments, as the fire crackled in the great hearth, and Epione decided that the two men must feel that they had tied up all loose ends in a satisfactory manner. In this, however, she was mistaken, as the spymaster suddenly said, "You may not be aware that I am an ordained vicar. It would be my honor to perform the marriage ceremony."

De Gilles rested his benign gaze on the other man. "I thank you for your kind offer, but I will arrange for a curé."

"Tonight?" Epione sincerely hoped not; she was a miserable mess, and was fading fast.

"Not tonight," he reassured her with a smile, brushing a fond thumb against her cheek.

"But tomorrow, perhaps. It depends on how quickly the arrangements can be made."

The grey-eyed man offered, "Allow me to provide transport, then; and my assurances that you will be delivered wherever you wish, in perfect safety."

"Thank you," said de Gilles in English, and it occurred to Epione, as she sleepily watched the fire, that the spymaster had never addressed de Gilles by name—or had even called him "Monsieur." Because he thinks he knows, she thought, and he wants de Gilles to be aware that he knows. But he is distracted by the cloak, and I—I see what is beneath the cloak, and am content with what I see. The cloak does not matter to me at all.

With a small smile, she closed her eyes, and contemplated the future. She'd come full circle, back to the place where everything had gone horribly wrong, only now with the certain conviction that all wrongs would—at long last—be made right again, or at least as right as they could be made. She would be patient—indeed, she'd been patient all her life, and had learned, stitch by stitch, to keep faith; it was why her husband had fallen in love with her. And that same faith told her that he'd return safely, to live out the remainder of his days here with her, in this quiet, isolated place. It may not be happily ever after—he was a wounded man, beneath his cloak—but she was uniquely able to provide a balm to his wounds. We were both adrift, she thought, but now we are bound to each other, and to this place. I shall miss him, but I have work to do, to bring *Desclaires* back to life again, before he returns— I'd best make myself a decent sun bonnet. With a happy sigh, she drifted off to sleep.

Made in the USA
San Bernardino, CA
01 June 2018